Unbidden Guests

Unbidden Guests

Martin Wilson

Copyright © 2013 Martin Wilson

The moral right of the author has been asserted.

Apart from any fair dealing for the purposes of research or private study, or criticism or review, as permitted under the Copyright, Designs and Patents Act 1988, this publication may only be reproduced, stored or transmitted, in any form or by any means, with the prior permission in writing of the publishers, or in the case of reprographic reproduction in accordance with the terms of licences issued by the Copyright Licensing Agency. Enquiries concerning reproduction outside those terms should be sent to the publishers.

Matador
9 Priory Business Park
Kibworth Beauchamp
Leicestershire LE8 0RX, UK
Tel: (+44) 116 279 2299
Fax: (+44) 116 279 2277
Email: books@troubador.co.uk
Web: www.troubador.co.uk/matador

ISBN 978 1783060 825

British Library Cataloguing in Publication Data.
A catalogue record for this book is available from the British Library.

Typeset in StempelGaramond Roman by Troubador Publishing Ltd
Printed and bound in the UK by TJ International, Padstow, Cornwall

Matador is an imprint of Troubador Publishing Ltd

For Julia, my wife, my daughters Becky, Anna and Alex
and my little grandson, Ben.

An unbidden guest is worse than a Tartar
– Russian proverb

CHAPTER 1

Frank Grinder woke with a stiff neck and a dry throat. He took a sip of water from the tumbler on the bedside table, put on his glasses and swung his legs out of the bed. It was becoming a worryingly typical start to the day: regretting how much he had had to drink the night before. Blearily, he walked to the window, pulled back the curtains and stared out at the drizzle suffusing the garden with a grey light. He glanced back at the face of his still sleeping wife. A short lock of black hair lay across her cheek as if positioned deliberately, accentuating the child-like quality of her features.

He put his forehead against the cool glass. The wooden furniture at the bottom of the garden was beginning to show signs of mould, bad enough for him to be able to see it from here. He would have to try to do something about it; scrape it off or buy some sort of product from the DIY store. And he would have to collect up the leaves which had started to fall from his neighbour's horse chestnut tree and which the wind had swept into soggy, mottled piles in the corner by the fence. Perhaps he should get someone in to do it for him, but it seemed ridiculous and pretentious to employ a gardener for such a small area, with no lawn and only narrow strips of flower beds separating the paving from the damp-stained brick walls on either side. A blackbird settled on the back of one of the chairs and pointed its orange beak at him, cocking its head to one side. He didn't know how long they lived, but there was every chance that it had taken possession of its territory long before he had; it certainly looked as if it was challenging him. He stared back at it, and at the dismal garden, settling into a reverie until the growing need for a cup of tea distracted him.

She had not moved, but she stirred slightly as he took his dressing-gown from the hook on the door. He was about to ask her if she wanted him to bring a cup up to her, but she turned onto her other side, breathing slowly, quietly, and he crept out of the room and down the stairs. The kitchen was immediately below the bedroom, and as he waited for the kettle to boil, he went over to the window and looked out at the rain. At this level, he could not avoid seeing how uneven some of the paving slabs were. The moss which had grown between them tended to lessen the effect, but there were one or two places that could cause a trip. Was that something that he could repair himself or would he have to pay a workman to do it for him? He had no idea. He didn't even know who you would ask to do such a job. A builder? A landscape gardener?

Grey drizzle, a dismal garden, and nothing to do. He dropped a tea bag into a mug and took it over to the deal table, waiting for the tea to turn the dark brown that he liked. As he fished it out, the paper label detached from its thread and the bag dropped back into the mug, splashing the table. He went across to the sink, looking for a cloth. There was none there; she had tidied and cleaned the kitchen as she always did before going to bed. Where did she keep the cloths? Or the kitchen towelling? The stain was beginning to seep into the surface. He tried to dry it with the sleeve of his dressing gown, but succeeded only in making a mark on it. He went into the downstairs lavatory, there was always paper there, and a spare roll, neatly and unobtrusively ready.

Back in the kitchen he tried mopping the stain with a couple of sheets of dry toilet paper, and then with a handful which he soaked under the tap. The stain grew larger, without appearing to get lighter, and small, damp curlicues of paper were now embedded in the grain of the surface. Meanwhile the tea had turned black. He tried picking the bag out by its sodden string, but it was still too hot, so he went to the cutlery drawer and took out a teaspoon which, had he thought about it, he should have had ready before the kettle had boiled. After two attempts, when the bag splashed back into the tea, he managed to balance it on the spoon, lift it out and then dropped it onto the table. With the aid of the spoon and more paper he got it into the sink and sat down to contemplate the, probably permanent, mess that he made.

Yesterday's newspaper was on one of the chairs, where she always left it when she cleared up, because she knew that he liked to go through it again before the morning's delivery, looking for articles that he had missed and seeing whether he could fill in any more of the unfinished crossword puzzle. He spread it out, guiltily, over the wet patch whilst he took the milk from the fridge. He checked that it had not gone off: they didn't get through much, he, because he liked his coffee and tea very strong and because he had an aversion to breakfast cereals, and she for cultural reasons. But, of course, it was fine; the insistence on fresh food was another characteristic of her background.

He looked out at the garden again. The rain had stopped, and there seemed to be a faint glimmer of sunshine behind the clouds. He ought to get out and do something. It seemed much easier for her, she could occupy herself for hours tidying the house up, cooking, reading the magazines that were sent regularly by her family. Her temperament was much better suited than his for taking apparent satisfaction from the mundane. Perhaps, if he took the car down to the local supermarket, he might see something that they needed at home. It was a pretty big one; perhaps it might even have a gardening section and he could buy some mould killer and a rake. But first he would make her some tea.

There were several small boxes of Rickshaw Brand Oolong tea in the cupboard, behind the teabags that he liked. He had no idea where she got them from. Did they come from the supermarket or were they also sent from home? He had never thought to ask. He boiled the water again and made her a cup, this time using the spoon to fish the bag out. She was beginning to sit up when he went in to the bedroom, but her eyes were still closed. For several seconds, he gazed at her perfect, even features and tousled hair.

'Hallo, F'ank,' she said, looking at him, as if his stare had woken her. 'How's my man today?'

'I've brought you some tea, love.'

'No milk?'

'No, it's your tea. Where do you get it from?'

'You got it. From kitchen cupboard.'

'No, I mean, where does it come from? Where do you buy it?'

'I don't remember. Maybe my mother send it.'

He handed her the cup and sat down on the bed.

'Listen, love, I think that I'll go to the supermarket.'

'You?'

'Yes, there's got to be a first for everything.'

'O.K., but how about you get dressed first?' she said, and put her hand on his knee.

'Oh, and I'm afraid I made a bit of a mess on the kitchen table. I dropped a teabag on it and I couldn't get the stain out. I'm sorry.'

'*Mo man tai*, don't worry,' she said. 'You're tired because you get up too early. Maybe, that's why you so clumsy. I'll clean it up,' and she laughed as she added, 'When you shop.'

The car park at the supermarket was enormous. Grinder had never seen one as big, other than at airports. He wondered whether there was a shuttle bus to the building as he reversed the car into a space which seemed a very long walk to the entrance. He saw that there were trolleys, jammed together in covered bays and went over to one. He struggled with it until he saw that it was attached to the one in front by a small chain with a coin slot. He searched his pockets, but could not find a £1 coin. He vaguely remembered stories of people being stopped by security staff for going round supermarkets without a trolley or a wire basket, but he could not see any baskets in the bay, or anywhere else in the car park. It was all a bit of a puzzle, but he would walk over and chance it.

As he went through the automatic sliding glass doors, he was astonished. It was huge. A giant hall of commerce: banks of check-out tills and beyond them a bewildering scene: rows and rows of display shelves with a throng of trolley-wielding people in the aisles between them. And he was taken aback by the level of noise: voices, announcements and music. He abandoned his earlier notion of wandering round, picking up the odd item that appealed to him or which he thought might be needed at home, and decided that he would just look for some moss-killer, or whatever it was that he needed. He walked past the café – he had not realised that there would be one – and the sign to the toilets, and the newsstand and, surprisingly, a book stall, and rows and rows of clothes, and found himself amongst piles of fruit and vegetables. Then it was bread, stacks of loaves of all possible shapes and then chiller cabinets with frozen ready meals and huge tubs of ice-cream, and then meat, and then fish, and then tea and coffee – no sign of Oolong – and then he was in the household section, washing powder and dishwasher salt and dozens of bottles of bleach, and then a haven of relative peace where there were only a few shoppers examining the labels on wine bottles and comparing the prices of spirits, and then again into the hubbub, where there were tins of soup and baked beans and, further along, cold shelves with cheese and yoghurt. And then he found himself near the back of a queue at a check-out and he saw that he was near where he had come in. He considered, for a moment, going back in again, retracing the start of his route but, this time, taking care to look for clues, but his head was beginning to throb again and he thought that he should have had something to eat before leaving the house. His wife would have been aghast if she had known that he had gone out without any breakfast; although she probably would, by now, have realised that from the absence of any mess in the kitchen, other than that which he had left on the table. Perhaps he should, at least, go back to the cleaning-products section to see if there was anything that would remove tea stains from a wooden surface; but she probably had got something at home and he would only get the wrong thing, even if he could find it.

Grinder had never had to go into a supermarket in the last twenty or so years; that was something that the succession of Filipina domestic helpers did, as well as cooking and cleaning the apartment and taking the dog for a walk, but he was sure that they were much better laid-out over there. He had never heard the amah complain, when she struggled through the door with several laden plastic bags of groceries and carboys of distilled water, that she had had any problems trying to find what was needed.

He decided against a coffee and a bun in the café. He would just go home, taking with him a sense of frustration and of having wasted his, he had to admit it, no longer valuable time. This was all confirming what he had dreaded might be the outcome of his retirement back to

England. After many years working in the firm of Chan, Grinder, Yeung & Lam, Frank had gradually begun to question whether there was a future for him in the Far East and had come to the conclusion that it would be better to come home with his young Chinese wife. He had over the years, of course, been back to England from time to time to see his shrinking circle of relations and had been conscious that things were changing and not always for the better. When he returned he had so readily slipped into his hard-working but comfortable and, above all, convenient routine that he soon looked back on these trips to England with an almost wistful fondness; but he was still conscious of how much change had been wrought since he had answered the advertisement in the Law Society Gazette, all those years ago, to join an established firm and had gone to live and to prosper in what he had, at first, thought might be just a colonial outpost. But, once he had begun to think about leaving the partnership he had pondered more and more about what was the right thing to do. As the local English-language newspaper would have said, he mulled it and, having mulled it he had asked Winnie if she would be content to settle down in the town where he had spent much of his early life. Of course she had said yes, so the decision was made.

He took off his steel-rimmed glasses and polished them with his handkerchief. He was conscious that he was sweating slightly and could see in the reflection that his ruddy complexion was more than usually flushed. He had wondered, before leaving the house, whether a tweed jacket was a bit too protective on this mild early autumn day but that was part of the trouble: you never could tell what the weather would do and he did not know how cold it would be in a supermarket. The tie, he thought, might have been a bit too much, no other man seemed to be wearing one, but it was hard to break the habit of more than two decades; it was a weekday and he went out properly dressed. He also noticed that his hair was in need of a cut. There was plenty of it still, grey and straight, but he did not want it to get so long that he might be mistaken for the presenter of an arts programme on television.

And that was another thing, where could you get your hair cut in England that wasn't either ruinously expensive or one of those places where tattooed, gum-chewing, belly-pierced girls whizzed through with scissors and clippers and left you looking as if you had been attacked by a combine harvester? He recalled, fondly, the relaxing hour-long sessions in 'The Hair Piece' in Queen's Road, when pretty girls – usually called 'Iris' or a similarly endearing old-fashioned name – would shampoo and massage his scalp until he was in a state of soporific contentment and then, slowly, meticulously, snip away around him whilst sitting on a wheeled stool and murmur 'that better, that much more better'. Their limited English a positive advantage as there was no inane chatter.

He walked back to his car, slowly, because there did not seem to be any need to rush. The sky had clouded over again while he had been in the supermarket and a few drops of rain touched his forehead. He wondered whether a quick visit to the pub near his home might be in order, but it was much too early for a pre-lunch drink and he was all too conscious of the perils of trying to cure ennui with alcohol. There were several old soaks whom he had left behind in the Far East, spending their afternoons, and their pensions, in the Club; indeed, they were a significant factor in his decision to come back to England for retirement. He would drive home, and perhaps go out for a drink when the hour was more respectable. As he got to his car his gloom was worsening and the thought, again, bubbled up from the murky layers of his sub-conscious mind that he needed something constructive to do with his, now copious, days. He certainly wasn't going to go back into legal practice, even on a part-time basis, even if that were possible which, in any event, he doubted. Perhaps some charity work? But he had a feeling that that wouldn't do for him: too intermittent, too worthy, too much like the resort of someone who was unable to fill his time properly; and, anyway, he knew no-one who was involved with any charity that might want to use him. What about applying for a job as a bursar in some local private school? But all those posts were probably filled, and with long lists of people waiting for the incumbent to drop off his perch. Cheltenham must be overflowing with retired solicitors and accountants who were trying to fill their hours and boost their incomes; and that sort of work would tie him to the office hours that he had so recently been glad to say goodbye to. Nor did he, truly, need to boost his income, and there was a degree of impropriety, he persuaded himself, in taking a job which others might need or want more, much more, than he did. And how would someone who had led such a different life fit in to that routine? Because his life had been quite unlike how it would have turned out had he stayed in England. There was no question, the Far East had an allure, a fascination that Gloucestershire did not, otherwise there would not be quite so many people over here asking him about what it was like over there.

Then, as he turned the ignition key, the idea came and, like a light being switched on in a darkened room, his mood lifted. That was it. He would write his memoirs.

But there was a stream of slow-moving cars preventing him from backing out of the parking space and, by the time that someone stopped and flashed his lights to let him out, his neck was aching with strain of peering behind him. He waved grudging thanks and edged forward until he got to the lane which led to the exit. It was jammed with cars queuing to get out of the car park. He turned on the windscreen wipers and listened to the screech of vulcanised rubber as they smeared an arc of dust, oil, rain and bird crap across the glass. Another driver let him through, and he joined the next line as it inched forward. His mood lowered again. Christ, he thought, who the hell would want to read about the life of a solicitor? It's not as if my work had anything sensational about it; no murders or frauds or celebrity corruption cases, just well-paid administration of corporate structures and high end property deals. He was not even sure that he would get any satisfaction from writing about it. It was not as if he hankered after his working life; on the contrary, he was glad that he had retired when he did. This was a tedious experience, thought Grinder. It was bad enough having to trudge around a soulless supermarket looking for things that you couldn't find, whilst inane announcements broke into the dreadful music – why did they think that playing stupid pop songs would improve the experience, and why did the women have such asinine voices? – but it really took the biscuit (in the unlikely event that you could locate a packet of biscuits in the infernal confusion of aisles and overhead signs), that having paid for the bloody shopping you wasted more time getting out of the car park than you had spent inside the store. That was the trouble with modern life in Britain, things were so poorly organised, so little forethought went into planning and here he was, stuck in a traffic jam when, he now realised, he rather badly needed to have a pee. It was just one instance of the many things which he had found irritating since he had come back. It was raining hard now, and the water was beginning to clean the muck from the windscreen. And then the light came on again. Bugger the memoirs, he thought; what was needed was a book about the things that annoyed him. He could write proper sentences, unlike so many journalists, and he had a sense of humour of a sort, so maybe someone, somewhere might want to read what he had to say and, even if no-one did, it might be a satisfying way of venting his thoughts. That was it: he would write a small book about what made him angry.

CHAPTER 2

'F'ank, sweetie, do you get your shopping?'

'Not really, Winnie. I couldn't find what I was looking for.'

'That's a shame. O.K, how about maybe I start cooking?'

'Fine. I'm going upstairs to the study. I've got something I want to do.'

'O.K., F'ank. See you later.'

Grinder went and sat at his desk. Through the window he could see the row of Georgian houses on the other side of Suffolk Terrace. The plane trees were beginning to shed their golden-brown leaves which lay in damp clumps on the pavement in what had become late afternoon sunshine. An elderly woman, dressed in a well-cut, navy blue coat and pale blue scarf was pulled along by her red setter which paused from time to time to examine the base of a tree and sniff it. In a window immediately across the road from him and at the same level, a curtain twitched and there was a flash of reflected light.

Grinder pulled open a drawer and took out an exercise book, a pencil, a ruler and a rubber. He opened the book at the first page, drew a straight line near the top and wrote "A Book of Irritation". He thought for a moment or two and then began to write an introduction.

Not bad, for a start, he thought. But there were so many things that annoyed him about modern life in Britain that they formed a miasma, a background theme against which he was now playing out his existence. He had not previously tried to list them and he did not now know whether it would be better to do so or whether it would be simpler and more effective, at least for its therapeutic benefit, to go with the flow of his thoughts. After a short period of contemplation, during which he gazed from his desk across the road and thought he saw the flash of light again at the same window, he decided that a stream of consciousness would suit his mood best. He would start with what had frequently irritated him, television production and, on the previous evening, and to Winnie's perplexed concern, had him shouting at the screen.

The smell of a roast had begun to drift up to the study. He looked at his watch. It was already nearly 7 o'clock, well after the usual hour for his first gin. He put his pencil down and massaged his aching fingers. It had grown dark outside and the street lights were on. A light rain was pattering against the window. He would leave the topic of post-production to another day. He turned off his desk light and went downstairs.

'That smells good,' he said as he went to the cupboard and poured himself a drink. Winnie had already brought in a tumbler with ice and lemon in it. 'That really does smell good, Winnie.'

She was still in her early thirties, small and delicate. Her hair was cut in the page-boy style which suited the small Chinese face so well and which Frank had always found irresistible. Her hands, which until they had moved back to England, had, aside from cooking, performed hardly any domestic chores, were immaculately manicured. He had noticed her hands when they had first met at a wedding party in the International Grand Hotel; later, that evening, she had told him that she did not like her job and wanted to work in a lawyer's office.

'I follow the recipe. You know, in the book by Oliver Twist.'

'Oh, really?'

'Yeah, quite easy,' she said.

'Aren't you going to have a drink?'

'Yeah, maybe,' and she went into the kitchen and came back with a Coca Cola.

They sat together in companionable silence. Then she said 'Supper not long now'.

And then:

'Because...'

Frank sighed inwardly. If all the years amongst native Cantonese speakers had taught him anything, it was that this literal translation of the term *yan wei* was the harbinger of an announcement that he would not want to hear. His secretaries would greet him with 'Because... we did not file that defence in time', he would receive a call from his travel agent saying 'Because... all the flights are fully booked' and once he was telephoned by his bank: 'Mr Grinder?' 'Yes, speaking.' 'Mr Grinder, because... your account is overdrawn.'

'F'ank, because...I have invited my family to come and visit.'

'When did you invite them for?'

'Maybe, three weeks ago.'

'No, when did you invite them to come?'

'I told you, about two weeks ago.'

'Well, are they coming?'

'Yeah, they coming.'

'When are they coming?'

'On Sunday.'

'What, you mean in two days time?'

'On Sunday.'

'What! How many are coming?'

'Not many.'

'What do you mean, not many"?'

'*Bah-ba* he not coming.'

'Who's he?'

'My father, Ah-Leung. He can't come. Too busy in his shop. Says cannot find time for a long holiday.'

'What,' expostulated Frank. 'How long is a long holiday?'

'Because...maybe a month.'

Frank groaned inwardly, but tried not to upset his wife. It had, he knew, been a long time since she had last seen any of her relations.

'So, not your father. Well, who is coming?'

'*Mah-ma*. But she can't come by her own. English not good enough.' She hesitated, and then seemed to have nothing more to say.

'Well, who's coming with her?'

'Younger sister, Winsome,' Winnie replied.

'That's alright, she's very nice. I met her once, at dinner, do you remember, just before we were married? And, of course, she came to the wedding.'

'Yes, and she speaks good English. More better than me.'

'O.K. Your mother can have the spare room and your sister can sleep in the box room, if it's not too small for her. I'll clear some of the junk out tomorrow,' he said, somewhat relieved. 'As a matter of fact, I have been meaning to get rid of a lot of that stuff from there. It's been there since our furniture was shipped over and, anyway, it's mostly packing cases. It'll be a good opportunity to go through it and have a clearance session. I'll get started tomorrow morning. I should be able to get most of it to the tip, even if I have to make several trips in the car. You know, it's funny, but it takes something like a family visit to make you do something like that. You live with stuff for almost two years without noticing that you haven't used it and, if you haven't used it, then I say that you don't need it.'

'And Rambo' she said.

'What?'

'Younger brother, Rambo. He also coming.'

'Why,' asked Frank. 'Isn't he at college?'

'He got chuck out.'

CHAPTER 3

Saturday morning. Grey skies and drizzle again. Winnie had gone out early to buy something new to wear for her family's arrival, taking the car. A good time to get on with the little book. He carried his mug of coffee up to the study, and sat down. The exercise book was still open where he had left off yesterday evening. He had just written 'Post Production' when the 'phone rang.

'What?'

'Hallo, is that Frank?'

Pause.

'Oh, er, Frank, er, it's Aubrey...'

Another pause.

'...Aubrey, your brother-in-law.'

'Yes, I know who you are.'

'Yes, of course you do. Erm, how are you, Frank?'

'All right.'

'Good, good.'

A long pause.

'What do you want, Aubrey?'

'...erm, are you, busy at the moment, Frank?'

'Yes.'

'I mean, right at the moment, Frank, er, I didn't mean,

erm, in your life generally, I meant this morning. Have you got twenty minutes?'

'What do you want, Aubrey?'

'Well, it's a bit difficult, but something has happened and I wanted to have a word with you about it. Could I come and see you? Say, about 11.30. For coffee.'

'I suppose so.'

'Thanks, Frank. See you soon.'

As soon as he put the 'phone down, Grinder felt that familiar remorse that his brother-in-law usually caused him shortly after they spoke. It had not, he knew, been necessary to be quite so curt with him, but you could never get him onto the point or, once on, off it. Aubrey was what was now styled a 'Team Vicar' at a group of parishes at the suburban edge of Cheltenham. He had been married to Grinder's droopy younger sister, Celia, since before he had gone out East, and they had two portly sons who, from their early teens, affected waxed jackets and flat caps. If Grinder had ever wanted to distinguish between them, he would have found it difficult. His private collective name for the Spindle family was 'the Puddle'.

At least, there was still enough time to get something down and continue from where had had left off on the previous evening, before the visitation of the Reverend Brother-in-Law, M.A. Now that he had got started, it was better to use the computer.

The bell rang. Grinder looked up and saw that it was now raining hard. For a second, just a second, he relished the thought of leaving Aubrey to soak on the doorstep, but he got up from his desk and went downstairs.

His brother-in-law was wet. Grinder reflected that he had, from their first meeting, characterised him as more than averagely soggy, but this morning he was literally so. Sopping clothes hung from his gangling frame, and straggles of sparse, dun-coloured hair stuck to his forehead. He peered through the rain-blotched lenses of his glasses.

'What on earth has happened to you?' asked Grinder, as he opened the front door. 'Have you fallen into something horrible?'

The Team Vicar took off his spectacles and attempted to dry them with a sodden handkerchief. He stepped inside and began to soak the doormat.

'I came by bus and there was a long wait at the stop and, er, unfortunately, I got off at a stop too soon for your house and had to walk from there.'

'Why did you come by bus? Has Celia taken the car?

'No, not at all. She has gone with a friend to a coffee morning, I'm not sure where. No, when I went to the car, I realised that I had forgotten to bring an umbrella, so I went back to the house and when I got back to the car I found that I must have locked the door with the key still in the ignition.'

'How can you do that? I didn't think that's possible, Aubrey. You've got to use the key or the zapper from the outside to lock it, haven't you?'

'Well,' paused the vicar. 'Yes, erm, in theory. In point of fact, that is so. But there seems to be a fault with my car, because it happened once before, when I slammed the door and there was a sort of click, and then I couldn't open it again. On that occasion, I had to go and get the spare set of keys to get back into the car. I've been meaning to take it to the garage to have it looked at, but I did not, unfortunately, erm, get round to doing so. Rather remiss of me, I confess.'

'Why didn't you get the spare keys this time, then?' Frank asked, as always, puzzled by his brother-in-law's constant capacity to seek the least obvious solution to a problem.'

'Ah, that was the trouble. The front door slammed behind me and I couldn't get back into the house.'

'And,' said Frank, 'the house keys were on the same ring as the car keys...'

'Quite,' replied Aubrey.

'Forgive my asking you this,' interposed Frank, 'but don't you have a mobile 'phone?'

'I do. It's very difficult to perform the team ministry without one, I regret to say, these days.'

'And Celia, I know she's got one. She calls me from time to time.'

'Indeed so, she has one and is familiar with it. Texting, and everything.'

'Then didn't you...?'

'I couldn't ring her ...erm...'

'Because?'

'My dear Frank, how could I ring her when my mobile 'phone was on the front seat of the car? I always make it my good practice to put it on the front seat as soon as I get into the car, in case of emergencies. Of course, I don't answer the 'phone when I am at the wheel, but I find some convenient and safe place to stop if get a call and...'

'So, hang on, Aubrey,' interrupted Frank, 'you're telling me that, parked outside your house is your car with the key in the ignition, your front door key hanging from it...'

'And the back door key, I always keep a complete set, it makes good sense...'

'And your back door key' continued Frank, 'and your mobile 'phone.'

'Yes, that's right.'

'Well, don't you think that you should 'phone Celia and tell her to go home and unlock the car and get them out?'

'Why. It hadn't occurred to me to bother her. The car is locked, as you know.'

'But anyone could smash the window, get into your house, steal whatever they want and drive it all away in your car, even getting your mobile 'phone.'

'And my umbrella. I noticed, when I realised that I had locked myself out, that it was on the back window ledge of the car, after all. May I use your telephone, please?'

After he had tried her on her mobile, and got her voice message, the Team Vicar rang his home and spoke to his wife, who had just got in and was wondering where he was. The car was still outside and intact. Grinder heard him say 'No, I've gone for a walk, my dear, and am thinking about next Sunday's sermon, but could you get my 'phone and the keys from the car, please,' before he hung up.

He turned to Grinder. 'I would rather that Celia didn't know that I have come to see you. Or, in point of fact, it would be more accurate to say that I don't want her to know what this is all about.'

Grinder groaned inwardly. Experience had taught him that the twenty minutes that his brother-in-law had mentioned on the 'phone earlier was unlikely to be anything like that. Most people used the term as kinds of bait, as it was too short a period to justify an outright refusal to talk to them. He had lost count of the times, in his working life, that clients had booked a short session with him – 'all I need is a ten minute chat with Mr Grinder, just for some quick advice, perhaps before he starts his morning's appointments' – only for him to start wondering whether he would manage to get in his usual coffee break and, later, whether lunch would have to be abandoned. Twenty minutes? It normally took the Reverend Aubrey Spindle M.A. longer than that to get his hat and coat off.

'And Winnie – is she not to know either?'

The vicar paused in the process of peeling himself out of his dripping jacket and dropping it onto the mat.

'Ah…erm…I think that I'd rather that she isn't made, erm, privy to it, just for the moment, if you've no objection, Frank.'

'How can I have any objection? I've no idea what this is all about. Look, you'd better come upstairs to my study.'

But, of course, he did have an idea or, at least, a shrewd suspicion. All his time with Chan, Grinder, Yeung & Lam, he had managed to spend Sundays at the Gentlemen's

Recreation Club, or go horse racing, or have dinner in the evening with friends without being importuned for free advice. As soon as he returned to England, he seemed to have been transmogrified into the local branch of the Citizens' Advice Bureau. If what he suspected was true, this would not be the first time that Aubrey had sought his opinion on an area of law in which he was as ignorant as any layman. But Aubrey was not alone; Frank had recently ceased to use one of his local pubs for fear that he was doing more business on his side of the bar, albeit unpaid and unwillingly, than was being done on the other side.

Aubrey settled into the chair opposite Frank's desk. From his jacket, he produced a damp envelope from which he extracted a piece of printed paper. It was headed 'Gloucestershire Constabulary'. He passed it over to Frank who looked at it, and said,

'Well, this a Notice of Intended Prosecution issued under section 1 of the Road Traffic Offences Act, 1988'.

He nodded sagely. At least, he thought, he had demonstrated that he was literate.

Aubrey looked impressed.

'I thought that you would know what it was,' he said.

Grinder did not offer the opinion that anyone, presumably including a clergyman, who was able to read would have come to the same conclusion as to the document's nature.

'But it's not in your name; it's addressed to an Alistair Spindle. Is that a relative of yours?'

'Alistair is my elder son, your nephew.' There was a hint of frigidity in the vicar's tone.

'I'm sorry, of course he is,' replied Frank, struggling to remember what the other boy was called, or which one was which.

'Well, let's see what he appears to have done.'

Frank read on.

'Why, it's only speeding. Is he worried about losing his licence? Has he been caught before?'

The vicar inhaled, rather sharply. 'No certainly not. Alistair assures me that this is his first brush with the authorities and he is deeply, deeply ashamed of it.'

'As you know, I was a commercial lawyer all my life, and I don't know much about the sharp end of criminal law…' said Frank.

The Reverend M.A. cringed.

'…but I wouldn't have thought that he has anything much to worry about. It says here that he was doing 36 m.p.h. in a 30 zone and if he hasn't got any penalty points on his licence he won't get disqualified for that. It'll just be a fine.'

'No, I have tried to reassure him of that.'

'Well, what are you worried about? I'm always glad to see you, Aubrey,' Frank lied, 'but what is it that you want from me? Surely not my advice on this. Because if it is, I'd say that, assuming that he can plead guilty by post, he should do so.'

'As a matter of fact, I do want your advice, Frank. As I said, I think that Alistair is very embarrassed.'

'Well, he shouldn't be. Most youngsters would consider it a rite of passage.'

'Maybe so, but he was driving my car…'

'What, with the keys in it?'

Aubrey ignored the interjection. 'Well, it actually isn't my car, strictly speaking…'

'Aubrey, you don't mean to tell me that it's a stolen car. I am impressed. When did you steal it?

'Please, Frank, this is most serious. Although the car is mine to use, the funds for its purchase were raised by my parishioners and, strictly, it belongs to the Church. I have told him that if it gets into the press that an ecclesiastical car was involved in a motoring offence, well, Heaven only know what the consequences will be.'

'Look, Aubrey, I think that you're worrying unnecessarily. Let him plead guilty, pay the fine, keep quiet and forget about it. There's no reason for anyone, not even Celia, to know if you don't want her to. I wouldn't have thought that the press would be remotely interested.'

'That is a reassurance, I must say,' said the vicar. 'But would you mind talking to Alistair about it? As I say, rightly or wrongly, I have told him that it is very worrying.'

'Why don't you just tell him what I've said to you?'

'I cannot help thinking it would be for the best if it came directly from you. I sometimes wonder whether he takes me altogether seriously.'

Grinder resisted the temptation. Instead, he said,

'Look, this weekend's going to be pretty busy for me, but if you want to send him over later during the week, I'll have a chat with him.'

He got up from behind his desk and, after a pause and then a look of revelation, his damp brother-in-law took the hint. They went downstairs together just as Winnie was letting herself in. She looked, puzzled, at the small pond that had previously been the doormat recess, but said nothing.

'How are you, Winnie my dear?' said Aubrey. 'I'm just on my way out.'

'O.K. fine,' said Winnie.

Grinder considered whether to do the decent thing and offer to run his brother-in-law back to his home.

'And I'm just back upstairs,' he said. 'I'll be in my study'.

There was just time before lunch to add a grumble about historians on television who never use the past tense.

CHAPTER 4

On Sunday morning, Frank took a coffee up to his study. This might be the last time for a while that he would have a quiet moment in the house. Winnie had promised him that she would take her family out as much as she could (this promise had come as the emollient not long after the 'because') but he expected that there would be a domestic upheaval and that he would have to exercise some self-control. With a mixture of Martin Chuzzlewit and Zen Buddhism he tried to persuade himself that he might gain some merit from the experience of behaving kindly towards his in-laws, and that he would feel enriched by doing so successfully. In the meantime he would cherish the calm and get in another section of his book. There was just enough time, he hoped, before he and Winnie had to drive to London Airport, for him to deal with journalists' inaccuracies.

The telephone on his desk rang just as he was finishing and startled him; he picked up the receiver. Before he could say anything, a croaking, half-whispering voice spoke.

'Ullo, iss thet Frenk Grroindre?'

'What?' said Frank.

'I arsked iss thet Frenk Grroindre. Iss thet you, Frenk?'

'Yes, I'm Grinder,' he replied, wondering what the accent was.

'Who is that?'

'My name iss Theodore Van der Vuyl Nuthatch, but it iss easier for most pipple to coll me Theo. Lissen, I must spik to you. Iss verry, verry important.'

'What's all this about?'

'I need to mit you to tell you. Um not tokking on the phone.'

'Well, I can't talk to you now, I'm just about to go out and I won't be back till much later today. Who are you?'

'I tell you already, mon, um Theo.'

'If you don't tell me what this is about or, at least, who you are, I'm going to hang up and I certainly won't meet you.'

'O.K. lissen, um a private ditictiff and thet's all um going to say on the phone. Excipt thet iss in your interrists to let me tokk to you. Will you coll me beck litterr?

'Pardon?'

'I orsked you to rring me when you git beck 'ome. Heff you got a pin? Good. Thess iss moi numpre.'

Frank took a moment for interpretation and then jotted down the number on the bottom of the page that he had just written.

'O.K. I really must go now,' Frank said and he hung up. This is bizarre, he thought.

CHAPTER 5

The arrivals hall at Terminal 3 at Heathrow Airport was seething with noise. Drivers sent to collect passengers held up placards with the names of companies and passengers in block letters – ALPHA RESOURCE PROCESSING, Mr IVANOV, JAMES O'REILLY, Mr ABDUL KARIM. Several family groups crowded the barriers waiting to meet travellers from India, each comprising at least one grey-haired and sari-clad grandmother, two brothers, a sister and several small children, and a big-shot with a gold Rolex wristwatch and an impressive stomach. Others stood or leant in ones and twos, with small children who would, from time to time, break away to run, dashing amongst laden luggage trolleys and throw themselves at dazed-looking long-haul passengers, newly but not freshly arrived, hugging fathers returning from business trips and sisters from gap-year travels. Occasionally there was a traveller, peering round from behind piles of suitcases, disappointment turning to anxiety, searching for the person who was supposed to be there to meet him, and blocking the flow of the passengers behind him as he rummaged through his hand luggage for his mobile 'phone.

A woman of about thirty, pale and dishevelled, wearing jeans and a loose cheesecloth top, stood with two very young children, one in a pushchair, and a trolley piled high with suit cases, balanced on top of which was a brightly coloured, shiny bag, crammed and overflowing with a plastic bottle, a packet of biscuits, two soft toys, a pack of disposable nappies and a grubby towel 'Don't worry, Daddy will be here in a moment', she said. 'He's probably stuck in traffic'. A famous (in his own estimation) young Pinoy rock singer, with a black straw trilby perched at the back of his head and white silk shirt, black trousers and white loafers donned a pair of dark glasses, paused and looked around, disappointed by the absence of photographers for *The Philippines Daily Enquirer* for whom he had practised partially shielding his face with his hand and saying, 'No photo, no interview, till I'm at the Dorchester'; then he walked towards the Taxi sign.

Frank Grinder and Winnie were by now by the barrier, she peering at the labels on the cases of the stream of passengers as they came through under the 'Strictly No Entry' sign.

'What are you looking for?'

'Cathay labels'.

'They won't be here yet'

'But, sign says 'Landed at 16.02'.'

'Yes, but that's only five minutes ago.'

'O.K., so we here.'

'But they'll have to get through Immigration and then collect their luggage and go through Customs. They could be another hour yet.'

'Better we here now,' said Winnie, firmly.

Frank shrugged, and so they waited whilst the scene before them changed continuously and yet remained constant – the same roles, with different players; bronzed, fit-looking couples back from visiting families in Australia; suited businessmen returning home or coming to Britain for a meeting, families from all over Asia and America and Africa; more Indian families arriving and being met in large numbers; a few children travelling with airline escorts; small, grey-haired Chinese ladies over-towered by trolleys laden with packages encased in fraying, striped, plastic material, like wind-breaks, with boxed electrical goods balanced aloft, rice steamers and microwaves; overweight tourists wearing baseball caps and straw hats, still wearing the flip-flops and t-shirts in which they boarded the flight at some tropical airport; magnificent West Africans in brightly coloured head-wraps and caftans, immense alongside the other passengers; young couples returning from their honeymoons, still clinging to each other; perspiring Egyptians wheeling their luggage. Frank felt Winnie's body tense beside him. Her hand was waving frantically a few inches from her face, palm out, fingers spread wide.

'Mummiah, Daddi,' she called.

Coming towards them was a group of Chinese. The Wong Family. Ah-leung, Ah-ma, Rambo and Winsome. They pushed towards the barrier and hugged Winnie.

'F'ank,' she said, 'This are my family. My father, my mother, my younger brother, my little sister.'

'Yes, Winnie, but I didn't realise there would be four of them. I thought you said that your father wasn't coming?'

'No, we don't want to leave Daddi and I told you Rambo coming.'

'Yes, but how are we going to get them all into the car?'

'Because, we squeeze. And put cases on the roof.'

Rambo looked about nineteen. He had a shock of hair, dyed light brown at the front, sticking from underneath his baseball cap. He grasped Frank's hand.

'Don't worry, man, we're not Big Belly Wongs. We'll squeeze in.'

'Pardon?'

'No, we're Three-Stroke Wongs,' and he laughed, too loudly. Frank noticed a touch of an American accent and wondered whether this was an affectation or the result of nurture by Filipina housemaids.

Frank shook the old man by the hand and tentatively kissed his mother-in-law and sister-in-law on the cheek. It was odd that he had never met her parents before; but the wedding ceremony had been a low key affair, which took place not long after he had realised that he was smitten by his secretary; and Winsome had been the only member of her family present. He looked at Winnie's face, her eyes sparkling with pleasure at seeing her family, and thought what a very attractive woman she was. He often wondered why she had never suggested that he come with her on her not very frequent visits to see her family when he and she still lived in Hong Kong; he could see no cause for embarrassment now that they were all together. And Winsome really was aptly-named: a younger version of her sister, with a very fetching, demure downward glance.

And just like Winnie, she put her hand in front of her mouth when she laughed. This visit may not turn out to be too bad, he thought, as he ushered the party towards the lifts.

'Do your parents speak English?' he asked Winsome.

'Maybe a little. Mother better than Father.'

'But you do, I know that?'

'I do. Because, Rambo, he speaks it too much.'

Rambo guffawed again.

'So, are you all ready to drive home?' asked Frank, 'Or do any of you want to use the toilets before we set off?'

'Is there anywhere to buy something to eat here?' asked Rambo. 'I'm starving.'

'Didn't you eat on the plane?'

'Yeah, of course, but Winnie said it takes about two hours on the road, and I don't think that I can last that long.'

'I'll tell you what, let's get out of the airport and we'll stop at a service station on the way.'

'O.K, but not too long, please.'

A man in a well-cut sports jacket, with a small badge in the lapel, and neat grey trousers appeared wheeling a small suitcase towards the gap in the barrier. He wore rimless glasses and a dark blue silk tie. His greying hair was neatly brushed back from his forehead. A black leather bag was slung over one shoulder. As he strode out, looking for the yellow overhead signs for taxis a look of slight puzzlement crossed his face as he saw a cardboard sign with the words 'MR IVANOV'. He walked up to the man who was holding it.

'I am Ivanov,' he said.

'Mr Lev Ivanov?'

'Yes, I am Lev Semyonovich Ivanov.' His accent was just perceptible.

'Did you have a good flight, sir?'

'Yes, excellent, thank you. No delay.'

'That's good, sir. Can I take your bag?'

'That is very kind. I was not expecting to be met.'

'Oh, I was booked to collect you. Just follow me and I'll take you to the car. I'll have to pay for the parking first.'

At the car park, Rambo watched as Frank struggled to get the some of the suitcases onto the roof rack.

'Give me a hand, please,' Frank said.

'I'm very tired,' he replied. 'I didn't sleep on the plane. And I'm hungry.'

'Look, just put as much as you can in the boot and I'll manage with these.'

Rambo grinned, and slowly began to put the hand luggage in, one by one. Then he got in to the back seat of the car.

'It's not a very big car. It's going to be very tight.'

'I didn't realise that so many of you were coming. And, actually, it is quite a big car by British Standards. It's the biggest that Rover makes.'

'I thought you would have a Mercedes or a Bentley. Ah-ma says that you're a rich lawyer.'

'I'm not rich. And I'm not a lawyer any more. I'm retired. That's why your sister and I live in England.' He did not care to explain which of those conditions was the reason for his return. 'Look, just squeeze up and make room for your parents. I think that Winsome will have to sit on your lap.'

'Man, this is a small car,' groaned Rambo.

They all got in. Ah-leung and Ah-ma, looking dazed from the flight, sat beside Rambo; his younger sister managing, somehow, to pinch herself in so that she could sit on the back seat, compressed between her mother and brother. Winnie in the front passenger seat. Frank noticed how the car had sunk ominously.

'God, I hope that the suspension will bear all the weight,' he said to Winnie. 'I'm going to have to take it easily.'

'Not too slow,' said Rambo from the back. 'I need to eat something.'

Frank waited whilst a man in a black anorak, wheeling a suitcase, followed by a smartly-dressed man, walked in front and got into a car with a taxi sign on it, and then he, gingerly, drove to the barrier and inserted the ticket. The engine stalled; he restarted it and, listening for scraping sounds, began the journey out of the car park.

They reached the M4 motorway. The sun was just beginning to set as Frank turned westwards. He lowered the sun visor, but the glare managed to escape round the edges and bore into his eyes. Traffic was building up in both directions and a stream of heavy lorries thundered by on the next lane, trapping him behind a slow-moving van, bearing the slogan 'Our Solutions for your Logistic Issues'. He snorted and made a mental note of it, whilst looking for a gap in the traffic. After a long time, he saw what he thought was enough space for him to pull out and he indicated and moved the over-laden car sluggishly to his right; there was a flash of headlights and a blaring lorry horn and he swung back, behind the irritating signage.

'This is going to be slow going,' he said to Winnie. Her mother leant forward and spoke to her in Cantonese. Frank thought he recognised the word *chi-saw.* His heart sank.

'Because, Ah-ma says Daddi want to use the toilet.'

'Well, tell him I can't stop here'.

'And I'm hungry,' contributed Rambo.

'Tell them that we've got to wait till we get to a service area. Look, I was going to go onto the M25 and the M40, but the M25 might be snarled up, so I'll carry on along the M4 and we'll stop at the Reading Services.'

'What numbers you say I should tell them.'

'No, there's no need. I was just telling you. Just say that we'll stop at the first services we come to.'

'I think, maybe, it would be quicker along the M25 and the other one,' said Rambo.

'Have you ever been to England before, Rambo?' snapped Frank.

'No, but that's what I think.'

'Well, we're doing what I said.'

'O.K. you know best' replied Rambo. 'I suppose.'

There was more conversation in the back in Cantonese.

Rambo said 'Daddi wants to know how long.'

Frank could feel irritation rising, like dyspepsia. This is no good, he thought, I mustn't start off on the wrong foot. He looked at the reflection of Winsome in the mirror. She was smiling, calmly.

'Yes,' he said, after a pause, 'I understand how he feels. Would you tell him that it is difficult to say, because I don't know how bad the traffic is going to be but, at this rate, it should be about twenty minutes. Will he be alright till then?'

Rambo spoke to his father.

'Yeah, he says he will be O.K. and will think of fire and not water. But I don't know if I can last that long.'

'Why, do you need the lavatory as well?'

'No.'

Eventually, Frank managed to lumber the car into the middle lane and there they stayed, past the M25 junction, past Windsor Castle, through the edges of the Reading suburbs until they saw the blue and white sign 'Services 1 mile'. He pulled to the left and, with relief, said 'We're almost here.'

He drove into the crowded car park and reversed into a space, using his wing mirrors as the rear window was obscured by faces and by packages on the shelf. Rambo was already opening the rear door.

'Wait a minute,' said Frank. 'Who else wants to use toilets?'

There was a hurried conversation in the back. Winsome said 'I don't and nor does Ah-ma.'

'Do you, Winnie?'

'No.'

'O.K,' said Frank, 'I'll take your father and show him where it is. Come with us, Rambo; you'll be able to buy a sandwich at one of the shops. The newsagents sell them.'

It was only when they got out of the car that Frank realised how slowly Winnie's father walked. He couldn't have been that old, he'd got a late teenage son, after all, and was probably not much older than Frank himself, in fact, possibly younger, but he moved with that self-nurturing concern that sometimes affected Chinese when their children had grown up. He seemed not at all driven by the needs of his bladder; but Rambo was getting visibly agitated.

'Look,' said Frank, 'I don't think you need to wait for us. I'm sure that you'll be able to find W.H.Smiths. You just go ahead and get yourself something to eat and we'll see you back at the car.

'Thanks, Frank, you're a friend,' and Rambo ran off towards the buildings.

Frank realised that he had taken the old man by the elbow and was gently leading him through the parked cars. They went through the big glass doors and, very slowly, moved towards the lavatories. He realised that he, too, needed to go now and wondered how it would seem if he applied some forward pressure to the arm. Eventually, they got there.

Frank waited in the corridor for Ah-leung. Then, even more slowly than before, they made their way back to the car. The three women were standing outside, talking. Even before he opened the back door, he was aware of a repulsive smell. Sprawled on the backseat, with a contented grin on his shining face, Rambo was holding a cardboard box in which was a triple cheese-burger and a mound of chips. In his other hand was a half-litre tub of

Coca Cola and ice which he was slurping noisily down to the bottom through a straw.

Frank withdrew his head. He went to Winnie.

'The car is going to stink all the way back to Cheltenham,' he complained, 'and it'll probably take weeks to get rid of the smell. It's worse than fish and chips. What was that he said to me about not being 'Big Belly Wong'? What did he mean?'

'Our family name is Wong', said Winnie.

'I know that.'

'Well, you say Wong the same way but it can be written with two different Chinese characters. One looks like a man with two legs spread out and a big stomach and the other is three lines joined together by another. We are the one with three strokes. Not Big Belly.'

'Well, I can see that none of you have got big bellies, but Rambo deserves to have one. I hope it sneaks up on him when he's older.'

'Alright,' he said to the girls, 'are we all ready to carry on?'

And so they all got back into the car, Frank feeling that, somehow, there was now even less room at the rear, and that the car was even more laden, rejoined the motorway and headed towards the A34, Oxford and Cheltenham.

At Terminal 3 a man in his fifties had just come through the barrier. He wore a pale brown corduroy jacket with leather patches at the elbows and leather strips at the cuffs. His luggage was a rucksack, bulging with what appeared, from their shapes, to be books. His hair was fairly long and straggly and merged with his beard. He wore heavy, horn-rimmed glasses. He paused, and looked anxiously around and then pulled his bag off the trolley and opened the top, rummaging around until he removed a crumpled paper which he studied closely, having pushed his spectacles onto his forehead. He put them back and looked around again at the line of drivers' placards. He looked at the paper again.

There was a triple bell tone from the public address system.

'Mr Ivanov. Calling Mr Ivanov. Please make your way to the information desk.'

He looked around and then above his head, and saw a sign with the word 'Information' and an arrow. At the desk a young woman in a dark blue uniform was trying to help a group of people whose language she, evidently, neither understood nor could identify. She smiled hard and uncomprehendingly at them as she tried to push back a letter, handwritten in an unknown script, which they kept sliding over the counter to her. With a bright grin she repeated, slowly and deliberately 'I am so sorry, but I can't understand what you want.' Her expression softened with relief as he approached and she turned to him.

'May I help you, sir?'

'You have, mnym, mnym,' munching his words, 'message for me.'

'And you are?'

'Yes, I am Lev Petrovich'

'Let me see...no, I don't think we have a message for a Mr Petrovich'.

'But, mnym, you call me on radio just now'.

'No, the only person we called was for a Mr Ivanov.'

'Is me, Lev Petrovich Ivanov.'

'Are you sure?'

'Yes,' he replied patiently, 'I am sure I am me.'

'I think that I better have some identification. May I see your passport, please?

The group next to him passed the letter over the counter again and watched as he opened the top of his rucksack and produced a maroon covered booklet, bearing the word *ПАСПОРТ.* They nodded enthusiastically and began speaking volubly to him. He replied to the man who seemed to be in charge of the group and pointed, and they moved away. The desk clerk smiled dazzlingly at him.

'Would you mind telling me what they wanted?'

'They wish to know where casino is in airport.'

'What did you tell them?'

'I show them sign.'

'What sign? There isn't a casino here.'

'One with picture of roulette table,' and he pointed at a yellow sign.

'That's the prayer room. It's supposed to be a chapel. Well, never mind, they've gone. May I see your passport?

He passed it to her.

'There. My picture. Is me.'

She looked at the picture.

'Of course it's you. But I can't read the name.'

'Mnym, the name is English also.'

'But it doesn't say 'Petrovich'.'

'No. Says 'Lev' and 'Ivanov'.'

'But you said 'Petrovich',' her smile now in a fixed rictus.

'Please, I said 'Lev Petrovich Ivanov' and is me. Please, what is message?'

'Well,' she paused, 'I'm not sure...'

'Please, you call for Ivanov. I am Ivanov. My passport say 'Ivanov'. Why I come to your desk if not Ivanov?'

She seemed unimpressed by the logic, but then a better reason occurred to her.

'Well, I suppose, as no-one else has come up. I'll give it one more try to cover myself, though,' and she spoke into the microphone on her desk, summoning, by name, the man who was standing in front of her. She lingered for a moment with her hand on the mouthpiece. 'No-one else has answered, so I'll give it to you,' she said graciously.

She handed him a typed sheet of paper. He pushed up his glasses and read 'Lev Ivanov. Please take the Heathrow Express to Paddington and check into the Medved Hotel in Praed Street. A room has been booked for you. Will meet you in the lobby at 20.00'.

CHAPTER 6

It was already dark when Frank turned the car into Suffolk Terrace and pulled onto the driveway. A fine drizzle had started and the reflection of the yellow street lights gleamed on the boot and roof. An acrid, ominous smell of scorched shock-absorbers had begun to compete with the cheeseburger and he was glad to get out. He stood by the driver's door for a moment, stretching his back and turning his neck. As he did so, he noticed a light go off in an upstairs window across the road.

Winnie got out and opened the rear passenger door.

'Come out, we're home,' she said in English. 'Come look at our house.'

Rambo, Winsome, Ah-ma all struggled through the other door. The old man remained where he was.

'Come on, Daddi, *fai-dih, fai-dih*.' He did not move.

'*Yah-plaih*, Daddi-ah, come into the house. We eat soon.'

Still no movement.

Frank looked into the back of the reeking car. The old man was wedged back in the corner, upright, eyes closed. Christ, he thought, it must have happened on the journey and didn't have room to fall forward. He leant in, but recoiled from touching the body.

'*Aiyeeah*, this is a BIG house,' Rambo was shouting. 'You live in all of it?' Winsome said something to him in Cantonese and they both laughed.

'Mummiah, what do you think of this house?' said Rambo.

'Wah, is really big.' For a moment, Frank wondered why she had not spoken to him at all since they had met but was now speaking to her son in English; but more pressing matters came to the fore. He stepped back and walked round the front of the car.

'Winnie,' he said quietly, 'come away from your mother. I need to talk to you.'

'What for, F'ank?'

'Your father.'

'Yeah?'

'I think there's something the matter with him. We've got a problem.'

'What do you mean?'

'Well, you have a look at him.'

They both went to the side of the car and looked in. The old man had not moved. Frank noticed that his glasses had slipped and lay crookedly astride his nose; his mouth hung partially open. Frank put his hand into the car but, again, hesitated.

'Winnie, what do you think?'

He moved back, respectfully, to allow her to lean into the car. Gingerly, she stretched out her hand, paused, and then touched the old man's forehead.

'Wah!' he shouted. 'What you want? Why you wake me?'

Startled, Frank felt his heart thumping. It was only after a few moments that it sunk in that Winnie's father, apparently, could also speak English.

'Daddi, we're here. We're home. You get out now.'

Ah-leung straightened his glasses and cleared his throat noisily.

'*Sik fan, ma?*'

'Yes, Daddiah, we going to eat. We going to have supper now.'

With surprising agility, the old man got out of the car. Without looking round him, he walked briskly up the steps to the front door, waiting to be let in. Rambo, Winsome and their mother joined him. As soon as Winnie unlocked it, they pushed into the house.

'Would you mind giving me a hand with the luggage?' called Frank.

Rambo put his head out of the doorway. 'Later, after we've eaten,' he said.

The drizzle was turning to steady rain as Frank struggled to unclip the elastic luggage cords from the roof rack and prevent the metal ends from leaping across the top of the car. With stinging fingers, he slid the suitcases to the edge and eased them, one by one, towards his chest and then to the ground. Then he opened the boot and took out the rest of the cases. A sharp pain began to spread in his upper body as he lugged and slid them across the drive to the porch. Breathless, he went back to the car to lock it. The remains of Rambo's snack would have to wait until tomorrow. Someone had shut the front door. Fumbling with aching, wet hands he found his keys, opened it and began to shift the cases into the hallway.

The aroma of cooking greeted him, and laughter and Cantonese, machine-gun chatter. He was always astonished at the speed with which Winnie could get a meal on the go. From the smell, it seemed as if the rice had already steamed and the vegetables and chicken were ready. He looked into the kitchen; seated round the long pine table, his wife's family was eagerly watching her as she ladled out the rice into bowls.

'Ah F'ank', she said, glancing across at him. 'Supper's ready. Sit down.'

'Actually, I'm not very hungry.'

Rambo looked up at him and gave him a quizzical stare from under the peak of his baseball cap, but could say nothing as he was already holding his bowl to his lips and shovelling rice into his mouth with chopsticks.

'No, look, I'll go up to the study. I have some things to do. Maybe I'll make myself a sandwich later. This way, it'll give you a chance to catch up with your family. And I'll let you sort out whose sleeping where. I'll see you all later. Oh, Rambo, the cases are all in the hallway, so I'll leave it to you to take them upstairs when you know where you're all going. See you all later.'

Rambo, nodded at him through a mouthful of soya chicken. The others all waved, 'O.K. Bye-bye.'

At last, thought Frank, I might get in a bit more of the book. He went upstairs sat down at his desk and turned on the Anglepoise lamp and then his computer. As he was waiting for it to boot up the telephone rang. He waited, hoping that Winnie would pick up the 'phone in the kitchen, but she was, obviously, too involved with her family. It was odd that she usually left it to him to answer when he was in the house. She was quite confident of her English and it wasn't, anyway, as if all calls were for him; she had made quite a few friends, amongst both English women of her age and in the local Chinese community. After about five rings, he picked up the receiver.

'Yes.'

'Hello, Frenk, why effen't you colled me? This iss Theo.'

Frank remembered the baffling conversation earlier that day.

'Theo, I told you that I was going to be out all day.'

'Yiss, but you'ff bin beck for quite a fahl.'

'Quite a what?'

'A fahl.'

'What?'

'Corn't you onderrstond English, mon? Doppleyew, haitch, oy, ell, ee,' he explained, and added, audibly, '*Die hel en stront*, this iss luk tokking to a orff-vet.'

'Look,' said Frank, 'I'm pretty busy at the moment. And did you just call me a half-wit?'

'Nah, Oi sed you'rre luk vun. Oi dudn't say you vere vun. But lissen, Oi tell you that we need to tokk. Ven con vee mit?'

'Pardon. Oh! Possibly tomorrow. I don't know. But, hey, how did you know how long I've been home?

'Oi sorre you.'

'You what?'

'*Stront*! Oi said Oi sorre you.'

'No, I understood what you said; I just want to know how you knew what time I got back.'

'I already tolt you, um a private ditictiff, I know diss dings; iss my job.'

'Did you see me?'

'Lissen, et dussn't metterr, I just want a mitting.'

'O.K. Look, I'll call you tomorrow morning.' Frank glanced at the paper on his desk. 'I've still got your number. Please don't ring me again this evening; I've got a lot to do. We'll arrange something tomorrow.'

'Eff you don't, arl coll you again to rremoind you. Iss forr yourr binifit.'

'Right,' said Frank. 'Good night.'

He wasn't certain whether he was more perplexed than disturbed, but it certainly was a bit unsettling. However, he was beginning to find that writing had a something of a calming effect on him, and so he turned to the fruitful topic of clichés in television drama.

After a while he looked at his watch. It was nearly 9.30 pm. He saved what he had written, and turned off the computer. He went across to the window. It was still raining. The light across the road had come on again. He realised that he was now quite hungry.

Winnie was in the kitchen, clearing away the remains of the meal. The others had all gone.

'I'm sorry, Winnie, that took me longer than I thought. I meant, at least, to say good night to your family.'

'No problem. They were all tired. Gone to bed. How about you want me to cook something for you?'

'No thanks,' he said, 'I'll just make myself a cheese sandwich. That will do me, and an apple.'

Winnie looked pityingly at her husband. You think you know the *gweilo*. You live amongst them and even marry one of them. She sighed and wondered how they managed to get by on so little food.

CHAPTER 7

Frank was at his desk early the next morning. He felt quite pleased with the progress he had made the previous evening; the bit was between his teeth and he felt ready to tackle the next topic – on the misuse of the English language – but he felt uneasy about getting carried away by it and appearing (well, actually, more than appearing) to ignore Winnie's family. But there was another short subject – uncontrolled children – which he could probably manage to finish before breakfast. And he must not forget to ring this Theo fellow.

He went downstairs. They were all at the kitchen table, coming to the end of what looked like an enormous breakfast. The remains of bacon and eggs were stuck to the plates and they were now attacking a large pile of croissants which Winnie must have got out of the freezer last night.

'F'ank, you come down too late. Maybe you want me to make you some breakfast?'

'No thanks, love,' he replied, 'I had a coffee when I got up this morning. And a yoghurt. That's enough for me.'

Winnie's family all looked up at him, the same astonished expression on each face.

'You know, you got to take care of that old body of

yours,' said Rambo. Frank was preparing himself to go into his familiar explanation, that the metabolism of the occidental was different from that of the Chinese when he was spared. The telephone rang.

'I'll get it, it's for me' he said, thinking how persistent Theo is.

'Yes, I was going to call you. I told you I would,' he spoke sharply at the 'phone.

'Er, were you, um, I mean did you? In point of fact, I have no recollection,' said Aubrey.

'Oh, it's you.'

'Oh dear, you sound disappointed.'

'Not at all,' lied Frank, 'I'm pleased to hear from you, as always. It's just that I thought it might be somebody else. Somebody I promised to call this morning.'

'Er, yes, that's always happening to me. I forget to ring someone back or I make an appointment but omit to, er, as you would say, jot it down and then its slips my memory. Indeed, only last week I was supposed to meet the Churchwarden to discuss the state of the roof and whether any repairs were needed immediately (I expect that they will be) and even though it was really a rather important matter, as I am sure that you would, um, agree, I hadn't written down where or when we were seeing each other and I had it in the back of my mind that it was to be in the vestry on Saturday morning and he rang me on Friday to ask where I was and, in point of fact, I should have been in the churchyard then. So I can well understand your predicament.'

'It's not a predicament' Frank said curtly. 'The man is

a bit of a nuisance and I said that I would call him back and I will, but I thought that he was getting impatient.'

'Yes, I know, I often find that people get impatient with me in similar circumstances.'

'Aubrey, I told you that I wanted to call someone. What is it that you want? Do you want to have a chat with my father-in-law, perhaps?'

'No. No certainly not. Well, it's not that I don't want to talk to him. In fact, I'm sure that it would be very nice to have a chance to have a conversation with him. I'm sure that he is a charming gentleman. But isn't Winnie's family in Hong Kong?

'No, they arrived here yesterday. Are you sure you don't want to talk to him?' Frank savoured an impious image of the Team Vicar M.A. and Ah-Leung exchanging observations on the salient problems confronting the world.

'Are they? I do hope that they had a good flight. It must be very tiring coming all that way. I remember when Celia and I had our trip to the Holy Land we were quite exhausted by the journey. And the flight from Hong Kong is much longer.'

'Yes, I rather suppose it is.'

'Indeed, er, it must be. What is it? It must be at least double.'

'Yes, at least. What do you want, Aubrey?'

'Ah, yes, I'm so sorry. In point of fact, you may remember my talking to you about Alistair.'

'Yes.'

'Well, I wonder if it would be convenient if I were to

bring him over to see you tomorrow. I really would like him to have the benefit of your sound advice before his problem weighs too heavily on him.' He pronounced the word 'problim', a habit picked up, no doubt, at theological college and now ingrained after being much exercised in the pulpit. 'I would so much like to have him properly prepared before the, um, inevitability of his having to disclose it to his mother. And before it gets into the media.'

'Look, I told you, it's not going to get into the press.'

'But, Celia. I greatly fear that she will be very annoyed…' The thought of his sister inspiring any form of dread intrigued him. She could be frightened by a lettuce. Frank was impressed that there were any people who might be in awe of her, even though, in order to achieve that state of affairs, she had to marry one and give birth to the others.

'Aubrey, I'd like to help, as you know, but there may be a bit of a difficulty about tomorrow. Hang on a moment…' and he put his hand over the mouthpiece.

'Winnie, what are you planning to do tomorrow?'

'Because, I was going to ask. Maybe, tomorrow, I take the car.'

'Where do you want to go?'

'I thought I take Ah-ma, and Rambo and Winsome to the seaside. That O.K.?

'What about your father?'

'He said he not want to go. I already ask him. He'll stay here. Maybe there's racing on teewee.'

Frank seized his opportunity.

'That's fine. If you father doesn't mind being left, I can get on with some work. But can you take my nephew with you?'

'Yes. Company for Rambo.'

'Good idea. Where do you want to take them?'

'That Weston place. Where you took me before.'

'Sounds good.' He took his hand away from the 'phone.

'Aubrey.'

'Yes, I'm still here. I, er, hope that this isn't causing, how shall I say, domestic inconvenience.'

'No. Not at all. But Winnie is taking her family to Weston for the day and she wondered whether your son would like to come along.'

'Well, it could only be Alistair as Percival has his cello lesson after lunch. At least, I think he does. I'm sure I've made a note of it. Well, fairly sure.' Not for the first time, Frank wondered what inspired his sister and the vicar to burden their younger son with that name. Perhaps Percival, was the patron saint of the incurably timid.

'No, there wouldn't be room in the car for both of them. But if you got here early, I could have a chat with Alistair before they set off.' Things were looking up: he would be able to fulfil his promise to talk to the boy, then get rid of him in short order; he would demonstrate consideration for Winnie and her family by letting them go on their jaunt whilst he minded the old man; and he would be able to get in some real work on the book.

'Indeed. And I'm sure that Alistair would find it a most rewarding experience. It will be extremely, er, educational, one might say, erm, for him to spend some time in the company of young people who are from a, how shall I put it, different, er, er, um, cultural complexion…'

'Aubrey, come on, I never put you down as a racist.' Frank chortled to himself.

'No, no, no, of course I'm not.'

'But you were talking about their skin colour.'

'Perhaps that was an infelicitous choice of word. I meant, of course, their cultural background. The fact that they, er, might, um, possibly be described as, different, that is to say…'

'Chinese?'

'Quite.'

'Aubrey, you don't have leanings towards any organisation that I wouldn't approve of, would you?'

'Frank, how could you even suggest such a thing? It is all a misunderstanding, based on an unfortunate, one might almost say, yes, I do say, regrettable use of…'

Frank decided that the vicar-baiting had gone on long enough. More importantly, he wanted to get him off the 'phone.

'Don't worry, Aubrey, I won't tell Celia. Can you get him round here at, say, about nine? I'll be here and we'll have our chat.'

'That is very good of you,' replied a more relaxed Spindle, 'and it will fit nicely into my schedule, as I'm due at a conference in that big hotel just outside Cheltenham at ten. It's definitely ten. I wrote it down.'

'Is that to do with the Church?'

'No, no. It's horticultural. Or, rather, agricultural. Or I suppose one might postulate that it is a blend of the two.'

'I didn't know you were interested in farming. I thought that your flock was human. Have you got some sheep?'

'No, no. It's doesn't concern ovines. Or bovines.' Aubrey paused to emit an archly stifled laugh, evidently considering that he had been very witty.

'Well, what's it about?' asked Frank, intrigued in spite of himself.

'The cultivation of *beta vulgaris*.'

'What on earth is that?'

'Erm, it's beetroot. That's its Latin name.'

'Good God, oh, I'm sorry, bugger me, I didn't know you were interested in beetroot. You do lead an exciting life.'

'Do I detect a note of sarcasm there, Frank?'

'No, just surprise.'

'Well, you shouldn't be surprised. Beetroot has many qualities. It is a rich source of antioxidants and protein and its nutritional benefits are such that the Church has a great interest in promoting its cultivation in parts of the world where people are deprived because of their cultural disadvantages...'

'Aubrey!'

'No Frank,' he replied sharply. 'This is nothing to do with the colour of people's skin. This is entirely a matter of poverty and lack of education. It can apply to anyone of any ethnic group, as, er, I believe, you well know.'

'Oh, I follow. The Church takes the view that if everyone eats enough beetroot we'll end up the same colour, and then we'll all love each other.'

'Frank, I really do not think that this is a matter for drollery. There is much hardship in the world and undernourishment is the cause of a great deal of it and...'

'Yes, I see, Aubrey', interjected Frank. 'Look, I really must make that 'phone call. I'll see you tomorrow when you bring the boy,' and he put down the receiver.

All this exchange had taken place in the kitchen, against a background of Cantonese. Frank thought it would be best to go up to his study to make the call to Nuthatch. After one ring, the 'phone was answered.

'Yiss, Van der Vyl.'

'Am I speaking to Theo?'

'Yiss.'

'I thought that your surname was Nuthatch.'

'Thiss morning, iss Van der Vyl.'

'It's Frank Grinder here.'

'Yiss.'

'You wanted me to call you.'

'Yiss.'

'So I'm calling you.'

'Yiss.'

'You're not being very communicative today.'

'Lissen, mon, volls heff irrse.'

'What?'

'*Die hel.* Look, snooperrs. Iffsdropperrs.

'Oh, walls have ears.'

'Iss vot Oi said.'

'So?'

'So, vee mitt. Today iss O.K.?'

'Well, I'm pretty busy, but I could manage a short while around lunchtime.'

'Foin. Mebbe, vee mitt at the pop you go to.'

'What, you mean 'The Unicorn'?'

'Yiss.'

'How do you know which pub I go to?'

'I toll you, iss moi job.'

'Can you get there for lunchtime? Are you in the area?'

'Yiss. Acrrorss the strritt. See you at tvulff.'

Frank looked at his watch. Was there time for one more short topic? He could make a start, at least. As the Canto-chatter filtered up from downstairs, he sat at his computer and put down his thoughts on chewing gum.

CHAPTER 8

The hotel was not quite in Praed Street, but in a gloomy mews, off a side road, which did not even have the help of newsagents, cafés or printer-cartridge shops to relieve its dismal appearance. It was a three storey building which had been converted from a late nineteenth century house. After leaving Paddington Station, it had taken Lev Petrovich several enquiries and false turns before he had found it. The sign outside said both 'Medved Hotel'and 'ГОСТИНИЦА МЕДВЕДЬ'. He was slightly surprised to see this, but also reassured. Strange, he thought, to give it such a name. His rucksack was now feeling very heavy after his having trudged it up and down trying to locate the hotel and it was with an effort that he climbed the steps to the front doorway.

Inside, the reception consisted of a small desk made of dark wood, behind which a fat, bald man in a shabby blue suit sat reading an English tabloid newspaper.

'I was told room has been reserved,' he said. 'In name Ivanov.'

'Yep. Sign here, mate. '

'Do wish see my credit card?'

'Nope. It's all been taken care of. Everything will be charged to the bloke who booked it.'

'Everything?'

'Yep. This is your key. Best to drop it off when you leave the hotel.'

Lev Petrovich was not sure that he understood whether he meant just when he checked out, but was now too tired to carry on much conversation in English.

'Please, do you speak Russian?' he asked the fat man.

'Nope. Why should I?'

'Because, mnym, signpost in Russian.'

'Oh, no, that's just the owner. Him and his missus are Russkies, I mean, Russian.'

'Is good, thank you,' said Lev. 'Is there elevator?'

'Yep, but it's not working. Never mind, your room's only one flight up. Staircase is over there,' and he pointed down a dimly-lit corridor.

Lev struggled his bag up to his room. It was small and sparsely furnished, with a rust-stained washbasin in the corner. Floral wallpaper. Faded prints of fox-hunting scenes hung on the walls. He put his rucksack on the floor, kicked off his shoes and lay on the bed; he would just have a rest before finding out where the lavatory was.

The telephone beside his bed rang. He woke with a start and felt the nausea of interrupted sleep. It had become dark outside, but there was enough street light coming through the window for him to be able to find it.

'Hallo, yes.'

'There's a couple of blokes down here want to see you.'

'Tell them I come in minute.'

Downstairs, standing by the small desk were two men.

They were both in their forties, one with a dark, almost southern European complexion and the other fairer. Both were carrying briefcases. Apart from their colouring, there was a sameness about their appearance and an anonymity which would have made it difficult to identify them afterwards. They approached Lev Petrovich as he came along the corridor.

'Mr Ivanov?' said the darker of the two, and extended his hand, 'I am Mike Green and this is John Black.' The other moved forward and also shook Lev's hand as a momentary look of surprise passed across his face.

'I understand that you speak very good English,' said the one calling himself Green.

'Mnym, mnym, is good, I hope.'

'This isn't your first visit to England on a trip of, er, this nature?'

'Of course.'

'Sorry, do you mean you have or haven't been here before?'

'I have. Before, I go to another conference. How you call? Mnym, a symposium.'

'What?'

'A symposium. A conference of scientifics.'

'Well, that's a bit different from this, isn't it?'

'No, it was also about production of beetroot. We have much expertise in Russia.'

'Oh', said Green, 'I get it. Beetroot!' and he smiled, and nodded at Black, who smiled knowingly at Lev. 'That's very clever.'

'No, is just branch of science,' said Lev.

'I can see that we're going to get on very well,' said Green. 'But let's not go into things now. You must be very tired. John and I only wanted to make sure that you had arrived all right and to touch base with you. You don't think that anyone saw you arrive, do you?'

'Well, yes, London is full of peoples and there were many in street.'

'Oh, I like your sense of humour,' exclaimed Green. 'We really are going to do business. But look, you get yourself something to eat and have a good night's sleep and we'll call for you tomorrow morning. I would suggest that we took you out for a meal, but we don't want to attract attention, do we? There's lots of small places to eat around here, and I'm sure you'll be O.K.'

'So what time you come tomorrow?'

'Let's say around ten.'

'So, how far is Cheltenham from London? How long it take?'

'Why? Have you got someone to see in Cheltenham? Are you combining business with pleasure on this trip?'

'No, mnym, but conference in Cheltenham. Perhaps I not say it properly.'

'No, you said 'Cheltenham' O.K, but conference, what conference?...oh, I get you. That's good,' and Green laughed and nodded at Black again. 'See you tomorrow, and I hope that you sleep well.'

They both shook hands with him and walked to the doorway. Lev, feeling that he had not quite understood what had passed between them, put it down to his tiredness. He went up to his room for a wash, brushed his hair and beard, found his wallet and went out into the night in search of something to eat.

Lev Semyonovich Ivanov settled back in his seat, behind the driver. His initial surprise that they had sent a car for him soon subsided into a feeling of comfort. It was a very pleasant change from the usual arrangements at airports, when he had to find his own way to the usual nondescript, dismal hotel. A four hour flight and with a three hour time difference could be quite tiring and it really was very pleasant to have the stress taken away. His clients were generally so obsessed with cautiousness; he had grown used to the first encounter being in some furtive corner, away from the public gaze. This was a relaxing variation of the usual routine. His eyelids became heavy and he shut them for a moment.

The driver's voice woke him.

'Sorry, I'm going to have to take it slowly, sir, the sun's dazzling me,' he said.

'Excuse me?'

'I said that the sun is so strong that I'm having to go slowly. It's got below the sun visor.'

'That's all right. I am not in a hurry.'

'That's good, sir. It'll be better soon. We should get you there in under an hour and a half from here.'

Lev Semyonovich was now fully awake. They were on a motorway and the sun was shining very bright ahead of them. They were travelling westwards.

'I'm sorry, why are we going in this direction? I think London is east of Heathrow Airport.'

'It is, sir, but we're not going to London.'

'Where are you taking me?' he asked, with a slight feeling of alarm.

'It's a conference centre, well a hotel, just outside Cheltenham.'

'A conference centre?'

'Yes, sir.'

Lev Semyonovich studied the back of the driver's head and then his face in the mirror. He seemed straightforward enough.

'Are you sure? It seems a strange place to meet the clients.'

'I've no idea about that, sir. I'm just a taxi driver. I don't even know who you're clients are. I was just booked to collect you and take you to the hotel.'

'Who booked you?'

'It was the hotel. I do quite a lot of work for them.'

'So, where is your company?'

'I'm on my own, sir. I'm based in Cheltenham.'

This is all very puzzling, thought Lev, but he felt more confident as the driver spoke. He appeared to be honest, and had not said anything threatening. He realised that he was leaning forward in the seat. He sat back.

'Perhaps I have time for a little sleep before we arrive. It has been a long flight. My body clock tells me that it is getting towards bedtime.'

'Of course, sir. I'm sorry if I disturbed you. I'll let you know when we are there.'

'Thank you.'

It was dark when the car pulled into the driveway of the hotel.

'We're here, sir'.

Lev Semyonovich was already awake. They were outside a large white building, standing on its own. Beside the doorway was an illuminated sign: 'Madrigal Hotels, Cheltenham Country House and Conference Centre.' The driver took his case from the boot and escorted him to the reception desk.

'Have a good stay, sir, and I'll see you at the end of the conference.'

Lev found a ten pound note and proffered it. The driver made the universal gesture, hand raised to signify reluctance to accept, without meaning it.

The lobby was large and well-lit. The reception area consisted of a long, light-coloured wood counter, rising from an expanse of pale carpet, and several comfortable looking and new easy chairs. There was a large arrangement of gerberas and white calla lilies on a table in the middle. Behind the counter were a young man and a young woman in smart uniform.

'I am Ivanov', he said to the young woman. 'Is there a message for me? Is someone to meet me here?'

'Mr Ivanov,' she replied brightly. 'You're here for the horticulture conference, aren't you? I don't think that there are any messages for you.' She looked towards the young man, who shook his head.'

'I don't think that there's anything to worry about,' she went on. 'The conference proper doesn't start till Tuesday morning, but there is a get-together of the principal speakers tomorrow evening. That will probably be in the Festival Room. We'll show you where that it is tomorrow.'

This was unlike any first encounter Lev Semyonovich Ivanov had ever known.

'You're in room 207. We'll have your bag taken up to your room. Would you like to reserve a table in the restaurant or would you prefer to have room service?'

'I will have a wash first and then will decide,' said Lev.

'Well, just let us know and we'll be delighted to oblige. Would you like a morning call and a newspaper?' and they both flashed smiles at him.

CHAPTER 9

'The Unicorn' was on the corner of two white-fronted Regency terraces. It was not exactly Grinder's 'regular' – he would not have liked to have been thought of as an habitué of any particular pub – but its small size and quietness appealed to him and he had occasionally dropped in for a solitary beer in the evenings before supper. For some reason he had never taken Winnie there and so it provided him with moments of nostalgia, a reminder of his life as a young man before he had answered that advertisement. The bar was an old-fashioned wooden counter, and the well-worn tables and chairs had a shabby dignity which he found comforting. Come to think of it, he might have become a regular without realising it, as he always sat at the same table, in the corner, and took the same chair. He pushed open the door, went up to the bar and ordered a half a pint of Campden bitter.

'Ah, *Côtes de Cotswolds*, certainly, Sir,' said the irritating landlord. 'And how are we today?'

Frank was reminded why he did not come into the pub more often, and he paid in silence and turned toward his table. Sitting in his chair was a gaunt man of about fifty, wearing a slate-grey anorak. He had on old-fashioned horn-rimmed glasses, which partially covered extraordinarily bushy eyebrows. He had a pint glass of beer in front of him. Frank began to move away.

'Pssstt!' said the man.

'Pardon?'

'Oi said 'pssstt', iss me, Frenk.'

'Are you Mr Nuthatch?'

'Ass a metter of vect, now, Oi em.'

'I wasn't expecting you here yet,' said Frank, glancing at his watch, 'I thought I'd get here early.'

'Me too.'

'How did you know it was me when I came in? Have you been keeping watch on me?'

Van der Vyl said nothing.

'Lissen, Oi toll you, coll me Theo.'

'O.K, Theo. Just tell me this: did you choose this seat for any particular reason?'

'Well, iss quiet, and this iss vere you usually sit.'

'How do you know that? I've never seen you in here before. Were you in disguise?

'No, but maybe Oi em in disguise now.' He looked round at the empty bar, and then whipped off the glasses, taking the eyebrows with them. Then he put them back on. 'Just sit down, pliss.'

Frank took the seat opposite him.

'Look, Mr...er.. Theo. Please tell me what this is all about. I must say that I'm not comfortable about all this. What is it that you want?

Theo swept the bar again through the spectacles and leant forwards.

'Oi don't vont anything. Except to prevoorrn you.'

'Prevoorn?'

'*Ach, die hel*, to toll you, to vorn you, to teep you orff.'

'What about?' in spite of the ludicrousness of the figure across the table from him, Grinder was beginning to feel uneasy.

'Am I in some sort of danger?' he asked.

'Not rreelly, daincher, not fizzikol, no, but it could be comprromising for you and also for your voyff.'

'My what?'

Van der Vyl Nuthatch sighed.

'De Choiniss leddy you arre merrrit to.'

'Do you mean Winnie?'

'Vell, Oi tekk it det you only eff vun voyff. Yis, Vinny.'

'You're not threatening me, are you? Because, if you are, I know exactly what to do...'

Theo interrupted him.

'Look, mon, diss iss not a thrrett. Berliff me, Oi em doing diss in your interrorists, not moin, not ennyvun ilse's. Oi just don't fill goott about vot iss 'eppening and Oi vont to prevorrn you.'

'Well you'd better explain.'

'Oi vell, eff you litt me,' replied Theo with a hurt air, a shrug of one shoulder and sharp upward movement of his chin.

So, with frequent interruptions when Frank could not penetrate the accent, he told his story.

Theo pointed out that, although Frank had probably not realised this, he was not English but was from South

Africa, where he had been in practice as a private detective ever since leaving the police force. He had not reached the heights of his profession which he had hoped for when he started and had mostly been engaged in divorce work and in making video recordings of claimants in personal injuries cases, on behalf of insurance companies who suspected them of faking or exaggerating their disabilities. Although there was a certain amount of satisfaction in tracking down the subject, taking up a covert position and watching him (for it usually was a man) getting out of his wheelchair and washing his car, or playing soccer or helping his son-in-law to construct a lean-to, or timing her (for it usually was an errant wife) as she slipped into an apartment block and later came out again, checking her make-up and hair in a mirror, Theo had never been able to comprehend why his career had not really taken off. He prided himself on his ability to adopt a non-descript camouflage (an 'oltrra iggo', as he described it) and to merge into the background, and he believed that he had excellent communication skills and, of course, he had his background in the police (albeit mostly in the traffic division) and yet, and yet, he had never seemed to get into the high quality work that he hankered after. So when, almost a month earlier, at a time when he had been going through a particularly quiet patch and was spending more time in his office, wearing his raincoat and trilby and with his feet on the desk, in what he hoped was a passable impression of hard-bitten nonchalance, than he was in detecting, the telephone call had been very welcome. He was no more suspicious than was usual in this line of business; clients, particularly in divorce cases, were often reluctant to reveal too much detail about their motives and identities and it was not unusual for them to adopt a strangulated, adenoidal or whispering voice or a fake accent on their first telephone call to him, and so he did not find anything to alert him in the fact that the caller had a very peculiar way of speaking, with a strange pronunciation of vowels (Frank suppressed a snort), and long pauses mid-sentence as if he were munching something chewy, nor when he, eventually, asked if Theo would be available to conduct some investigative work at short notice. When, in a subsequent telephone conversation, the caller used a term which sounded like 'S. Spinach', which he assumed to be a codename, and referred to Moscow, he realised that there was a Russian connection. On reflection, he realised that no-one had actually mentioned it but, he had assumed that, as he had been approached in South Africa, and that, like most of his compatriots, was aware of the threat posed by cubic zirconia and other synthetics coming onto the market from that part of the World, the sleuthing in which he was to be engaged was connected with diamonds. Once he had been offered business-class return flights to London and a substantial cash down-payment, he had not been able to resist the prospect of such a classy elevation in his practice. He did not go into much detail about the number and nature of the calls and meetings he had with his new client but Frank had the impression that there were not many and that the lure of both the fees and the promotion to a more impressive level of detective work had been impossible for Van der Vyl (or was it now Nuthatch?, he forgot) to resist.

Theo paused and Grinder noticed that he was staring at his empty glass.

'Would you like another beer?'

'Vell, vusky vould be bitterr.'

'Sorry, do you want another bitter?

'*Stront*, nah, I said vusky. Luk a Pils. '

'Sorry, do you want a lager. Is that lager you're drinking? I thought it was bitter.'

Theo exhaled his exasperation.

'Heffn't you hearrd off Pils Vuskey? B…E..L…L…S, or a Grraass would do.

'A what?'

'Cheesus Krroist, mon, this is Brritain. Don't you eff Femmous Grraass in dis contrry?'

Frank went to the bar and came back with a double scotch and a small jug of water. Theo raised the tumbler in acknowledgment and continued.

He had had only had one face-to-face meeting with the client and it was either the man who had spoken with him on the telephone or someone with a very similar accent and manner of delivery. That meeting was shortly before he left for England and was very brief. The man came to his office, handed over a packet containing a substantial amount of cash, return air tickets and contact details. It also included an open return train ticket to Cheltenham Spa. Theo had looked up Cheltenham in the battered atlas that he had retained from his schooldays and had noticed that it was only about half an inch from Birmingham, which he had heard of. He had Googled Birmingham and found that it had a famous Jewellery Quarter and so, in his mind, it all began to fall into place and when he opened the package and saw that the air tickets were 'bizniss clorrss' he realised that he was, at last, dealing with something big time.

Shortly after arriving in the United Kingdom he had received an email telling him that the target of his investigation was, indeed, in Birmingham, and that he was to move into an apartment in Cheltenham because it was far enough away not to draw attention to what he was doing but had a direct rail link to Birmingham. He had gone to the estate agents named in the email and, sure enough, he was told that a furnished flat had been taken for him, and he was given the keys. On his own initiative, he had taken a trip to the Jewellery Quarter. On the following day he received a 'phone call from a man with a very different sort of accent, telling him to go for a meeting at New Street Station and he had done so and, in the concourse, had been approached by an oriental-looking man who had taken him for a coffee.

It was then that he had learned that his commission had nothing to do with investigating artificial diamonds and that what he was expected to do was to gain access to a factory somewhere in the city where it was believed that a substitute for a Chinese sauce was being manufactured. He could not recall clearly the name of the sauce but he gathered that there was something immoral about it.

'An immoral sauce?' asked Frank, who was about to suggest a connection with devilled kidneys, when he thought better of it.

'Vel, 'e said something about doing something wrong. Something luk 'Oi sin'.'

'Well, what did you think was immoral about it?'

'He medd it prrutty clear that the idea vos either to still the vorrmula or set voirr to the vectorry.'

Theo had immediately become very uneasy. He had always tried to keep on the right side of the law and had never been engaged in anything more sinister than inserting a match into a valve, in order to deflate the tyre of a target in a suspected fraudulent claim in a personal injury case, so that he could retreat behind some bushes and take a photo of the man changing the wheel. He had, nevertheless, decided to carry on for the moment and see what his next instructions might be. The next day, he had received a call from what he took to be the same man, telling him that he was to keep watch on a family who lived across the street: a European man with a Chinese wife, and to make a record of who visited their house and for how long.

He had made his observations for some days. He had seen Frank and a very attractive younger Chinese woman (whom, he admitted he liked the look of) but he hadn't seen anyone come to the house apart from a dripping wet clergyman and, yesterday, a family of Chinese. He had also started keeping a *tep* on Frank's movements.

'What, do you mean following me?'

'Yup.'

'I didn't see you.'

'Vel, Oi voss in disgoise.'

Frank was perplexed; judging by Theo's current endeavour to make himself inconspicuous, he could not understand how he had failed to notice either him or the curious throng who must have formed around him; surely there would, at least, have been a few teenagers expressing their derision in their monosyllabic grunts.

Instead, he said 'I'm impressed' and Theo made a self-deprecating gesture, patting the back of his head and slightly dislodging his glasses and eyebrows.

The apprehension had begun to grow that not only had Theo been engaged to do something illegal but also that he had been set on the wrong target. He had seen Frank going to the local supermarket and to the pub that they were now in and had watched him drive off with his wife (discreet enquiries at the newsagents had revealed not only that she was his wife but that also her name was Winnie) on a few occasions, but they were never away from home, apart from yesterday, for any length of time and they usually came back with bags of shopping. There was no sign at all that Frank was engaged in any business activity or had meetings with anyone. Also, he was very struck by the fact that, on Friday, Frank had gone to the supermarket. At first he thought that that might have been a rather clever form of *rronty-foo* until he saw that he was actually pushing a trolley between the aisles and did not speak to anyone, except, from what he could see from his viewpoint behind a stack of on-offer cardboard boxes of detergent, seemed to be in irritation. Also, his detective's instincts told him that it was improbable that anyone engaged in serious counterfeiting or *industrrial s.spinach* would be out doing his own grocery shopping. Finally, what had clinched it, was seeing the party arriving yesterday in Frank's car. Whilst the Chinese connection was obvious and it did, for a moment, seem as if, after all, this could be the real deal, it had not taken him long to come to the conclusion that no-one, not even as a cover, would bring along a whole family including what looked like a geriatric and an oriental punk. The only possible offset was the young woman, who was really *regtig mooi*, even prettier than Winnie and he knew about these trreps...

'Treps?'

'Yis, you know, with jem or marrmalate, or something. Vot iss it colled? 'Unni trreps, dets it...'

...but she looked too nice and innocent and all the other circumstances outweighed the possibility that she would be used as bait. Even before the family had arrived he had come to the conclusion that he should get out of the job, and should warn Frank of the danger he and his wife might be in and that is why he had called him on Sunday morning. Now that he had seen the family arrive, he had no doubt that he was doing the right thing.

'What danger?' Frank asked. 'We aren't involved in anything to do with industrial espionage. The only diamonds I have been involved with are in Winnie's engagement ring, and we got that from Hoi Lee Fook, in Queen's Road, Central, in Hong Kong, and I can assure you that they're not Russian synthetics. I used to act for their holding company, the Ten Thousand Lucky and Perpetual Riches Group, and their principal shareholder is Loon Hang Bank and ...'

'Vor Chroissek, mon, diss is not to do vit a benk or diamonds ... Hey, did you jost toll me that there iss a shop colled 'Holy Fuck'? Wow! Ess there another colled 'Blutty Good Sheg?' and, for the first time, Frank saw him smile, a smirking, self-satisfied stretching of his thin lips and a short, single exhalation, 'Hah', just discernible as a laugh. 'No, lissen, I toll you biffore det vos moi misstek, it vos some Chinese-type sauce.'

'Well, how does that concern me or my wife?'

Theo said that he was not sure, but as he had been told to keep observations on an Englishman with an oriental wife and from that particular flat, he assumed that it was him.

'O.K., so they've got the wrong man, or made a mistake about us, but why danger?'

Theo wasn't certain, but he had an unhappy feeling that, what with the Russian connection and the oriental sauce, it was probably the Chinese Mafia, although he didn't have anything positive to go on and he didn't want to risk it by asking any of these people directly. Of course, he didn't have enough information to know where to start making even discreet enquiries.

'The Triads?' suggested Frank, who was beginning to find the drift almost as difficult as the accent.

'Mon, you moss be mett. Oi admit that oy em out off moi depff, but um not stupit. Vot do you think Oi should do, put an announcement in 'The Gloucestershire Echo' arrsking forr inforrmation?'

'No, I said 'Triads'. There isn't a Mafia in China. Nor in Russia, for that matter. The Mafia is an Italian organisation. The name is an acronym for *Morte Ai Francesi Italia* which means 'Death to the French in Italy'. It was a resistance movement before the unification of Italy.'

'Luk, arre you lissening to me or giffing me a cheogrraphy lesson?'

'History, actually,' said Grinder, and instantly regretted it.

Theo paused, said nothing and adjusted his glasses which had slipped so that one eyebrow pointed downwards and the other aimed at the ceiling. Frank was unsure whether this was the result of the earlier laugh or a current fit of pique.

'I'm sorry, Theo, I didn't mean to be rude, please carry on.' He touched his own spectacles in what he hoped might be taken as a gesture of solidarity, even though he was fairly certain that they had remained in their usual alignment. He then regretted that action; either Theo would not have noticed it or, more likely, might see it as mockery. Theo still said nothing.

'Please go on, Theo,' he said. 'What did you actually discover?'

In a low voice, Theo said that he that he wasn't sure how much he should tell him because of the rules of client confidentiality. Frank was about to about to explain that no such rule existed for private detectives, particularly when the client had asked him to do something illegal and, anyway, he had already disclosed quite a lot but, just in time, he thought better of it. Instead, he asked him about his first trip to Birmingham, when he had gone to the Jewellery Quarter.

Theo said that he had found it very interesting. He had not realised how big it would be nor that there were so many shops that were manufacturing jewellery and so many small, old factory buildings. He had noticed that many of the shops had gas jets flaming at the back, and had wondered what they were for until he realised they were all set on workbenches and that there were workshops at the back behind the display areas. In fact it was while he was looking through a shop window that he was nearly rumbled.

'Why, what happened?' asked Frank, now thoroughly intrigued.

Theo explained that he had caught the train to Birmingham whilst in disguise because, at that stage, he still thought that it was all to do with artificial diamonds and that it would be a good idea to make himself familiar with the area without anyone knowing who he was.

'Like you've got on now?'

'No, Oi 'ad a fig.'

'A what?'

'A fig. On moi 'ead.'

Frank was mystified; he could not see the logic in travelling on public transport and wandering around the streets beneath a piece of fruit in order to avoid drawing attention to himself. Then he realised what Theo meant.

Theo continued, saying that it was a hot day and the air-conditioning on the train wasn't working and although he knew that he was sweating he did not realise that his yellow hair-piece had slipped forward over his forehead. When he was staring through the jeweller's window he could see his reflection, but his dark glasses must have prevented him from seeing himself too clearly and it was only afterwards, at the police station, when he was escorted to the lavatory, that he looked at himself in the mirror and saw what had happened to it.

'At the police station?'

The problem had arisen, said Theo, because he had been so fascinated by the workshops that, for a moment, he had forgotten what he had gone there for and, thinking that some of his friends back home might be interested, he had been standing for quite a long time taking photos through the window of this particular shop where he could see someone at a workbench at the back, when a couple of big black guys came out and took hold of him and the owner called the police.

Frank endeavoured to assume a sympathetic expression and said that it must have been an unpleasant experience. Theo said – as far as Frank could understand him, although he was not altogether sure of the last bit – that it was quite the contrary. The Birmingham police had been very kind, although they spoke with a very strong accent that made it difficult for him to follow what they were saying, and he wasn't certain that they knew what he was saying, and they had given him his camera and wig back, once they had sorted it all out. When he was in the police they would have kept the camera and given him some attention with a truncheon and a Rottweiler. Maybe the explanation was that he had eventually told them that he had been a high ranking police officer, himself. They gave him a sympathetic look and a cup of sweet tea before he went, and even asked if there was anyone looking after him, which he thought was a very decent way to treat a stranger in this country.

Anyway, he went back and then, later, he received the instructions about this sauce thing.

'So you realised then that it was nothing to do with synthetic diamonds?'

'Yiss.'

Theo turned away and there was another long pause. An impression flitted through Frank's mind that he had offended him again, but then he saw that Theo was scrutinising four men who had come into the pub together and had gone up to the bar. They all wore dark suits and ties.

'And?' said Frank.

'Vett.'

'Sorry?'

'Vett. Shhh.'

'What's the matter?

'Oi'm chicken.'

'What are you scared of? Do you know those men?'

'Voi do you think um scared. Nufferr sin them before.'

'I'm sorry, I thought that you said that you were chicken.'

'Oi did. Um chicken them out. Um vunderring what the blutty hull they arre doing here.'

'It's a pub,' said Frank, trying to suppress any hint of exasperation. 'They've come, I should think, for something to eat and drink,' and, noticing that Van der Vyl was again staring at his empty glass, 'Would you like another?'

'O.K, but just an orrf off butter.'

I'm beginning to crack this, thought Frank, and went to the bar and asked for two halves of bitter.

Other customers were beginning to come in, but Theo was still staring at the group of men in suits. When Frank got back with the drinks, Theo briefly inclined his head to indicate another table a few feet further from the bar and they moved to it. He was sitting with his back towards the bar, and took the proffered beer in silence. Frank sat down, opposite him.

'Go on. Please.'

Theo resumed his narrative but so quietly that, even though he leant forward across the table, Frank could hardly make out what he was saying.

'Sorry,' he said, 'Could you speak a bit louder.'

Without a word, Van der Vyl got up and took his glass to an empty table at the far end of the room. Frank followed and sat down next to him.

'What's the matter?' said Frank.

'Vun off those men iss stirring at us,' Theo replied. 'I think, maybe, he's on to us.'

Frank was about to offer the suggestion that, if the man was staring, the likely explanation was Theo's appearance. During the short interval when Frank had been at the bar ordering the drinks, Theo had exchanged his glasses for a pair of large, round, orange-framed spectacles of the kind favoured by film directors and fashion editors. The false eyebrows had also gone, but as if to balance the overall hair effect, he had donned a luxuriant flaxen toupée, which must have been the Birmingham fig. Frank could see the edge of the canvas lining where the front came to an abrupt meeting with or, rather, fractionally off Theo's forehead. The central parting was dead straight, and looked like a field of corn which had been ploughed with a single furrow.

'I don't think they're watching the two of us,' said Frank. 'Certainly they're not at the moment.'

'You corrn't be to surre. Look, Oi'm not 'eppy with this place now, therre arre too many pipple. Cen we go somevhere olse?'

Frank Grinder made a show of looking at his watch. The truth was that he was becoming embarrassed at being seen sitting at a table with someone who looked as if he had escaped from a mental hospital and, on the way, had burgled a fancy dress shop. He certainly did not want to leave 'The Unicorn' in his company and have to walk through the neighbouring streets with him.

'Actually, I didn't realise what the time was. My wife is expecting me home for lunch. As you know, we've got her family staying with us and I don't want to seem to be avoiding them. Is it possible to meet again, say, tomorrow? Would that be convenient for you?'

'Yup,' replied the spectre. 'I toll you vot. I'll come to your 'orse.'

'My house?'

'Yup, vot tarm sholl I come?'

'Actually, that's not a good idea because...'

'Voy not? You von't heff anyvun ulse in your 'orse. They'rre orff to the seaside.'

'How the hell do you know that?'

'Iss vot Oi do.'

Frank was, momentarily, taken aback. Perhaps this man was not such a fool.

'Well, no, I don't think that it would be a good idea because Winnie's father is not going with them. He'll be at home.'

'Oh, ollrright. You can come to moi flett. Say tvulff.'

'Tvulff?'

'Oi didn't min repit vot I sed. I sed 'say' minning: 'ow about? 'Ow about tvulff o'clock?'

'Yes, that's O.K. What's your address?'

'Shhh. Neffer guff it out loud in a pop,' and Theo produced a battered note book from one pocket and a stubby pencil from another, wrote it down, tore the page out and slid it across the table to Frank.

'Vee mossn't liff together. You go vurrst. See you tomorrow.'

When Frank got home, they had started lunch without him. What was left of several dishes of rice, vegetables, noodles, chicken, prawns, beef and bean curd, were scattered over the table, looking as if they had been attacked by a swarm of particularly ravenous locusts

He went over and kissed Winnie, who was sitting at the head of the table, and nodded at the rest of the family. Ah Leung's eyes were already closing.

'Sorry I'm late, love. I got held up over some business.'

'Because, we start without you. Rambo was very hungry.'

'Not just me,' protested her brother, and he belched in what was, to him, a very satisfactory manner.

'No, no, you were quite right to start without me. Look, I'll just have some of those noodles,' – Rambo gave him a penetrating, puzzled stare – 'and then I'll go upstairs as there's something I must do.'

Back at his desk, Frank wrote his chapter on the misuse of English.

The mood had taken hold of him. He had both time and energy for another, this time on restaurant critics.

CHAPTER 10

The thin Monday morning light filtered through the dusty fanlight above the door of the Medved Hotel. The fat man was still behind the desk, perspiring slightly as he prepared the bill for a young, Central European couple, apparently tourists visiting London on a tight budget who were anxiously counting their small wads of sterling. With an air of resignation, borne of almost daily repetition, he was trying to explain to them why tax was added to the bill and why it had cost so much to make a short telephone call home from their bedroom.

The men were standing, quietly, in the lobby when he came down the stairs. This time, it was the fairer of the two who came forwards.

'Good morning, Lev,' he said. 'John. I hope that you had a good sleep.'

'Yes, I remember you are Mr Black, and this is Mr Green.'

'Better just to call me Mike,' said the other. 'Are you ready to go?'

'Mnym, yes.'

'O.K., well, first we'll take you to a quick meeting. I've just had a call from him. He's waiting for us.'

They left the hotel and walked a short distance to a

side street where cars were parked at meters. Green clicked open a black Mercedes and got into the driver's seat, ushering Lev Petrovich to the seat beside him. Black sat behind.

They drove the short distance into Lancaster Terrace and then turned off right until they got to a square where they parked in a bay, outside a graceful terrace of white, five-story houses. Black got out of the car and went to a door and, after a short while, beckoned the others to join him. The door was already open when Lev and Green got there. A uniformed maid ushered them into a lounge, where they waited, all of them standing as if, by unspoken agreement, it was inappropriate for them to sit on the elegant furniture.

The door opened and grey-haired Chinese man walked in. He was wearing a perfectly cut grey, pin-striped suit and dark blue silk tie. Lev noticed a slight limp as he came towards them and shook each of them by the hand.

'And this is Mr Ivanov?' he asked Green.

'Yes, sir.'

'Mr Ivanov, it is a great pleasure for me to meet you.' His accent suggested an English public school education. 'I have heard a great deal about you. I hope you had a pleasant journey. You arrived yesterday, I believe.'

Lev Petrovich glanced down at his unpolished, misshapen shoes and noticed that one of the laces was almost undone. He compared them with his host's gleaming footwear.

'Is good for me, mnym, to meet you also, but you are who?'

Black and Green exchanged glances and smiled. This man was really very good: he had plainly projected himself into his role and was playing it flat out.

'Me, who am I? Shall we say that you may refer to me as Mr Li. And without putting too fine a point on it, I am paying for your services. That is why I wanted to meet you before you started work.'

'I understand,' replied Lev Petrovich, not understanding at all.

'Mr Ivanov, you are, of course, Russian.'

'Yes. From Russia'.

'I wish to satisfy myself of one small detail. It may seem quite trivial to you.'

'Trivial?'

'Yes, it may. You see, where I come from, the country is so vast and there are so many dialects that people from one region cannot understand the spoken language of another region. As you know, it is only the written language, the characters, that is universal. We have a widely used dialect, which is called *Putonghua* but not everyone speaks it and people usually converse with others from their region in their local dialect.'

'Characters?'

'Yes. Now, you see, I have absolutely no desire to make myself seem impertinent but...'

'Impertinent?'

'It is not necessary to repeat everything I say,' said Mr Li, his urbane smile belying the slight edge of his tone. 'I just wanted to be reassured that the same problem may not arise. Russian is a vast country...'

'Vast?'

Mr Li decided to ignore the probable question mark and to take it as merely confirmation of the adjective.

'...Yes, and it occurred to me that because, as far as we are aware the, how shall I call them? – the opposition – largely consists of Russians, there may be a risk of their speaking to each other in a regional dialect with which you may not be familiar, when you are listening in.'

'Mnym, mnym.'

'Of course, there may be dialects and you may be able to understand all of them. I would rather tend to expect that someone of your reputation in the field would be multilingual...,' Mr Li glanced at his immaculate pale blue shirt cuff and flicked off a speck of dust, whilst checking his slim wristwatch, '...and conversant with the vernacular of different provinces – if there are any – but my real question is, are there different versions of Russian or does everyone speak, more or less, just the same language? You will, I am sure, understand my wanting some reassurance on this.'

'Just same language?'

'Good, well, that's settled. Is there anything else?' Li addressed Mike Green.

'No, I don't think so. I think we're ready to go, aren't we, John?'

Black nodded his agreement.

'Then,' said Li, 'I will leave you to your own devices and will wait until I hear the results of your, er...research. Thank you so much for calling on me this morning.'

He had not invited them to sit down and now he walked with them to the front door.

'Goodbye, then' he said. 'Until you contact me Mr Green. Or Mr Black.'

As they walked back to the car, Black said 'That went very well. I think he's impressed with you. I imagine that he was expecting some smoothy but could see how much better you will be able to slip in and out. Well done.'

Lev Petrovich followed none of that, nor what the purpose of the brief meeting had been. But it was too complicated to ask. He wondered whether he might still be suffering from jet lag. He was certainly feeling quite sleepy and, sitting now in the back of the car, he found it hard to stop himself from dozing off. He was aware that they were going through some congested streets with long pauses at traffic lights and then round a lake in a big park, and that the two other men were talking quietly to each other without seeming to involve him in their conversation. He must have nodded off, because he realised that they were no longer in the park, but were crossing a bridge over a wide river and to his left he could see a tower which he had seen in photographs and, in the distance, there were some very tall, oddly-shaped modern buildings which he did not recognise.

Over the bridge, and he saw a sign to a cricket ground. He had heard about cricket and was curious to see it being played but there was no sign of anything happening as they passed; it was almost as if the players were cemented into position. They continued past houses which were much smaller than the one they had come from and rows of shops, all with cars parked outside them. He closed his eyes for a short while.

He woke because the car was turning off to the left and then, slowly, down a side street of shabby houses and through some open gates with a dirty, white sign with the words 'Milford Road Industrial Estate' in peeling black paint. A rusting car, jacked up on bricks, its wheels gone and its windows smashed sat just inside the gates. Opposite was a small group of buildings, some not much larger than sheds, each in a small square of litter-strewn and oil-stained concrete.

'We'll leave the car here,' said Green, turning towards Lev Petrovich. 'It should be alright for a moment. Have you brought your camera?'

'Camera? No. Is in hotel.' He pronounced it 'khotel'.

'Probably a shrewd move,' said John Black. 'I don't think we should be drawing attention to ourselves.'

'Excuse me, please,' asked Lev, 'is this Cheltenham?'

'You really are very good, you know' replied Black and both he and Mike Green laughed.

'Look, I think it's best if we do this quickly, we'll just take you over to have a look at the building.'

They got out of the car and walked a short distance past the sheds, and turned a corner where a slightly larger building stood on its own. Its corrugated metal roof was loose at one corner and banged as a gust of wind hit it. Three of the windows were boarded-up on the outside and the other two had dirty, grey sheets hanging on the inside like drawn curtains. There was no appearance of activity but a surprisingly clean and well-written sign announced it to be 'Camberwell Light Engineering Company'. A large dog was urinating against the front door.

'Well, this is it,' said Green. 'This is one of the two places where we think that things may be going on. It doesn't look like much, but this may be where the sauce is being manufactured. So we'll have to try to get you in and you can get hold of the formula, or disable the operation, or both.'

'But, please, my, mnym, speciality is beetroot.'

'Oh, that's brilliant,' said Green. 'I didn't know that you have been involved on a beetroot investigation before. That's great. So you'll be familiar with what can be done with beetroot, apart from turning your pee bright red, that is. I didn't realise that you knew that we believe that beetroot might be being used in the manufacture. You've certainly done your homework.'

'Yes, beetroot. Also, as you say, peas. Those my special studies. But, mnym, not know of red peas.'

The dog had finished and now moved, in a leisurely fashion, towards them.

'Look,' said Black, eyeing the dog nervously, 'I don't think that we should hang around. Let's get back to the car. We'll bring you back another time, probably when it's dark, if you think that's best, and then you can give the place a proper going-over. We just wanted to give you a preliminary feel for the set up.'

They walked back to the car and got in, Lev sitting in the back again.

'You say, mnym, mnym, I think,that there are two places?'

'Yes, that's right,' Green replied.

'The other place, perhaps, is Cheltenham?'

'There you go again,' laughed Black. 'The other place is in Birmingham. We'll go up there tomorrow.'

They set off, Black driving, retracing the route by which they had come. Lev Petrovich was more awake now, partly because his curiosity was aroused. As they were crossing the bridge again, he asked the pertinent question.

'Please, what are we doing?'

'Do you mean, where are we going?'

'No, I mean why do you show me building and want me to go in?'

Black and Green spoke quietly to each other for a moment and then Green turned back to Lev.

'Look, John and I can't see any harm in you knowing the bigger picture. What is going on at that place or in Birmingham or, perhaps, both, could undermine the monopoly our client has. It's like liquid gold.'

'This is about gold?'

'No, not gold as such. It's a condiment or some sort of sauce that is important in Chinese cooking. It's like... what is the most widespread flavouring in Russian food? What is it, would you say, that makes otherwise plain or inedible food enjoyable to eat?'

'In case of Russian food, vodka,' replied Lev. 'Or, better, being drunk.'

'It's something as important as that,' continued Mike Green. 'So if it was being counterfeited and the oriental market flooded with a cheap substitute, well, you can imagine the loss it would cause to our principal. That's why your expertise is so important.'

Lev Petrovich looked thoughtful.

'Yes, mnym, I had not thought of making vodka from beetroot. Has possibility.'

'No,' said Green, 'we're not asking you to make it. We're asking you to find out what is happening, and where. You're a specialist in espionage, after all.'

Lev Petrovich looked puzzled but said nothing. Then he nodded thoughtfully.

'So tomorrow we go to Birmingham, yes?'

'That's right,' said Black.

'Then from Birmingham we go to Cheltenham?'

'What is this thing you've got about Cheltenham?'

But Lev had nodded off in the back of the car.

Lev Semyonovich Ivanov had just unscrewed the top of a small plastic bottle of Scotch which he had taken from the mini bar in his bedroom and was looking for some ice when the telephone rang.

'Mr Ivanov?'

'Yes.'

'Hi, I'm Dick Worthy. I think that you were told that we are having a pre-conference get-together of speakers this evening. If it's O.K. with you, we'll be meeting downstairs in ten minutes.'

'Yes. Shall I meet you in the bar?'

'No, no, I don't think so. I've booked one of the small conference rooms. It's called the Shergar Room. Could you make a note of it? It's on the ground floor, not far from the bar, in fact.'

Lev Semyonovich saw that there was an ice bucket in

the alcove above the mini bar. He emptied the bottle into a tumbler, dropped in a couple of lumps and took his drink over to the window. What he had thought were lawns when he arrived yesterday had turned out to be a golf course. He watched as a two late golfers teed off towards the sinking sun. This was all getting a bit strange. He had been in England for more than 24 hours and no-one had even begun to identify the target to him. He thought that he had misheard the chauffeur when he mentioned a conference, but the receptionist had said the same thing and the call he had just received confirmed it. What did they mean by other speakers? Well, he had better go down and find out what it was all about. He swallowed his whisky, put on his jacket and took the lift to the ground floor.

The Shergar Room was panelled in the same light-coloured wood. A long table stood in the middle with chairs upholstered in the material matching those in the reception area. Bottled water and tumblers, writing pads and ball point pens were laid out. The large windows on one side of the room overlooked the golf-course. Four people were sitting at the table, three of whom turned towards the door as he came in and the other, a man in his late thirties, stood up.

'Hi,' he said, 'I'm Dick Worthy. You must be Mr Ivanov. It's great to meet you. I've heard so much about you. I don't know if you've been told, but I shall be the Moderator at the conference. It was my idea that the speakers should meet each other for a chat beforehand. I gather that you haven't made the acquaintance of the others, although you probably know them by reputation. I know this is going to be a great conference. It's going to be awesome. With four iconic figures like you.'

Worthy smiled a lot and his handshake was excessively firm. Lev thought that he seemed wrapped up in his own importance or maybe was just an enthusiastic young man. Or both. He turned towards a woman with iron-grey, frizzled hair. She was wearing a tweed suit.

'This is Eleanor, Eleanor Landarbeiter. You must have heard of her. She is our specialist in organic production. She has just finished a project for Unesco in Africa.'

'How do you do?' she said, rising slightly and taking his hand almost as fiercely as Worthy had. 'Yes, I'm Organics. Cow shit and all that sort of thing. Glad to meet you at last. One of your articles was reproduced in *Organic Husbandry* magazine and I was very impressed. Oh, by the way, don't be misled by name. I'm as British as overcooked vegetables. You're the only distinguished foreigner amongst us.'

Before Ivanov could take in what she had just said about him, one of the others, a slim, epicene, young man with rimless glasses, stood up.

'That's not right. I'm American.' He looked at her archly. 'Unless you meant that I'm the only one who isn't distinguished?'

'Oh, rot!' said Eleanor. 'Of course I didn't mean that. I forgot that you're a Yank.'

'I think that this might call for my services as Moderator', Worthy interjected, 'Our *very distinguished* American friend is Taylor Siccita. His field is irrigation. Oh, excuse the pun.'

Lev Semyonovich was perplexed. For the first time since his arrival, his English had failed him. But the whole thing was becoming mystifying. He leant across the table and shook Siccita's hand, and wondered whether the other man's role might let some light in. He was a red-faced and portly, in his mid-fifties. He wore a pale grey suit that shimmered slightly as he moved. Lev noticed what looked like a very expensive, very large, clumsy gold wristwatch as he stretched out his hand.

'I'm Johnny Walker. You've heard of me of course.' He chuckled loudly and the flesh beneath his chin wobbled. 'No, it really is my name. '

'Johnny is our expert on logistics. He runs a very successful business here in England and he will be talking on communications and distribution,' said Worthy. 'But you, of course,' he continued, turning to Lev, 'are our expert of particular interest to the conference.'

'Am I?'

'Of course, your knowledge of beetroot production is, I believe, unparalleled. Please, take a seat.'

Lev Semyonovich considered this for a moment and came to the conclusion that there were three possibilities: that this was a highly sophisticated operation with an elaborate front, part of which was now unfolding before him; or that he been brought to the conference so that he could learn something about the production of whatever it was that he had been hired to investigate (but if either of those was the case, why would he be thrust, without warning, into the role of an expert on beetroot?); or that there had been some awful mistake and that he was in the wrong place. Whatever the true explanation was, it would be best to try to avoid giving the game away.

For the first time Ivanov noticed a pile of printed leaflets on the table in front of where Worthy was now sitting.

'These are the flyers we've had printed,' he said. '*Beetroot Production for a Hungry World.*' That's quite a snappy title, don't you think? That was my brainchild. Look, I won't trouble you to look at it now, but it's got the agenda in it, with the times we've allocated for each of you to talk. I would only ask you, now, to check that the time-table suits you all ...No problems?' He paused for a moment and raised his eyebrows in a brief, concerned gesture. 'Good, then I think that we can move onto the final phase of this evening's get-together.'

He reached behind him for a bottle of screw-top Chardonnay and poured out five glasses. As he did so, Lev Semyonovich caught sight of the name 'Ivanov' in the pamphlet, and looked closer. Against the description of one of Russia's leading botanists was the name: Dr Lev P. Ivanov. '*Chyort Voz'Mi!*' he muttered to himself.

'So, is everyone happy with that timetable?' asked Dick Worthy.'Good, then we'll stick to it as far as we can. No-body is going to expect you to keep to it to the minute, but it would be normal to leave a period at the end when we can throw it open to questions. I've organised similar conferences before and, indeed, you, Eleanor, and you, Johnny, have been speakers.' They both nodded. 'Well, I think that this is going to be the best yet. Really worthwhile. But for the benefit of Taylor and Lev, when we come to questions, there's a man in a dog collar who usually turns up, and he raises some really stupid points. Just be warned.'

CHAPTER 11

Frank Grinder could not sleep. The light streaming through the gap between the curtains must have woken him. He lay, looking at the beautiful, childlike face until she moaned quietly and turned away from him, deep in that slumber which she achieved so easily and which, so often, eluded him. He got out of bed and looked into the sunlit street. The curtains in all the houses across the road were still drawn. At least, he thought, it should be a lovely day for their trip. For a moment, he wished that he was going with them, but then thought of her father, and the chance to get some more writing done and, of course, his promised meeting with Theo. It was only six-thirty in the morning. A cup of tea, perhaps, and then he would start on a new topic.

Still in his pyjamas, he took the tea up to his study. This is not a bad time of day to write, he thought. Perhaps a shortish topic before Aubrey and Alistair turned up.

He realised that he had had no breakfast. He went downstairs. It was still only seven-thirty. He took from the fridge a pot of strawberry-flavoured Bifidus ActiRegularis (for that is what the yoghurt pot said was in it) and, thinking of the possibility of a chapter on pseudo-science, went to make himself another cup of tea, when he heard the sound of car doors slamming.

The doorbell rang.

'Good Grief, I mean, hallo, Aubrey. And hallo, er....'

'Good morning, Frank,' said Aubrey. 'I see that you are still in your night attire. I hope that we are not disturbing you.'

'Yes, well, it is a bit early. No-one else is up yet. You'd better come in.'

'I so regret inconveniencing you but, as I think you know, I have to get off to a rather important seminar at which, I expect, I shall be invited to make my, ahem, little contribution and I want to get there in good time so that I can settle myself in, so to speak. I was, in point of fact, considering leaving home rather earlier than we did, but I did not wish to impose ourselves on you at an inopportune hour.'

'Very considerate of you,' muttered Grinder through his clenched teeth.

'Yes, well, I am comforted to know that you think so. Come along, Alistair. Don't stand there on the doorstep.'

The boy was wearing a green waxed jacket and smartly creased fawn trousers. Under the Barbour, Frank could see a shirt and tie. Just the job for a trip to the seaside on a sunny day, he thought.

'Would you like a cup of tea, Aubrey? What about you...er...Alistair?

'No thank you,' replied the Team Vicar. 'Not for me. I had better be getting off. I don't want to risk getting caught for speeding,' and he looked darkly at Alistair. 'I'm sure Alistair would like a cup, though. Milk, no sugar, please, for him.'

Frank showed Aubrey to the door.

'I'll collect Alistair sometime this evening, if that is convenient to you. I will telephone when I leave and give you an approximate indication of my E.T.'

'Your what?'

'The time I expect to be here.'

'I think that's called an E.T.A, Aubrey. E.T was a creature from Outer Space – oh, never mind. Can I just ask you something?

'Of course.'

'From what you said, I gather that you're going to spend all day at this conference.'

'Seminar. Yes.'

'So, you're not going to Church.'

'No.'

'Or visiting the sick and needy of your parish?'

'No.'

'Will you be conducting some sort of service, like blessing the seminar before it starts or saying a concluding prayer, or something?'

'No, why do you ask?'

'Well, I just was curious about why you've got your dog collar on. I would have thought that, off duty, you would want to be in mufti.'

'Oh that,' replied the Reverend M.A. 'I find that it tends to draw attention, so that it is useful for catching the Chairman's eye.'

He turned back towards his son, who was still standing in the hallway.

'Now, have a lovely day, Alistair and you make sure that you listen to what Uncle Frank has to say.' And, for a few hours, he was gone from the life of the older of the Spindle boys.

'Come into the kitchen, Alistair,' said Frank, 'and let's have that tea. I could do with another cup, myself. You don't mind me in my pyjamas, do you?'

'No.' said Alistair.

'Well, come and sit down. Actually, it's probably a good thing that you've come before anyone is up. It'll give us a chance to have a little chat. Take your coat off. Make yourself comfortable. I don't think you need your tie on, either.'

'But Father said that I should wear one. He said that we might be going to a smart restaurant for lunch.'

'You do know that it's Weston-super-Mare that you're going to?'

'Oh yes, he told me. And he told me that you would give me some legal advice about my motoring problem.'

'Good, but you didn't need to wear a tie for that. Not many lawyers see clients when they're still in their pyjamas, so you can take it that this is a friendly chat from your mother's brother and nothing else.'

Alistair looked confused.

'How old are you, Alistair?'

'I'm eighteen, Uncle Frank.'

'Well, you've got a driving licence, obviously. I assume that you weren't driving without one.'

'Oh no, Uncle, I wouldn't have done that.'

'Right,' said Frank, 'my advice to you is: live a bit more. As you youngsters say,' or perhaps, in your case, he thought, don't say, 'get a life.'

'What do you mean, Uncle?'

'All I am trying, perhaps not very successfully, to say is that you shouldn't let yourself get so worried by small things. A speeding offence is hardly on a par with armed robbery or treason or insider dealing or,' he added, for good measure, 'criminal damage.'

'I see,' said Alistair, politely, but Frank thought that he did not.

'In essence, I'm suggesting that you should behave like most eighteen-year olds. Don't be afraid to take a few risks. The best teacher is experience.'

'F'ank,' called Winnie from upstairs, 'are you in the kitchen?'

'Yes.'

'Who you talking to?'

'It's Alistair. Aubrey has been and gone.'

'Ah, O.K. maybe I better get my family up and we can go off early to Weston. Can you start making some toasts? Quite a lot.'

CHAPTER 12

Winnie drove the car slowly into the outskirts of Weston-super-Mare. The road led past rows of houses and supermarkets and small industrial estates. Rambo was sitting beside her, leaning forwards slightly, ready to give her directions.

'This does not look much like the seaside,' he said. 'I can't see any sea. You're going the wrong way.'

'Shut up, Younger Brother,' said Winnie. 'I'm following the signs to the beach.'

'This isn't the way to the beach,' said Rambo.

Alistair, sitting next to Winsome and Ah-Ma at the back, thought that, perhaps, Rambo was right, because they seemed to be heading out of town and back towards the direction of the motorway. Best not to say anything yet, if at all. Winsome seemed to be asleep now and the old lady was concentrating on a paper packet of seeds which she had been continuously popping into her mouth and cracking with her teeth ever since they had got into the car.

And suddenly, there it was. An expanse of mud-coloured sand with rows of vehicles parked on it, and a promenade, lined on both sides with stationary cars.

'See, Rambo, here it is,' said Winnie, with a note of triumph. 'I got you here. To the seaside.'

'It's just mud. I can't see any sea. It must be an inland beach. Probably the only one in the world.'

'Look over there,' Winnie said.

About a mile away, across the mud flats, and where the grey coast of Wales was dissolving in the mist, lay a stretch of water.

'No, it's just a big river,' Rambo argued.

'No, my husband told me that the tide might be out. You have to wait till the sea comes back.'

Rambo, incredulous, shook his head. 'I never heard of a place where the sea is there one day and gone the next. There would be some pretty angry boat people if that happened in Cheung Chau.'

Alistair said 'It's true. Weston has the second highest tidal range in the world.'

'How do you know?' challenged Rambo.

'I looked it up before we came. My father says that you should do your research before setting off to somewhere new. He says that you should fill your mind with information so that you can get the most out of an expedition.'

'Your father,' said Rambo, 'is, perhaps, a *fook-sui*.'

'A what?'

Ah-mah gave her son a warning in Cantonese.

'Your father is a...priest,' said Rambo.

'Yes, I know that, of course. Well, actually, he's a Team Vicar. Why did you mention it?'

'Look,' said Winnie, 'there's a space. I go in there.'

'You sure you can do it?' said Rambo. 'It's only about five times as long as the car.'

'Shut up, *Sai-lo*! You're the *fook-sui*.'

A bemused expression clouded Alistair's face. Why did she just call Rambo a priest? He remembered that his father had warned that there would cultural differences when his mother announced that her brother was going to marry a Chinese girl. This might just be an example of them.

They got out of the car. Rambo pointed out a nearby parking meter and Winnie went to get a ticket.

'You put it in the windscreen,' he explained to her.

'What is that building thing with the long bridge sticking out?' asked Winsome. 'Shall we go there?

'It's the pier,' said Alistair.

'What is it for?'

'You can walk along it as if you are going out to sea.'

Rambo snorted.

'And,' Alistair continued, 'they usually have things to do on it and more things, entertainments, inside the building. I expect that there will be some sort of concert hall or a theatre.'

'Will it have a restaurant?' asked Rambo. 'I'm starving.'

'I expect so.'

They set off along the promenade, in the direction of the pier. Rambo pointed to it and turned back to his mother.

'That's where we're heading, Ah-ma. Not too far for you? You can have a rest when we get there. And how about some food?

'You a good boy. I manage. But *mo fai-di*. Not go so quick.'

So, at her pace, they ambled along in the strengthening sun. They passed signs to the miniature railway and a putting green. Alistair hoped that one of them would ask him what they were so that he could explain but, instead, Winsome enquired:

'Aren't you hot in that coat thing?'

He looked down at his Barbour.

'Yes, a bit, I suppose, but my father said that I should wear something warm and rainproof because you never know what the weather will do at the seaside.'

'Well,' said Rambo, 'it's not the seaside... No sea.'

On their left, they passed another beach car park which was beginning to fill up. A camper van had taken up a strategic position, facing the distant water, and its occupants had set up a windbreak and five canvas folding chairs. A woman in a t-shirt and wide, flapping shorts emerged from the van with a tray of steaming mugs. Beyond the car park, a horsebox had unloaded its cargo of four depressed-looking donkeys, ears drooping, waiting for the start of another tedious day of short walks with screeching children astride them. Further along, seven or eight sari-clad women sat on the sand in a circle, listening to music coming from something that Winnie could not see.

'What's that?' said Rambo, pointing along the promenade.

'It's a Ferris wheel,' Alistair, quietly pleased, explained.

'What is it for?'

'You sit in those little cabins and you go round in it.'

'Why?'

'So you can get a good view.'

'Of what?'

'Of the beach and the town.'

'Why? I can see the beach from here.'

'Well, people like to go round in them, I suppose,' said Alistair, slightly crushed at not having impressed Rambo.

'They must be *moon cha-cha*.'

'Don't be rude, *Jai*,' said Ah-ma.

'I'm not being rude. I just don't understand what the point is.'

'Well, I've never been on one,' said Alistair.

'Shall we go on it then? Do you want to?'

'Not really...I'm not sure that my father would approve. He would probably think it was a waste of money. I know that he doesn't particularly agree with funfairs, and that's a bit like one.'

The crowd on the promenade was gradually becoming thicker. Tattooed, overweight men, some in singlets, others in soccer shirts, dodged electric disability scooters being driven amongst them. An elderly man wearing a faded, blue yachting cap. Couples with young children, some on their fathers' shoulders, some in pushchairs, walked towards them. Most of the men turned to stare admiringly at Winsome as they passed.

'They not see many Chinese here,' her mother explained.

A Punch and Judy booth had been set up. A semi-circle of small, chattering children squatted on the sand looking up at the drawn curtains waiting for the show to start.

'Hey, I need a pee,' said Rambo. 'Is that a lavatory over there?' He pointed to a shiny, grey capsule standing outside a fence which surrounded a derelict brick and cast iron building.

'It's one of the modern ones,' said Alistair. 'It's automatic. But you need to pay to get in.'

'Wah!' said Rambo, 'An automatic pee machine! Does that mean it does it for you?'

'No, of course not,' replied Alistair. 'They just flush and clean the seat after you.'

'But that would be good – a lavatory that would do the pee for you. Expect they have them in Japan. *Yiu!* There's someone in there.'

'Have you got the right change?' said Alistair.

'Change?'

'The right money. Coins.'

'I don't need money.'

'You do, look it says on the door, £1.'

'No need. You watch,' and Rambo went and stood close to the entrance, shifting uncomfortably from foot to foot. After a few minutes, there was a scuffling noise from inside and the door slowly slid open. A middle-aged woman stepped out. Instantly, Rambo leapt behind her into the cubicle and the door closed noiselessly.

'*Aaaeeiyah*!'

Rambo's scream could be heard above the sound of flushing water. Then silence. The door opened again and he emerged, the front of his trousers and his trainers soaking wet.

'You not make it in time?' Winnie asked him.

'The *ngong gau* thing sprayed me before I could do anything!'

'Don't swear!' his mother scolded him. 'Why I have to keep telling you?'

Alistair was curious to learn. 'What did he say?'

'He use not nice word in Chinese.' Alistair realised that this was the first time that the old lady had actually spoken to him.

'Yes, but what did it mean?'

'It mean something not good. Maybe you not good, too. It seem my son use bad words a lot when he with you. And he do bad things.' She gave him a hard look.

Although Alistair knew that that was unjustified, he was aware of a sensation of something akin to pride.

'Well, I'd still like to know what he said.'

'I not tell you.'

Rambo intervened. 'What is that stink?' he asked.

There was, indeed, a strong smell of frying fat. Queues had formed outside fish and chip stalls. People were sitting on the promenade wall and on the ground, eating with their fingers from polystyrene trays. Aggressive gulls approached them; it was far easier to catch food in this way than out at sea.

'That is awful,' said Winsome and she covered her nose and mouth with her hand. 'Do English really eat that stuff? Isn't there anything else to eat here?'

They were almost at the pier. Outside, a fibre glass pirate incongruously advertised the attractions of Cheddar Gorge. Beside it, a sign proclaimed 'Tour of India' and pointed to a two-metre high plastic elephant with steps which led to a small platform on its back; when you came down, you had completed the tour. A trio of laughing, obese women in singlets exposing their coloured bra straps, rolled heavily towards them, their stomachs wobbling with each waddled step. Rambo stared at them as they passed; from the back they looked as if their loose trousers contained boulders, juggled by an unseen, giant hand.

There was an ice-cream parlour at the entrance to the pier.

'I'm going to get something to eat,' said Rambo. 'Anyone want ice-cream?'

Winsome said, 'That smell has put me off eating for a bit.' Her sister and mother both shook their heads.

'I think I will,' said Alistair. 'Actually it's made me feel quite hungry.'

The women looked at each other and again shook their heads.

'I'll buy them,' said Rambo. 'What do you want?'

'Same as you're having.'

Rambo joined the queue. As he got closer he examined the illustrations.

'Two of those, please,' he said, pointing to a picture of a cone with a mound of ice-cream and a bar of chocolate sticking out of it.

'A Ninety-Nine,' said the bored young woman at the hatch.

'O.K.,' said Rambo and proffered a £1 coin. 'Keep the change.'

'No, that's £3. One-fifty each.'

'You said it was ninety-nine.'

'No, that's what it's called.'

'Is what called?'

'The ice-cream. Like what you asked for.'

'You have names for your ice-creams, or just numbers? That's funny.'

'Well, you've got numbers on the menus in your Chinky restaurants,' she said glancing coldly at him and at the queue behind him. 'Do you want them or not?'

'Yeah,' and he gave her a £5 note. She handed the ice-creams to him.

'Keep the change.'

She stared at him. 'Are you trying to be funny or what?'

'No, I mean it.'

'Well, thanks.'

'You're welcome,' he said and turned towards Alistair.

As he handed the dripping cone to him, a herring gull swooped and grabbed at Rambo's, sending the stick of chocolate flying, landing at the feet of an elderly man in a white, flat cap and beige, basket-weave shoes, who immediately stepped on it.

'You wait, I'll catch that bloody, that *diu lei* bird,' he shouted.

'I already told you. Stop swearing, *Jai*,' his mother rebuked him. Winnie repeated it in Cantonese and tried to look serious but Winsome laughed, her small, even teeth sparkling in the sunshine.

'You'll never catch it, Rambo,' said Alistair.

'Yes, I will. I can still see it.' He picked up a drinks can and threw it at the bird which had landed on the mud flat below the pier, its yellow beak still covered with ice-cream. It was a surprisingly accurate shot, missing by only a few inches. The bird rose, screeching, in the air.

'Careful,' said Alistair. 'You might have killed it.'

'That's what I want to do.'

'Then, what?'

'Then I eat it. I told you I was hungry.'

'You wouldn't eat a seagull, would you?' asked Alistair.

'Yeah. You know, we Chinese, we eat anything.'

'Well, how would you be able to cook it?'

'I'd eat it raw.'

'You wouldn't!'

Rambo grinned. 'Of course I wouldn't. Don't believe everything you hear,' and led Alistair further down the pier. The women followed. Alistair was not entirely certain whether Rambo's reassurance was limited only to uncooked seagulls.

'Winnie,' said Winsome, 'are there any shops on this place? I don't mean just restaurants, I mean proper shops.'

'I don't know. Maybe we take a look.'

'I don't want to go shopping,' said Rambo. 'Do you?'

'Not particularly,' said Alistair.

'How about, maybe, you three walk round this thing to see if there are any shops and him and me meet you back here in, say, half hour?'

'What will you do?' asked Winnie.

'O.K. We'll stand and look over the edge and see if the sea comes back.' Alistair did not understand why he winked at him.

'O.K.' said Winnie, and they walked off.

'Do you want some of my ice-cream?' said Alistair.

'No, I got a better idea. Look.'

Further along the pier was another kiosk. Above it was a sign with a single word: BAR.

'Let's have a couple of beers.'

'Oh. I don't think so. I don't drink very much. Actually, I don't drink at all. And, anyway, I don't think that I've got enough money on me.'

'No need. I'll pay,' said Rambo.

'No, well, I don't...I mean, that's very kind of you, but I don't think that it would be a very good idea because...'

Rambo interrupted him. 'Well I'm going to get one for myself, so why don't you try it. It's a sunny day. It's a holiday.'

'Yes, but, I don't think that my father would...well, I mean to say, if he had thought that I was going to buy a beer he might have given me a bit more money and...' and then he recalled what Uncle Frank had said to him that morning.

'Actually, why not? Yes, please.'

Rambo ordered two pints of lager. They were passed through the hatch to him in clear, bendy plastic containers. He and Alistair took them over to the parapet and leant on it, looking towards the water. Alistair had taken off his coat and hung it over the edge.

'Can you see, Rambo? The tide's coming in. The sea's got a bit closer,' he said. The sides of the unfamiliar tumbler squeezed in and he slopped beer over the front of his trousers.

'Yep, I can see. But look at you. Now we both look like we've wet ourselves. Drink some before you spill any more.'

Alistair took a sip, spluttered and swallowed. Then he took another sip and then, emboldened, a gulp.'

'Tell me,' asked Rambo, 'honestly, is this your first beer?'

'Er, yes.'

'What do you think of it?'

'Well,' said Alistair after a moment's pause and another gulp, 'it's got a bit of a funny taste, but it's quite nice. And it's thirst-quenching.' He took a long swallow.

'Better than ice-cream?'

'It is now. Yes, I think I'm starting to get used to it'. He drank some more and said, 'I think it's better than seagull, too,' and began to snigger.

'O.K.,' said Rambo. 'Finish that up and maybe we have time for another before they get back.'

But as Rambo walked towards the kiosk, he saw his family coming back, none of the three smiling.

'No shops here,' said Winsome. 'Shall we go into the town to see what they have?'

'I don't want to go shopping,' said Rambo. 'Do you, Al?'

'Not really,' said Alistair and he hiccupped.

'I not want to go, either,' said Ah-ma, 'I am tired of walking. I want to sit down.'

Winnie brightened.

'I got an idea. I look in the building before and they got gaming machines. You like a bit of gambling, Mummiah.

How about you go and sit at a machine and *Muih* and I go to town to look at shops and,' turning to the boys, 'you two can…'

'We'll find something to do,' said Rambo.

'Look,' said Winnie. 'Let's all go in together and find a machine for Ah-mah and then we can meet back there in about an hour.'

'Maybe, Alistair and I get something to eat. You hungry, Ah-ma?'

'No,' his mother replied, 'I ate already. I had some chips when those two were trying to find shops. Horrible!'

They walked together into the main building. As the glass doors opened, they were hit by a deluge of noise. Gaming machines, bumper cars, screaming children harnessed into the seats of a vertical ride, pinball machines, rock music, a ghost train emitting ghoulish laughter, glass enclosures with mechanical grabs hovering over tacky prizes, bells ringing, parents shouting, electronic fanfares as jackpots were struck, all together in a torrent of sound.

'This is a good place, here,' said the Ah-ma, her face lighting up as she saw an empty seat in front of a row of one-armed bandits.

'Do you know how to use it, Mah?' Rambo asked.

'Of course I do,' she said. 'Go, *Ah-Tsai*, I see you in an hour.'

'O.K, Mummi-ah,' said Winnie, 'Winsome and I go shopping now. You sure you be happy?'

'Yes, I'm glad to sit.'

'You've got enough money?' asked Rambo. 'I've got some £1 coins if you want.'

'Yes, I got. And will have more when you come back!'

'O.K. Then Al and I go to get something to eat.'

Rambo smiled at his sisters.

'Bye-bye *Sai-Lo*,' said Winnie.

'Bye-bye *Dai-Lo*,' said Winsome.

Impervious to the cacophony, the two girls walked off, arm in arm, towards the other end of the building and towards the town.

Rambo and Alistair went towards the door through which they had come and into the relative calm of the boardwalk.

'Actually, Rambo, I'm not really sure that I do want something to eat yet. In fact, I feel a little bit...'

'I'm not hungry, either,' said Rambo. 'What we need is that other beer.'

He left Alistair taking deep breaths of the sea air and went to the bar hatch. He came back with two more plastic tumblers of lager and joined Alistair as he leant over the parapet.'

'You O.K.?'

'Yes, I think so,' Alistair replied. 'Thanks for that. I feel bad about you paying, though.'

'You're welcome,' said Rambo.

They stared in silence for a while, Rambo trying to see if he could tell any difference in where the sea was from when he last looked.

'Rambo,' said Alistair after a while. 'Can I ask you something?'

'Yeah, O.K., man.'

'Well, it's this. Why does your family never call you

'Rambo'? They always seem to call you something else, but never your name. Why is that?'

'Rambo isn't really my name. Well, it is, but I gave it to myself.'

'How come?'

'Well, we Chinese, in the family, we usually call each other by what we are.'

'I don't follow.'

'Well, for instance, my mother calls me *Ah-Tsai* because it, sort of, means 'son' and Winnie calls me *Sai-Lo* because it means 'younger brother' and Winsome calls me *Dai-Lo* because that's big brother, because I'm twenty and she's nineteen. That's probably what you've heard them call me.'

'Did Winnie choose her own name?' Alistair asked and, perhaps emboldened by the beer. 'It seems a bit of an old-fashioned name to me.'

He laughed and hiccupped simultaneously, and then took a slurp of lager, spilling some down his shirt front.

'No. I don't think she chose it. I think that it was given to her by an old schoolteacher. A lot of girls in Hong Kong are called Winnie.'

'What about Winsome? Was that a teacher? I don't mean was the teacher called Winsome. I mean…' and he paused.

'Yeah, I know what you mean. No, that wasn't a school teacher, because I helped her choose it. She wanted an English name a bit like her older sister's and I thought that 'Win' sounded good. If a name sounds as if it's lucky then we believe that it can bring good fortune. She, of course, wanted to add something to the 'Win' bit and I suggested she should use something like 'plenty' and she liked that and was going to call herself Win a Lot until I found out that it was the name of some dog food. So then we decided on Win Some Money, and then just Winsome.'

'So, then, those are not your proper names. I mean, they are your proper names. I don't mean proper names, like in, er, Proper Names, I mean proper names, like your own names, er, I mean real names, except, I suppose, they are real names, er, do you know what I mean?'

'No,' said Rambo, 'I haven't got any idea what you're talking about.'

'Actually, what I mean is, do you, erm, do you have Chinese names?'

'Yeah, of course. Winnie's is Chi-fa. Fa means flower. Winsome is *Chi-saw*. No, that's a joke. It's really Chi-ming. Ming means bright.'

'So what about your name?'

'Well, we all have a family name. Ours is Wong. And then there's usually a generation name, that's like, all the brothers and sisters in a family, and our is Chi. And then there's the personal name. Mine is 'King', like royalty, only it means something different.'

'So, why did you call yourself Rambo?'

'Don't you see it?' Rambo said. 'I am Wong Chi-king. I thought that it was a pretty good name until I went to Senior School and the other kids said that it sounded like I was a cry baby. They started calling me 'Kentucky Fried Wong'. And that Rambo was a hero of mine and he was no coward. I'd seen his films, so I took his name. I did think of calling myself Sylvester Wong, but Rambo is better. So now, everyone calls me Rambo Wong. Except for my family.'

Alistair nodded. He felt a warm bond growing between him and Rambo. He didn't think he'd ever met such a nice chap. He wanted the day to last forever, except that he felt a little unsteady.

'Shall we have another beer?' he said.

Rambo looked at him. Alistair's shirt front was soaking.

'Maybe, later. Not for the moment. I think we had better go and check on Ah-ma, see if she's all right.'

They went back into the pandemonium and found Rambo's mother. She was sitting by the same gaming machine, frowning with concentration, her legs pulled back under the chair. The pile of coins had grown significantly. Rambo and Alistair went and stood behind her and Rambo touched her on the shoulder, but she continued to stare at the revolving images on the screen without looking up or otherwise acknowledge him. He touched her again and said,

'Mummi-ah.'

Without looking at him, she leant forward and pulled the lever. A trumpet blast issued from the machine, 'The Ride of the Valkyries' in electronic major. Lights flashed and twenty £1 coins clattered on to the tray. A momentary smile passed across her face as she added them to her heap of winnings and then she reapplied herself to the screen.

'Mummi-ah!'

She ignored him.

He moved alongside her and put his hand on her shoulder from the front. Angrily, she waved him away.

'Mummiah, I wanted to see that you were O.K. Are you happy to stay here for a bit longer?

She stared hard at the screen and pulled the lever again. Nothing happened apart from a flash of information about how many credits were left.

'So, Alistair and I will go and look around in here. We'll come back in about twenty minutes.'

Without turning away, she said, 'Because, you interrupt me when I am winning. Go.' She waved him away again.

'O.K. Al,' said Rambo. 'Let go. What is that over there?'

'Oh, Dodgems.'

'What's that?'

'Bumper cars,' said Alistair. 'Do you want to try them?'

After ten minutes of having their necks jerked, and of Rambo repeatedly being warned by the attendant not to dangle his arm out, and of being screamed at by a couple of teenage girls whom he targeted to the edge of persecution, they stopped the car in the middle of the rink, clambered out and, barely avoiding injury, dodged the between cars which were still colliding.

'Don't you two come here again, or I'll have the manager onto you,' the attendant yelled after them as they ran towards the bank of pinball machines which Rambo had spotted. They spent some time there, but gave up as Rambo was winning so often that he felt embarrassed for Alistair, who could not understand why the co-ordination of his hands and eyes seemed constantly to fail him at the last moment.

'Shall we have that other beer now?' he asked Rambo. He was not certain that he really wanted another one; indeed he was not certain of anything except his conviction that his new, Chinese friend was the most entertaining and heroic person he had ever met.

'Are you sure you can manage one?' asked Rambo.

'Yes, I think so. But let's find the toilets first. Oh, there's the sign.'

The doorway to the lavatories was in a corner next to the ghost train.

'Oh, look, what's that?' asked Rambo.

'It's the ghost train,' said Alistair. 'I'll tell you about it in a minute, but I've really got to go in there.'

He could not remember peeing for such a long time. He swayed slightly as the endless stream hit the porcelain with a pressure which, too, was unexpected. He grinned at Rambo, who was now standing beside him.

'Wow! Look how long I'm doing this for, Rambo! I'm better than a horse. That must be all of two minutes. That's me, empty for the rest of the day, I should think.'

'No, you'll need to go again soon enough.'

'Bet you I don't. Anyway, let's go and get those beers,' he said and turned away from the urinal towards the door.

'Aren't you forgetting something?' said Rambo.

'Oh, I'm not washing my hands,' said Alistair, giggling at his new boldness.

'That's up to you,' said Rambo. 'I just thought that you should put your *ban jau* away before you go.'

'Eh?'said Alistair. 'I haven't got a banjo. I don't get it.'

'Not a banjo. Look at you. You'll get arrested.'

Alistair looked at where Rambo was pointing, and hurriedly adjusted himself.

'And the zipper.'

'Oh shit!' said Alistair and laughed raucously.

They went out to the bar and bought two more lagers.

'You are the best friend I've ever had, Rambo' said Alistair, as they slopped them back to the pier's balustrade. 'I'm going to give you some money when we get back 'cos I'm sure you've bought at least two rounds. It's just I haven't got enough money on me. My bloody father didn't give me enough,' and he sniggered at his own audacity. 'I'll make sure you're alright, don't you worry. Oh, you asked about the ghost train. That's great fun. It's really scary – cobwebs and skeletons and things.

He hiccupped again.

'Shall we give it a try? But, I'm sorry, you'll have to lend me the money. I haven't got much. My bloody father didn't...'

'Don't worry. I'll pay. My pleasure,' Rambo said.

They tried to take their beers back into the building but, at the door, they encountered the man who had been in charge of the bumper cars.

'You can't bring those in here,' he said, suspicion written across his face. 'If you want a drink inside you'll have to buy one in 'The Captain's',' and he pointed to a cavernous fake pub on the other side of the vestibule.

'But, if you ask me, you two have already had enough. I've been watching you.' Alistair looked puzzled and was searching for a suitable response when Rambo took his elbow and led him back towards the parapet.

The wind was coming up and the mist had cleared completely. Mare's tail clouds were scattered across the deep, blue sky. Alistair stared at a gull perched further along the balustrade and watching him with an intensity that he had not previously noticed in seabirds. He wondered whether he could outstare it, whether anybody had ever tried to outstare a seagull; perhaps someone had conducted a scientific study about it. It was hard to concentrate on its eye, as it kept making little shrugging movements with its head and neck. Perhaps it did not like being stared at. It wasn't easy to know what it was thinking because he could only look at one eye at a time, sideways on. It wasn't like trying to outstare a human or even a cat. It wasn't easy to outstare a cat...

'You're right,' Rambo interrupted his meditation. 'The sea has got nearer. The space is filling up. Wah! I never seen that before. How close will it get?'

'I expect it will get right under the pier', said Alistair, and giggled, although he was not sure why.

'That's amazing, Al.'

That was the third time that Rambo had called him that. He liked it. It sounded tough. He thought that he might take to calling himself 'Al' from now on. His father wouldn't like it, he knew, and Percival might be a bit shocked. His mother probably wouldn't mind. She hardly said anything, anyway; he wondered why that was. Yes, it had a good ring to it.

'Come on,' said Rambo. 'Let's go and try that ghost thing.'

The bumper car man was no longer at the door when they went back inside and towards the ghost train. Exaggerated howls and screams were emanating from the entrance.

'It might be a bit scary,' said Alistair. 'Will you be all right?'

'I don't think it will scare me,' said Rambo. 'I like horror movies.'

After a ten minute ride in semi-darkness, during which their faces were brushed by sham cobwebs, and phosphorescent skeletons had swung towards them, and their ears had been blasted by electronic cackles and screeches, the carriage emerged into the bright hall. Rambo brushed fragments of fibre glass and dust from his hair.

'That wasn't very creepy,' he said. 'Are you o.k?' You look as if you've seen a ghost.'

'Actually, I'm not feeling too good.'

'Do you want to get some fresh air?'

'No, I don't think so. Actually, I think you were right: I need the loo again.'

'The what?'

'The toilet. I just need to get there.'

'Do you want me to go in with you?' Rambo asked him.

'No, I'll be alright, I think. I'll find you, but perhaps somewhere a bit quieter.'

When he emerged from the men's lavatory, Alistair was still pale but feeling somewhat better and a little less shaky. His head was throbbing, but he assumed that that was due to the noise and the harsh lighting. At first, he could not find Rambo, and then he saw him, staring at an upright glass case. There was a something that looked like a miniature crane inside, its claws hovering over a pile of trinkets, plastic balls and little, brightly-coloured cardboard boxes. He was half-crouching, staring through the glass.

'What is this thing?' he asked, turning towards Alistair.

'It's a grab game. You put a coin in there and you twiddle that knob and try and pick up a prize, and then you try to drop it down the chute.'

'Then what?'

'Well, if you get it in time, you win the prize.'

'Sounds easy.'

'I don't suppose it is, though.'

'Do you want to have a go?'

'No, I think I'll just watch you.'

Rambo put a £1 in the slot, the machine started to whir and the claws of the crane opened and began to descend.

'Go on,' Alistair shouted. 'Work the control!'

Rambo jiggled the lever and the crane went lower and then to the left, until it was just above a clear plastic ball containing a several coins. It was about two centimetres away, when the jaws closed, the whirring stopped and the grab moved back to its original position. He inserted another £1 and moved more quickly, aiming for the same ball. The jaws touched the edge of the ball and began to close over it, when the machine stopped again, skidding the ball to the other side of the glass enclosure.

'I think I am getting it,' said Rambo, 'but maybe that ball is too difficult. I'll try for this one next time,' and he pointed to a cardboard cube which gave no indication of its contents.

He put in another coin. The crane started up and he managed to get the claws immediately above the box, when they closed again.

'One more time,' he said. 'Perhaps it's easy to pick up that toy.'

There was a very small, bright orange teddy bear, with a miniature bow tie, sitting upright on a carpet of coins. One of its ears was beginning to come off. This time, he was faster, and managed to pick the bear up, only for it to fall from the claws as he moved it towards the chute.

'This is not fair;' said Rambo, 'but I'm going to make it fairer.'

'How are you going to do that?'

'If we lean this thing a bit to one side, the crane won't have so far to go down on the other side and it will give me more time to grab a prize. It's just geometry, Al. Will you help me?'

'I'm not sure...,' said Alistair. 'I don't know if that's such a good idea.'

'Come on, man, it's not that difficult. It just needs us both to lean against the side, then you hold it in position and I'll start the crane going. At least, let's give a try. If it doesn't work, I'll give up. Look, you put your shoulder there and I'll come round to your side and we can start pushing together.'

CHAPTER 13

Winnie and Winsome came back into the building. Winsome was carrying a Marks & Spencer bag but otherwise there was no indication of a successful tour of the shops. They walked towards the back, where they had left their mother and recognised the gaming machine; but the seat was unoccupied. The hubbub was just as loud as when they had left and it was, at first, difficult not to be distracted by the noise, as they looked around to see if they could find her. Some sort of incident seemed to have happened, because there were several attendants together at one corner. They wondered whether she might have gone to see what was happening, so they went towards it, but she was not among the onlookers who were watching someone sweeping up broken glass. They thought that they might catch sight of the boys, but they weren't anywhere to be seen, either.

'They probably gone to get something to eat,' said Winsome.

'But where's Ah-ma?' Winnie asked. 'She said she didn't want anything.'

They went back to the gaming machine. On the empty seat was a white plastic bag with the label of a duty-free shop at Hong Kong International Airport.

'She is saving her place,' said Winsome. 'She must have gone to the lavatory.'

They walked slowly round the arcade again, just to see if the boys had come back and were at any of the amusement machines. When they came back, the chair was still empty.

'Ah-ma doesn't usually take this long,' said Winsome. 'What can have happened to her? Do you think she's all right?'

'She said that the chips was horrible. Maybe she not feel so good. Maybe, because of the cold wind, she is getting a 'flu. We better look to see if she is in *chi-saw*.'

They went together towards the sign for the lavatories, beside the ghost train. The doorway led into a corridor, with 'Gents' on one side and 'Women' on the other. Winsome went in, leaving Winnie to wait outside, keeping an eye out for their mother and the boys. After a few minutes, Winsome came out.

'There are a lot of cubicles in there,' she said. 'Most of them weren't occupied and I looked under the doors of all the others. I think I could recognise her shoes. I couldn't find her.'

'Did you try calling her?'

'No. That's embarrassing.'

'Well, I think you should.'

'No, you do it.'

Winnie went in. She stood in the middle and called her mother in Cantonese.

'Are you alright, love?' came a voice from one of the cubicles.

'I look for my mother. Have you seen a Chinese lady?'

'There isn't one in here with me, me duck,' the voice replied and there were answering chuckles from some of the other cubicles. 'There isn't enough room. Although, I'd make an effort if it was man.'

A shriek of laughter came from nearby.

'You would, too, Annie. That would be just like you.'

Winnie, puzzled, called her mother's name again, but there was no reply; she came out into the passageway, just in time to see her mother emerging from the doorway on the other side. Winsome put her hand in front of her mouth.

'Mummiah, what have you been doing.'

'I had to go to the toilet.'

'But that's the men's *chi-saw*. What were you doing there?'

'Well, there's no sign. Just that English writing. Anyway, there weren't any men in there.'

'We were getting worried about you. Have you seen the boys?'

'Not since they left me. Anyway, I need to get back to my place. I'm having a good run. It's real *fat choy* for me today. I want to win some more.'

Winnie said to her mother that they ought to think about getting back as she did not want to get caught in heavy traffic on the motorway. She told her to remain at the same gaming machine while she and Winsome went to find Rambo and Alistair and then they would meet back there. They walked round the building again, checking every amusement machine and table and each queue. They went and stood by the ghost train exit for a few minutes to see whether Rambo or Alistair had gone on it, but when a group of laughing people came out, the boys were not amongst them. They checked to see whether there were any other entertainments that they might have gone to, but, apart, from the vertical ride, where, anyway, they could see all the occupants, there were none. They noticed the pub and, after a moment's hesitation, went in, uncomfortably, together and walked round the tables, ignoring the stares and offers of drink from overweight, tattooed men standing at the bar.

'Let's try the restaurants,' Winnie said.

'Yes, you're right; you know Rambo, when he's hungry, he'll have anything. He's not fussy, like Ah-ma. That's probably where they are,' Winsome replied.

They went back to their mother and told her that they were going to have a look in all the eating places on the pier; she was to stay where she was. On no account should she move as, once they had found the boys, they would bring them to her and then go back to where they had parked the car.

'I'm happy here,' said Ah-ma. 'Maybe another ten minutes, to get some more money.'

The girls went back to the pier entrance and looked into the ice-cream parlour. There were bright, clean tables and chairs inside, most of them occupied. Winsome was interested to see that it did not just sell ice-cream: there were plates of sandwiches with piles of chips beside them and, at several places, fat, shiny sausages with fried eggs and more chips. At every table there was a big, red, plastic tomato and a glass bottle of brown sauce. But no Rambo or Alistair. They came out again and began a methodical check of every café and restaurant on both sides of the pier. Although it was now late afternoon, they all were fairly full and, despite the different names and description of the establishments, almost all the customers were eating the same things – either fish and chips, or sausage and chips, or hamburgers and chips, or pizza and chips. Winsome noticed that they all had the same smell, a bit like McDonalds in Hong Kong.

'I'm getting worried,' said Winnie, looking at her watch as they came out of the last café. 'It's been more than an hour since we left them.'

'Yes, but you know what Rambo is like,' said Winsome.

'I know, but he wouldn't leave Ah-ma. I don't know where they can be. Surely, they haven't gone into the town.'

'Perhaps, they're down by the sea,' said Winsome, who had noticed that the tide had come in. 'You stay here and I'll go down to the water and take a look.'

She went down the steps by the sea wall and walked towards the water's edge. Winnie watched her as she went across the mud, leaving her footprints in the damp sand. The wind was stronger now and she realised that she was beginning to feel cold. The small figure of her younger sister got closer to groups of people along the shore, and scampering dogs, and she watched as she came back towards the pier. Winsome looked up at her and gave an expressive shrug of her shoulders.

'Have you got Rambo's mobile 'phone number? We better see if we can call him,' said Winnie.

'I've got his number, but it's a Hong Kong 'phone. I'll try it anyway.'

Winsome searched in her bag for her smart 'phone and brought up Rambo's name. A woman's recorded voice told her, in Cantonese, to try again later.

'If he's not got his 'phone switched on there's no point sending him an SMS or an email. Not if we want to talk to him now. But it's very odd; he usually has his 'phone on all the time, even when he's in bed.'

They stood for a moment, side by side, looking towards the sea

'So, what do we do now?' Winsome asked Winnie.

'I think we better go to the Police,' she replied.

They went back into the arcade to collect their mother who was, with her open hand, shovelling £1 coins into the white plastic bag. A contented smile had spread across her face.

'I've finished now,' she said. 'We can go now. Where is Rambo and that other boy?'

'Mummi-ah, listen,' said Winnie. 'We can't find them. There's no need to worry, because they're big boys, but we can't reach Rambo on his 'phone and we really should be leaving now. I am not very happy about driving husband's car when there is a lot of traffic. So, younger sister and I think we should go to the police station to see if they can help find them. Maybe they went into town and get lost and then the police will help find them.'

'O.K.' said her mother. She looked worried for a moment and then she brightened up again. 'You go to the police and then come back here. Maybe I'll have another quick game or two.'

'No, Mummiah,' said Winnie. 'You come with us. We don't know how long we are there.'

'But I'm tired.'

'No, you're not. You can't be. You've been sitting down for about two hours.'

'No, that's not true. I had to get up and go to the ladies.'

'Actually, you didn't, said Winsome, 'you went to the men's. But apart from that, you've been on this chair all the time. Come on, now.'

With much groaning and sighing, Ah-ma hauled herself to her feet and began taking very small, elderly steps. Winnie said:

'Come on, Mummi, you give me that bag...*aiyeeiah* it's heavy...and take my arm and Winsome's and we walk together. But *fai-dee, fai-dee,* hurry up, it's getting late.'

A young man was standing on the boardwalk as they left the building. 'You ask him the way to the police station,' said Winnie. 'Your English more better than mine.'

All three went up to him and he grinned broadly. Winsome asked him for directions. He gazed appreciatively after her slim figure and firm bottom as they walked back along the pier.

'Now, that's a nice young *gweil-lo,*' said her mother. 'Very helpful. Very polite. Not like that boy who came with us, that *tong sai lo* of your husband.'

'He's not a cousin, he's my husband-sister-oldest-son.'

'Well, who was the man who came this morning, wearing his collar back-to-front?'

'That was Alistair's father. He's a wicar. He is married to my husband's sister. She's called Celia. They got one other son, called Perky, or something.'

'I don't care what their names are. That boy is no good.'

'Why do you say that? He seems all right to me. Just a bit quiet. Perhaps he's shy.'

'Him? Shy? No, he's no good. Bad influence on my boy,' and Ah-mah assumed a sagacious, mother-knows-best expression, sucking in her lower lip and nodding her head, twice.

They walked on in silence until they came to the police station.

'I better deal with this,' said Winnie and she walked up to the counter, and approached a grey-haired man in uniform with sergeant's stripes on his sleeve. He smiled at her, kindly.

'Excuse me,' she said. 'I've lost my brother and his friend.'

'Is your brother, er, Chinese?' the sergeant asked, somewhat pointlessly.

'Yes, well he's a HKSAR citizen. He's from Hong Kong.'

'And is his friend, er, um, not Chinese?'

'Yes, he's *gwei-lo* – he's English.'

'And is the friend called Mr Spindle?'

'Yes, maybe. I think so. His first name is Alistair.'
'And is your brother called Mr Wong?
'*Wah*, how do you know that?'
'I'm very glad you've come,' said the sergeant.

CHAPTER 14

At about the same time as on the previous day, they were waiting for him in the lobby.

'Good morning, er, *Mayke*, good morning *Chon*,' Lev Petrovich greeted them. 'Where we go today?' I feel much better, had, mnym, good sleep.'

'We're off to Birmingham today. We're going to show you the other place,' replied Green.

They went to the car, which was parked in the same place, and drove to Edgware Road, and through Maida Vale, Kilburn and Cricklewood. Lev, more alert than yesterday took out a notebook and began to write down the names. They were very unusual and he wanted to be able to tell his colleagues about them when he got back. Green saw him doing this, and nodded silently, with approval. When they got onto the motorway, Lev Petrovich put the book away. He took it out again when they reached the edge of Birmingham and left it open, on his knee. He started writing when he saw signs for Stechford and Saltley and Lozells and Nechells and Sparkbrook.

Sparkbrook looked very much like the place in London that they had been to. The houses were similar, and after a few turns and diversions they were at another small industrial estate. This one, he thought, looks a bit better than the one yesterday.

'This remind me of Volgograd,' he said.

'Why's that?' John Black asked, as he turned off the satnav and removed it from the windscreen.

'Because, mnym, lot of rebuilding. Lot of new houses built after the Great Patriotic War. But still some ruins left. Was there siege here, also?'

'Not that I know of,' replied Black. 'But, then, I don't know this area. Have you ever heard of a siege here, Mike?'

Green shook his head. 'Not unless there was a skirmish between Bangladesh and Pakistan.'

'Why do you say that?' said Black.

'You'll see when we get out of the car. I've been up here before. Let's leave the car here.'

As soon as they were outside, Lev was aware of the most enticing smell. Wafts of fragrant, unfamiliar spices filled the air.

'What is smell? Is wonderful. Have never smelled before. Mnym, mnym, is this the sauce you talk about yesterday?'

'No,' said Mike Green, 'what you can smell is curry. Or rather, balti. We're on the edge of the Balti Triangle.'

They walked through the gateway and into the industrial estate. The roadway was crumbled and potholed from the passage of heavy vehicles. On either side were small, single-storey factories, built of brick and asbestos-roofed. Some were occupied by garages and car body repair shops. There were two printing businesses, a sign-writer's, a vibratory metal-polishing business called 'Master Bright' and a plastics extrusion company. Some of the buildings seemed to be unoccupied, but most had cars parked outside, and lights on inside. There was a tyre-fitter's with the shutter doors open, and as they walked past, Lev saw that there was a car perched on a hydraulic ramp inside. By a larger building, articulated lorry trailers were spaced closely together. Lev slowly read the writing on the sides and was about to ask what was meant by 'logistic issues' when Mike spotted a large wooden shed across the road – 'Proky's Caff', the sign read.

'Anyone fancy a coffee?' he asked, 'I could do with one. What about you, Lev?'

'Please, yes,' said Lev Petrovich.

'Might well be a Russian place' said Black. 'This could be interesting.'

'Why do you say that?' asked Green.

'The name; it's certainly not English. Possibly, it's short for Prokofiev.'

'Mnym, but, in Russia, nobody called Proky.'

'Well, let's go in and find out.'

Behind the counter was an overweight man in his forties, his large bald head accentuated by a comb-over which gave the impression of an oil slick floating on a pink ocean. He wore a grubby, off-white apron over his protuberant belly. A large steel urn, from which wisps of steam emerged at the top, stood beside him.

'There you are', said John. 'A samovar.'

' 'allo, gents, you allroit?' said the fat man. 'What would you loik?'

'Three coffees, please,' said Mike.

'Anythink ter eat? Oi'm doin' a special on bycon sornies. Boiy one, get one fray.'

Mike looked at the other two who both shook their heads – in Lev's case, in bewilderment.

'No thanks, well, may be a packet of crisps. Do you have any crisps?'

'Yeah. What flyvour? Oh, sorry, oi've only got plyne.' He elongated the word, dropping the tone in the middle and raising it to at the end.

'Plain will do.'

'Milk and sugar, gents?'

Green looked round again. 'Just white, no sugar, please.'

'Tyke a seat. Oi'll bring 'em over.'

They sat down at a formica-covered table, against a wall. A grimy window looked out onto a side street. Mike peered through it.

'That's the place, that's where we're going.'

'Where?' asked Lev Petrovich.

'Do you see that white sign with red lettering? Camberwell Fabrications?'

'Yes, yes I see. Like the name yesterday?'

'Precisely. You're certainly on the ball, Lev. We'll take a closer look after we've had our coffee.'

The fat man brought three mugs over to them.

'There you go, gents.'

'Tell me,' asked Green, 'are you the owner?'

'Yeah.'

'How come you're called Proky?'

'Oh that...that's a spelling mistyke. That's whoy oi 'aven't pyed the soign-wroiter.'

The delicious smell, when they got outside, was just as strong, if not stronger: cumin, coriander, ginger and fennel with an undercurrent of garlic and onions.

'I think that the wind has change direction a bit,' said Mike, 'but it seems to be always in the air. Just think about, it's a perfect cover for what they might be doing over there. You'd never know if they were cooking up a sauce there.'

They went and stood across the road from the building. It was less ramshackle than the factory that they had looked at on the previous day, but there was no sign of any activity. Here, too, drawn curtains hung inside the windows. Once again, the sign board was very clean and looked freshly-painted.

'Is like yesterday?' asked Lev. 'We don't go in?'

'No, that's right,' Mike replied. 'We just want you to have a look at it, briefly, and, perhaps, get the feel for it. Because it might not be John and I who come back with you. We tend to do day shifts, and you will probably want to come again, like at the other place in New Cross, when it's dark. This is more in the nature of a recce. Incognito. We don't, any of us, want to put our faces on offer. Today, it's best to keep a low profile, but you should have seen enough for you to know how you'll want to kit yourself up for when you come back.'

Lev nodded, as if in full agreement.

'I understand,' he lied.

'Have you seen enough?'

'Yes.'

'O.K., we'll go.'

'To Cheltenham?'

Mike and John laughed.

'No. It's alright,' said Black. 'You don't need to keep up the act with us anymore.'

'So, where we go now?'

'We'll go straight back to London and drop you off at your hotel.'

CHAPTER 15

The calm in the house was almost palpable. The only sounds now were birdsong from the garden, the occasional car being driven slowly down the quiet street and the muted voices coming from the television in the living room below, in front of which Frank had installed Winnie's father, waiting for the horseracing to begin. The sunlight which came dappling through the plane trees fell onto his desk. He looked at his watch; there was plenty of time before he was due to meet Theo. He turned on the computer again. Celebrity chefs and their impossible 'simple' recipes: that should keep him going for a while. After thirty minutes he got up and went downstairs.

'I'm going out for a bit, Mr Wong,' said Frank. 'I shouldn't be too long. Will you be all right by yourself?'

The old man smiled at him, revealing several gold teeth, but said nothing.

Frank Grinder crossed the sunlit Suffolk Terrace and turned right and then left into Prince Street and then left again into Bleinheim Road. He had recognised the name as soon as he had looked at the scrap of paper that Theo had given him; he had strolled along its tree-lined pavement from time to time, without taking particular notice of the houses in it, other than that they were buildings similar in age and style to those on his own street. He was vaguely aware, from the fact that several of them had doorways with more than one bell push, with names beside them, that they had been divided into apartments. Number 53 turned out to be one of those. He went up the steps, and pressed the buzzer second from the top; as the paper said, it was the only one with no name beside it.

The door opened instantly. Theo beckoned Frank urgently into the hallway and closed the door behind him. He then opened the door, looked up and down the road and shut it again. He looked very different, without his wig and glasses and with normal eyebrows, but the big, shambling frame was unmistakeable. He appeared to have cut himself whilst shaving, because there were small scraps of tissue paper adhering to his cheeks and chin. Frank wondered how he had managed to nick the end of his nose, but now knew better than to ask.

The detective put his forefinger to his lips and blew on it, as if he was cooling the barrel of an imaginary pistol, but by which gesture he was indicating the need for silence. Then, on tiptoe, and with large strides, he led Frank to the staircase, turning once to repeat the gesture. At the second floor landing, he took out a Yale key, opened the door and ushered Frank in.

In spite of the bright day outside, it took Frank a minute or two to accustom his eyes to the gloom in the flat and to understand the reason for it. The two sets of heavy, velvet curtains were drawn except for a small gap in the middle, through which the sunlight struggled. He took in the dark, functional furniture: a dining table with six chairs and a shabby, settee covered in a sombre, mauve fabric. On the table lay a plate with a couple of toast crusts and smear of baked beans. Steam rose from a half-empty mug of tea. It was obvious that Theo had not intended to invite him to stay for lunch, which was a relief. Theo went to a window and opened the curtains just sufficiently to enable him to peer into the street. He then did the same at other window.

'S'okay,' he said. 'Tek a sitt.'

Frank sat, gingerly, on the edge of the settee. A small cloud of dust rose from it. Theo sat at the table, pushing the plate to one side as he did so.

'Iss goot thet you were ebbel to come now.'

'Why's that?' asked Frank.

Theo got up and went to look out of the window again.

'Becorrse, Oi eff met a decision.'

'Oh yes?' said Frank.

'Yiss.'

Frank waited. Normally, he thought, when you tell someone that you have come to a decision, the next step is to say what it is. Instead, Theo was silently staring into his tea mug. It seemed to Frank that a minute had passed by.

'Aren't you going to tell me what it is?'

'Iss a spider. I thought voss a fly, but, no is differnertly not a fly. Look, iss got no vings,' and he got up and showed Frank a black object which was floating in the bottom of the mug.

'No, I meant, aren't you going to tell me what it is that you've decided?'

'Oh, thet. Um coming orrf.'

'Orrf?'

With an air of portentousness, like a prime minister announcing to anxious listeners that the currency had been devalued, he said, 'Um coming orrf the case. Oi eff decitet thet iss inconsistent with the dignity of my prrofession that I continue to rrun the rrisk off infolfement in neffrious activity.'

'Neffrious?'

You know, immoral, rreprre'ensible. Against the law. Oi thought that, ass a solicitorr, you'd know vot thet minns.'

'I've never been a criminal lawyer,' replied Frank, and then asked himself why he had said it.

'You'ff never been a criminal lawyer, always a 'onest one, I suppose,' and Theo smirked the same thin, straight smile that Frank had seen in the pub the day before.

'So, your leaving the case,' said Frank. 'I rather got the impression that you might from what you said yesterday. What are you going to do?'

'Vot do you mean, vot em Oi going to do?'

'Well, I mean, what are you going to do?' Frank wondered how he could explain himself further. 'You can't just stay on in this flat, doing nothing, presumably. What's your next step going to be?'

'Vell, the fursst thing is thet I shall mek contact with my client and toll 'im thet Oi corrnt ect fr'im any morre as moi perrfessional entuggrety vill be comppermised if

Oi find myself impelcated in, luk I sed, neffriuous skulduggery, and thet oi eff mussguffings about the 'ole effer...'

'Effer?'

'*Ach, die hel*, mon, you eff something wrong with your earring?'

Frank momentarily touched his earlobe in puzzlement when Theo continued,

'A-F-F-A-I-R, effer, and Oi am not perrparred to rrun the rrisk of being struck orrf by my prrofessional body...'

Frank wondered, simultaneously, what the professional body was, and whether Theo's client would understand him when he told him that that he was resigning.

'...and, therreforre, Oi em coming orrf.'

'So, you'll tell him – if you can find him – that you are resigning from the case.'

'Yiss.'

'And then what will you do?'

Theo shrugged.

'Oi effn't yet decided. Oi vill eff to go back 'ome, Oi suppose,' and he seemed wistful, 'and Oi certainly von't do any more spoying verrk, at least, not forr those bukkerrs, but Oi might chust kip moi oy on you ent yourr voyff.'

'Why would you want to do that?'

'Chust to mek surre you don't come to any 'arrm.'

Frank was alarmed.

'That is very kind of you, Theo, it really is. But I don't think that anyone can seriously think that Winnie and I are involved in any of this business. You said yourself, yesterday, that you could see that we weren't connected with it and...,' he paused to consider how he could put it diplomatically, '...whilst I appreciate that someone of your perspicacity,' he wondered, on seeing Theo's look of incomprehension, whether he should, in revenge, spell the word out, but then decency triumphed, 'will have worked it out before lesser men could, nevertheless, I think that anyone who has seen us would eventually come to the same conclusion. So I'm sure that we can manage without your help, kind though your offer is. And,' he added, 'I really couldn't put you to any further trouble, particularly when I'm sure that you will want to get back home as soon as you can. I bet that, since you've been here, the cases have been piling up for you and that your secretary will be waiting for you to come back and deal with them.'

He wondered whether Theo had seen through his attempt to flatter him; they didn't sound too convincing.

'Lissen,' said Theo. 'You von' efen know um there.'

'What about your return flight?'

'Ped forr. Open-intit rreturrn.'

Frank sighed.

'Look, Theo, thanks for that but I really don't think I'm going to need you.'

Theo looked hurt and he sniffed.

'Vell, um not doing it for you, then. Oi'll do it for Vinnie. She, at lisst, looks as if she vould be grretful for some discrrit perrtection.'

'I had better be getting back,' said Frank, looking at his watch although he could not read the dial in the dim light. 'Was there anything else that you wanted to discuss? You remember that you said yesterday that you wanted to continue the conversation that we were having in the pub.'

'No nothing,' and Theo sniffed again.

'O.K. then, I'm off. I'll see you, I suppose, or perhaps not.'

'You go down by yourself. Best ve're not sin together.'

'Suits me,' said Frank and, once again, regretted it.

When he got back to his own house, the racing had begun. The old man had moved his chair closer to the television and was staring at the screen, his glasses at the end of his nose. With a ballpoint pen, he was marking the list of runners in the newspaper, which lay folded across his lap. A steaming cup of Chinese tea was on a side table next to him.

'Hallo, Mr Wong, everything o.k?'

Ah-leung glanced briefly towards him and nodded.

'How about something to eat? *Sik fan, ma*?' asked Frank, using one of the important phrases that he had learned in Hong Kong.

'No, thanks, I make sandwich later,' the old man replied, haltingly.

So he can understand English, Frank thought. That would make things easier.

'Alright, just let me know if you want anything. I'll be upstairs in my study. Oh, by the way, have you heard anything from Winnie? Any 'phone calls?'

Ah-leung stared, blankly at him, then went back to the television.

CHAPTER 16

'What we shall do,' said Dick Worthy 'is to file into the hall in the order in which we shall be sitting. So, you'll go first, Johnny, and then you, Lev, and then me and then you, Eleanor and last, but not least, you, Taylor. I hope that you don't mind abandoning the 'Ladies First' rule, but there's not that much room between the seats and the edge of the platform and what I don't want is doing some sort of gavotte in front of the audience.'

'We live in modern times,' Eleanor Landarbeiter replied with a guffaw. 'Makes not a scrap of difference to me.'

They had assembled for coffee in the same room as the previous evening, for what Worthy had referred to as a 'pre-con pep talk'. A plate of biscuits lay on the table.

The organic Ms Landarbeiter was not wearing her tweeds today. Instead, she had on a cotton print full skirt and a purple blouse with a loose, floppy bow at the neck. Her iron hair was screwed back in a bun and she had, this morning, applied startling lipstick. Lev Semyonovich looked at her and wondered whether she was a victim of deuteranopia. Siccita, the young American, was wearing a beautifully cut, dark blue suit and pale blue tie. Johnny Walker was dressed as on the evening before. He looked at Lev, smiled and shook his head as Lev took out his packet of Java Solotaya cigarettes.

'Sorry, Lev,' he said. 'You can't smoke in here.'

'Really?'

It's against the law. Can't smoke in restaurants or hotels or public buildings. Even at work. It's like the bloody Soviet Union...sorry, I didn't mean that.'

'No, that is all right. Though, actually, you could smoke in the Soviet Union. In fact, you were encouraged to.'

'Is that right?'

'Of course. The Party wanted to promote the sale of CCCP cigarettes.'

'What were they like?'

'Strong. Very'

Dick Worthy moderated.

'Shall we get back to business? So, when we have all taken our places, I shall make a short, introductory address and then you can all make your presentations. You've all had a chance to look at the timetable I showed you yesterday?'

They all nodded.

'So, if no-one has any last-minute objections, we'll stick with that order: Eleanor, you first, this time; then Taylor; then, you, Johnny; and we'll finish up with you, Lev, as you're the star turn.'

This comment did nothing to lift the cloud of apprehension that had been hovering over Lev Semyonovich Ivanov since yesterday evening's meeting. A Java would have been very timely; but it couldn't be helped. For an instant, he considered feigning illness, but if they called a doctor and he found that there was nothing wrong with him, it would only complicate the problem even further. He could not afford to risk exposure, and its inevitable consequence: discovery of the reason why he had come to England. He had worked too hard, achieving dominance in his field; it would all be blown away if that happened. He would just have to improvise. He had been in tight spots before.

'Fine,' said Worthy. 'So, we'll go in, shall we?'

They left the Shergar Room and walked along the corridor. When they got to a pale wooden door, Dick opened it and ushered Johnny Walker in. Lev followed him onto the platform and sat down. He turned to his right and saw Worthy pulling out a chair for the surprised Eleanor, and Siccita sitting down beyond her. He then looked straight ahead.

The conference was much bigger than he had hoped. Nearly every seat was taken by, mostly, middle-aged men and women. His first impression was of cardigans and sports jackets and open-necked shirts. A few black faces; were there, African delegates, he supposed. In the front row was a thin, balding man in a dog collar. But so many people in the audience; could they all be interested in – he glanced at the paper which he had brought in with him – *Beetroot Production for a Hungry World*? And he was supposed to be the expert on beetroot. He smoothed the flyer on the dais in front of him and hoped that inspiration would come.

The moderator was on his feet and addressing the delegates. Ivanov heard the words 'urgent' and 'together' and 'sustainability' several times, he heard his own name and those of the other people on the platform, and 'crisis' and 'self-sufficiency' and, once, 'macro-economics'. He heard 'issues' repeatedly and 'nutrition' and 'super-food' and 'logistical', and then there was applause and Eleanor Landarbeiter was standing up and talking into the microphone.

She spoke briskly and, as far as Ivanov could tell, cogently, because there was much nodding in the audience. At one stage, he noticed, the priest was making notes and, in the rows behind him, a few others were also doing so. Her manner fell into the hinterland between forthrightness and aggressiveness; the way she grasped the edges of her lectern and thrust her upper body half-forward suggested that she would brook no dissent to the propositions that she was advancing. Her topic was, as she had indicated, organic production of vegetables. She enthused over the way in which the manure, which was readily available in Third World (no, she did not call them that, she said 'developing') countries, was horribly under-utilised. Ivanov took in some of what she was saying as he cast around for recollections of anything to do with beetroot. He was arrested, partly through the reaction of the audience, by her use of the expression 'bucket loads of their own shit', and her snorted laugh as she said 'but don't try this at home.' Suddenly she was onto the dangers posed to human health when this method of fertilisation was employed with lettuce and other shallow-rooted, edible-leaf plants and the superiority, in this respect, of *beta vulgaris*, with its inbuilt crap-filter. And then she said that, on that subject, they probably could have done with a crap-filter when listening to her and, to surprised laughter and much applause, she sat down.

Worthy thanked her and turned to the next speaker, whom he introduced as being a leader in the field of irrigation, excuse the pun, and he laughed, alone. Taylor Siccita rose and moved across to the lectern, smoothing his lapels and adjusting the already impeccable knot of his silk tie. He spoke quietly for twenty minutes, projecting Powerpoint diagrams and charts onto a screen to the left of the platform, his rimless glasses reflecting the images. At first, there were several requests from the back of the hall for him to speak up, but these subsided as the listeners sank into a stupefied torpor as he droned statistics towards the screen, almost never looking at the audience. Lev Semyonovich gave up trying to follow what Siccita was saying; there was absolutely no risk that he would unintentionally repeat any of it when it came to his turn to speak, and he was better employed trying to think of something to say. What could he remember about beetroot? He wished that he had taken more interest during *botanika* lessons in senior school.

There was a scatter of polite applause as Siccita resumed his seat. Worthy moved to the lectern and introduced Johnny Walker as an unusual speaker. He said that it was a breath of fresh air (if his more academic colleagues took no objection) to have someone from a business rather than a scientific background and he knew, from past experience, that he was quite a character. The members of the audience looked relieved and, when

Worthy pre-empted him by saying that, with a name like that, it was obvious that he would give a *spirited* talk, this time they joined in his laughter – at least, enough of them to avoid him more embarrassment.

Walker spoke without notes, without Powerpoint images, without making use of the presentation easel that stood behind him on the platform and, seemingly, without conscience. Even to Lev's distracted and unfamiliar perception it was apparent that he was plugging his own business in the hope that, amongst the delegates, there were representatives of aid agencies or foreign governments. The hypotheses of his talk were simple and two-fold: a great deal of potential in the production of beetroot was going to be lost because of inefficiencies in distribution; and it was only the group of transport companies with which he was connected (an obvious euphemism for ownership of the majority shareholding) that had the necessary expertise and equipment to solve the problem. He called the problems 'the logistical issues'. He spoke with an earthy charm, interspersed with several anecdotes, and had the audience's attention and laughter. He told them of how satellite navigation technology had led inexperienced drivers (not, of course, employed by his organisation) to destinations so far from where they intended, that they were actually in the wrong country. He spoke of the waste caused by duplication of instructions on the one hand and of the failure to maximise capacity with the 'full-load in, full-load out' principle. He told them how vitally important it was to have a network of spare-part depots, such as that which his companies had established in all developing countries; and how, just like in the HSBC advertisement, it was essential to be familiar with local customs and languages, something which, of course, he had instilled into all his employees. He concluded by telling his listeners that he happened to have brought along some information packs which would provide some detail (and contact information) which he had left in the place where, he believed, they were about to have coffee.

Lev observed the Moderator from time to time whilst all this was going on, and particularly during the last few minutes. His face was impassive. He had wondered, at the time, why they had not taken the break after the second speaker and now he thought, perhaps, that Johnny Walker had been deliberately placed to follow the tedious irrigationist.

Dick Worthy was on his feet again, telling the audience that, somehow, Mr Walker had read his mind, and that they would now be taking the coffee break in the room that led off the back of the hall.

'Fifteen minutes, please,' he said, 'and then our distinguished Russian guest, whom we've all been looking forward to hearing from. And do help yourselves to Mr Walker's literature which, as he said, is in the coffee room.'

He ushered the speakers off the platform.

'There's more coffee for us in the room we were in before,' he said. 'I thought that you might prefer not to have to mingle quite yet,' and he looked towards the cleric who seemed to be hesitating between approaching the platform and joining the throng.

'Let's move quickly,' he said, 'before we're caught.'

'I think I will just go to my bedroom for something,' said Lev. 'And then, maybe, for some fresh air.'

He went along the corridor with the other four, but instead of going back into the Shergar Room, he continued to the reception area and out through the main entrance. For a moment the idea of making off passed through his mind, but the thought of what the consequences might be overcame it. He stood on the gravel driveway and took out his packet of cigarettes. As he inhaled the first few draughts, an idea began to form. After five minutes, Lev Semyonovich went back the way that he had come, and turned into the room where the others were still having their coffee. Worthy turned towards him and looked at his watch.

'There's probably enough time for you to have a cup, Lev,' he said. 'That is, if you still want one.'

Ivanov thought that he detected more than a simple enquiry. He probably suspects that I've been for a slug of vodka, he thought, rather regretting that he had not.

'No thanks, I don't need coffee.'

Was that a knowing look that Dick Worthy gave him?

'I have been outside for some air. And a cigarette,' he added, to allay Worthy's suspicion. 'I am ready to start now, if you want.'

'Hang on a minute; I'll just see if Conference has re-assembled before bringing you all back in.'

He went out and came back a minute or so later.

'Yes, they're all back in their seats,' he said. 'So, if you're all ready, let's go.'

The delegates were, as far as Lev could see, sitting in the same places that they had been in before the break. Some had taken off their jackets or jerseys, although he did not feel that it was warmer; in fact, he felt slightly chilled. Perhaps the air conditioning above where the speakers were sitting was more powerful. He glanced at the others, but they seemed unaffected. Eleanor Landarbeiter smiled encouragingly at him and gave a thumbs-up sign. Worthy stood up.

'We now come to our final speaker this morning. I am sure that this will be a great treat for us all. I know that I have been looking forward to hearing from him. Dr Ivanov is a fellow of the State Technical University of Volgograd. He has, as most of you know, had a distinguished career in the field – there I go again – excuse the pun, of agricultural development and has made a specialty of the storage of carbohydrates in root vegetables. For the last six years he has concentrated his research on the nutritional properties of the *genus beta vularis* and has authored several papers and, I'm sure that he won't mind my saying this, the absolutely definitive textbook on the subject of the cultivation and processing of beetroot. I was going to call it 'the humble beetroot' but I am confident that, by the time that he has concluded his presentation, you will think of it as a noble vegetable. We are all very grateful that such a distinguished and busy man of science should take the time and trouble to travel from Russia to be with us at our conference. So, ladies and gentlemen: Dr Lev Petrovich Ivanov,' and Worthy resumed his seat.

There was animated applause as Lev Semyonovich rose and moved to the lectern.

'Beetroot, ah, beetroot!' he began. 'It is the soul of Russia.'

He rolled the 'R's and assumed a stronger Slavonic accent than when he had been talking to Dick Worthy and the others; and he spoke slowly. He saw Worthy give him a quizzical glance.

'Everybody knows how important it is to us. I suppose everyone here has eaten Russian salad and I pity those who may not have yet tasted our beautiful *borscht*, the soup which sustains us in times of cold and misery and also in times of celebration. My dear, dead mother used to make it with, also, carrots and celery and, when we could obtain one, the juice of a lemon, and then would add sour cream. You can eat it hot, or you can eat it cold. Perhaps with some black bread to help fill you up. Then you are in paradise.'

He paused, and wiped away a non-existent tear.

'Forgive me, but my English is perhaps not so good.'

A shaking of heads in polite disagreement in the front row.

'You are so kind. But when I remember my little *mamochka* and her wonderful soups it is difficult...'

He bowed his head in silence, and glanced at his watch. There was an embarrassed, sympathetic inclination of the heads in the front row.

'But it is not only for salads and soup that we use our beetroot. We use it also as a vegetable in our stews. And we get most of our sugar from it. And,' here he took a punt that no-one in the audience knew whether or not this was true, or even possible, 'we make a particularly delicious type of vodka from it.'

No-one appeared to demur.

'Because of all the sugar in it. Because it is very good against the cold. And we have a lot of cold weather in Russia. As Napoleon found to his cost.

'My mother,' he paused and looked down again, 'she made wonderful beetroot vodka. And beetroot *borscht*, but I think I have already told you that.'

Another pause.

'This conference is to address the problem of,' now glancing at the crumpled piece of paper, 'beetroot production in a hungry world. And everyone thinks that the hungry world is in hot countries, like in Africa and India. But that is not always the case. Of course not. In cold countries you can get very hungry, also. In fact, when it is very, very cold you get very, very hungry, unless you have some hot food. In Russia it can be very cold. That is why we like our beetroot soup. By the way, we also like cabbage soup. You don't have to put soured cream in cabbage *borscht.* But a piece of bacon goes nicely in it. My mother also, she made cabbage soup. Sometimes with bacon in it. Sometimes not. So it is not only in hot countries that beetroot is very good for nourishment of people. People think that a cheap source of food is needed only in poor, hot countries. But is also in cold countries. There are poor peoples in cold countries. Like in Russia. That is why we like our beetroot.'

There was a certain amount of restlessness in the first

few rows. The man in the dog collar crossed and recrossed his legs and shifted in his seat.

'So, that is why I now tell you this story: South east of Nizhny Novgorod,' he continued, guessing wildly, 'about two hundred kilometres from the city, there is an area famous for its beetroot production. The soil is very rich and most of the farmers there, I think you would call them smallholders, cultivate this vegetable. It is a wild and lonely place, and the wind can blow very cold there. Much of the beetroot is used for the production of vodka and it has to be taken to the big state-owned distillery (I am talking of the Soviet times) where it can be processed. By tractor and trailer is several days journey, there and back, and it is too far for most of the farmers to go, and too expensive for them. So, they use a co-operative system and buy together a tractor and some trailers and they chose one among them, usually a fit young man, to deliver the crop to the distillery and then he brings the empty trailers – I am sorry, Mr Johnny Walker, but they don't have your advice – and takes them back to each of the farms.

'The time I am talking of was, perhaps, forty years ago. The young farmer who had been selected to make the journey wrapped himself warmly against the wind and the rain, kissed his young wife goodbye on the doorstep of their warm, little house and set off towing several trailers loaded with his beetroots and the beetroots that his neighbour had dug up. He stayed, on the way, in *tavernas*, which are like a simple inns, and delivered his load. He made good time on the way back but, still, he had been away three days and nights. When he got to his village, he drove straight back to his house. It was now very cold and night had set in.

'His pretty wife heard the tractor coming along the lane and stood by the front door to welcome him home. She had lit a big fire in the kitchen and a pot of rabbit stew was cooking gently, giving off a wonderful odour. She had also baked some *chleb*, our Russian rye bread, and had put out a tumbler of vodka for him. As soon as he got in, she helped him out of his wet greatcoat, led him to a chair and pulled off his boots.

'He sat by the fire, very glad to be home, and sipped his vodka. Then, when he was ready, his wife ladled some of the delicious-smelling stew into a couple of bowls and set them on the kitchen table, with chunks of bread beside them. They had their meal in contented silence and, when they had finished, she cleared the table, poured her husband some more vodka and came to sit beside him by the fire. Only then did they begin to chat.

"Volya,' she said, for that was his name, 'how did it all go?'

'He told her of his journey. How it had been very windy and wet on the first day; how he had stayed at the same two inns that he had used previously; how the owner of the second one had tried to swindle him over the price of his meal by claiming that he had beer when he had only had vodka; how the men at the distillery had been very friendly and had helped him to unload the trailers so that he could make an early start back; and how only the foreman had been rude to him and made him wait till the beetroot had been washed before he would weigh them.

He told her about his return journey, making good enough time with his empty trailers to be able to avoid stopping at the cheating inn and to go straight to the other one, where, although he arrived very late, they were willing to give him something to eat and how, the next morning, he had found a rash over his back and chest and thought that he must have been bitten by bedbugs, although the itching had stopped now. And, of course, he told her how glad he was to be home, and he leant over and kissed her cheek. Then he asked her what she had been doing while he was away.

"Nothing special,' she replied. 'Oh, except something quite odd happened on the second night that you were away.'

"What was that, my love?' he asked her.

"Well,' she said. 'I had started to make the rabbit stew in advance because I know how much you like it when it has been reheated a few times.'

'He smiled at her and nodded.

"And,' she continued, 'it was an awful night, much windier than the night you left, quite a storm, with driving rain.'

'She told him how, just as she was going to sit down and have something to eat, she heard the sound of a car coming down the lane and stopping outside the house. She drew back the curtains at the window and saw a man opening the little gate and walking towards the front door, so she opened the door. In that short distance he got soaked; the rain was running in rivulets from the brim of his hat. So she asked him to come in and dry his coat by the fire.

'He was a big man, of about forty and with black hair and a well-trimmed beard. While his clothes were drying, she offered him a tumbler of vodka, which he took, gratefully, from her. They chatted of this and that and, after an hour had passed, his coat and hat were dry, but he showed no signs of going and, as she was hungry and wanted her supper, and felt that it would be wrong to start without inviting him to eat, she asked if him if he would like to have some supper.

"That was quite right,' said her husband, 'it would have been very rude not to ask him to join you.'

'So she asked him to sit down, and she gave him some of the rabbit stew, which he seemed to enjoy very much because he had a second helping. After supper, she made some black tea and they sat by the fire and drank a couple of glasses, and chatted some more.

'What with the rain and the wind outside and the smell of the wood smoke, she began to feel drowsy and wanted to go to bed. The man still showed no signs of getting ready to go; and she was in a quandary. She did not know whether to ask him to leave or whether it would be just as rude to go upstairs and leave him alone.'

"So, what did you do, my love?' asked her husband.

'She said that she had thought it over for a while, and then decided to ask him if he wanted to stay the night. He readily accepted the invitation. The only problem was that it would not have been very comfortable downstairs, as he would have had to stretch out on the stone floor beside the hearth and, also, it would have got cold when the fire died down during the night. So she thought that she had better ask him to come upstairs. Well, of course, there was only the one bedroom with the double bed in it.

"'So, I suppose that there was nothing for it, but for you to let him share the bed.'

'She said that that was just what she thought. There really was no alternative.'

Some of the audience were looking at their neighbours in uncomfortable puzzlement.

"'No, I suppose not,' said her husband. Then after a while he asked, 'Did you make love?'

'She explained that it really was very cold outside, and they could hear the wind howling across the plane and they had snuggled up together under the blankets, and so it seemed only natural to hold each other tight and then she found that they were having sex. Then they went to sleep, but early in the morning he woke her and they did it again.

"'Yes, I understand,' said her husband, 'it must have been very comfy in bed.'

'She said that the man had been very good at it, but that she did not think it would be right to do it for a third time, so she got up when she heard the cock crowing and went downstairs to draw some water from the well and to start making breakfast. The hens had laid some eggs, so she cooked them with some *kasha*. He came downstairs when he smelled breakfast, had a wash in a pitcher and sat down with her to eat. Then he finished dressing, put on his hat and coat and went back to his car. She had heard it as it drove slowly away, down the lane.

"'Did he say anything before he left?' her husband asked.

"'No,' she replied, 'nothing at all. In fact, he was really quiet in the morning.'

'Husband and wife sat silently for a while, looking at the fire.

"'Would you like some vodka before you go up?' she asked him.

"'No thanks,' he replied, 'I'm ready for bed now.'

'They sat for a while longer, then the husband asked her if it really was true that the stranger had said nothing that morning and she replied that, as far as she could remember, it was true; he had said nothing, except, now that she came to think about it, he had thanked her just before he left the house. And, yes, he had shaken her hand.

"'So,' said the husband after a while, 'I don't suppose we will ever find out what he wanted when he came to the house.'

"'I suppose not,' she replied.

'So,' Ivanov continued, 'that is a story about beetroot farmers in Mother Russia.'

An embarrassed silence filled the hall, broken only when Dick Worthy coughed nervously. Lev Semyonovich turned towards him, and then back to the audience.

'Yes, I see,' he said, 'I think that the Moderator is telling me that my time is up. Yes, I see it is,' and he ostentatiously looked at his watch.

'I regret, because there is much more that I would like to have been able to tell you about the growing of beetroot. Perhaps, is better if you read my books. Thank you.'

He sat down. There was a smattering of applause; politeness rather than enthusiasm. Lev could see several delegates talking to their neighbours and shaking their heads. Worthy was on his feet again.

'Well, yes, er, thank you very much for that most insightful and, um, moving, that is to say, amusing talk. Really informative. We are all so grateful to you and, er ...I think that we have now some time for a few questions. Yes?'

Although he vainly, desperately looked round the auditorium for any other raised arm, the only one belonged to the old conference-hand in the dog-collar. He pretended that he had not seen it, but could not maintain the fiction, particularly as, after an unconscionable pause, no-one else came to his aid.

'There is a question from the front row.'

'The Reverend Aubrey Spindle, M.A. My question is, in point of fact, for our distinguished Russian visitor. He paints a very moving picture of the loneliness of life in the countryside near, where was it...?

'Nizhny Novgorod,' interposed Lev Semyonovich, relieved that the priest could not remember the name.

'...and it is very interesting to hear about the uses to which *beta vulgaris* can be put. But I would like to learn from him a little more about the technique of cultivation of this most important vegetable. I happen to be very interested in it and have made something of a study and, if I may be permitted to say so, a contribution, albeit modest, to the learning on the subject. In fact, I, personally, have cultivated quite a successful crop, myself, in the small allotment that I have the privilege of using and, in the last few years, it would not be going too far to suggest that my production has been quite abundant, but that, of course, is in English climatic conditions, where we do not, in my experience, er, um, experience the extremes, and, in particular, the exceptionally cold weather, and from the sound of things, the bitter winds that...'

There was a commotion on the platform; Worthy had jumped to his feet.

'I'm sorry to interrupt you, sir,' he said, 'but it looks as if Dr Ivanov has been taken ill.

Lev Semyonovich had slumped forward onto the desk, his head resting on his folded arms.

'Are you alright, Lev?' asked Worthy, bending over him.

Lev Semyonovich opened one eye, and then the other, and blinked.

'I will be fine, I think, in a minute.' He had reverted to his normal English. 'Perhaps a little fresh air.'

'I think that you should go up to your room. You don't look well. Would you like me to call a doctor?'

'No, no. But I think you are right. I shall go to my room.'

'Conference,' Worthy addressed the audience. 'We'll take a five minute break and then resume the questions and answer session. But without Dr Ivanov, I'm afraid.'

A surprisingly gentle Eleanor had come over to Lev.

'Come on, old chap,' she said, 'I'll see you to your room. You look as if you could do with a lie down.'

CHAPTER 17

The telephone on his desk rang. Frank picked it up, expecting it to be Winnie. Instead, it was the Team Vicar.

'Er, hallo, Frank.'

Frank swore quietly; bang goes the rest of the afternoon, he thought.

'Er, did you say something Frank? Hallo, is there anyone there. Hallo.'

'Yes, Aubrey, I'm here,' he replied. 'And, no, I didn't say anything, at least, not *to* you.'

'I'm sorry, have you got someone with you? Am I disturbing you?'

'No and yes.'

'I don't follow you, Frank. What do you mean?'

'Never mind, Aubrey. What do you want? I thought that you were at your horseradish-fest.'

'No, it's beetroot. I told you, *beta vulgaris*. And it's not a festival. It's a serious scientific conference. An assembly of like-minded people who, in point of fact, have an interest in the cultivation of this most important root vegetable. Well, I say, cultivation, but the matters under discussion are not restricted, merely, to cultivation, because we have had most informative talks on irrigation and, indeed, on the problems of transportation; and also there was an interesting, talk by a Russian academic, although I say interesting, it was rather puzzling, because I am not *entirely* certain I followed his exegesis; although he was very moving when he described the loneliness and hardship of life in the tundra. Well, actually, I'm not certain it was the tundra, because he was talking about a region of Russia with which I am not familiar; actually, and in point of fact, I am not particularly familiar with any part of Russia, not having been fortunate enough to have visited that country, but...'

'You were, I think,' Frank interrupted him, 'about to tell me what you've called me for. You haven't finished already, have you?'

'Well, you've rather hit the nail on the head, Frank... Sorry, did you say you have got someone with you? You said something.'

'No, I haven't got anyone with me. I expect it's just my paranoid schizophrenia talking.'

'I am so sorry, Frank, I did not realise that you are unwell. Would it be better if I rang you back later? Would you prefer me to... ?'

'Aubrey, please tell me why you called.'

'Why I called? Called? Oh, I see, you mean, why have I telephoned you?'

'Yes.'

'Ah, that's most interesting. I have heard people use that term before, but that has, rather, been on one of those rare occasions when I have watched an American film on television. They say 'call', don't they, when we would say 'telephone'? Or we would normally say 'ring' wouldn't we? I mean, the verb rather than the noun. But then, it should not be surprising, should it, when we talk about a telephone call? But I hadn't appreciated that it had come into usage in this country. Of course, it may be that it is something you picked up in Hong Kong. Do they say 'call' over there?

'As far as I know, I never picked anything up in Hong Kong. Aubrey, what do you want?'

'Oh, I, er, *called*,' and Frank envisaged the arch smile, 'in order to tell you, as you so rightly surmised, that we have finished. It came to something of an abrupt end because the Russian academic whom, you may recall, I mentioned, was taken ill. Not, I think and, of course, devoutly hope, seriously, but enough to bring his part to an end. It was really most unfortunate because I was in the middle of asking him a question about the effect of climatic conditions on cultivation, and it would, I have the temerity to think, have elicited an extremely illuminating response because I had been formulating my enquiry with some considerable care before posing it and, had he been able to respond, it would have been of particular interest to many at the conference who, like I, had come along in the expectation of broadening our knowledge, not only for personal gratification, but also because so many of us were, I surmise, concerned for the wider picture, namely the alleviation of famine and concomitant hardship in less fortunate...'

'Aubrey.'

'Yes.'

'Why are you telling me this?'

'Because I wanted to let you know that I shall be leaving shortly. We carried on with some more questions and answers after the Professor had left the conference hall and, indeed, there were some useful adjuncts to what we had already learned from the others speakers, but the session did not last anything like as long as I had anticipated, and, but for the regrettable mishap, it would, I think, have lasted considerably longer. I had, in point of fact, made some notes for questions that I wanted to ask of the other speakers but, puzzlingly, try as a might, I just could not catch the Chairman's eye. In fact, two or three times he seemed to look straight through me, even though I had my arm raised. It was most curious, but then, I suppose, he probably was unsettled by that unfortunate occurrence when I had, indeed, managed to ask a question. So I shall probably have a quick chat with one or two of the other delegates and, possibly, a cup of tea. I suppose that they will still be serving tea, even though we did not get as far as the tea-break which was on the, er, menu,' and Frank could almost hear the smirk, 'excuse my pun. In point of fact, they ought to provide tea, because refreshments were included in the price of the tickets...'

Frank could not restrain himself.

'You *paid* to go?'

'Of course I paid. I couldn't ask the treasurer of the parish to fund my excursion which was to pursue an interest of my own. Anyway, I shall go and find out whether tea, and I would hope, some cake, or possibly biscuits, although cake would be better because, now I come to think about it, as a result of the disruption earlier – you know, of course, that I am referring to Dr Ivanov's unhappy episode – I did not manage to get anything for my lunch. Although, I should have done because luncheon was also included in the programme. Perhaps I ought to follow that through, although it does seem somewhat niggardly to complain about missing lunch when it was the result of the misfortune that was visited on that poor gentleman. I wonder how he is? Frank, I might just see if I can find the Moderator and enquire of him whether Dr Ivanov might appreciate a visit from me. What do you think?'

'I wouldn't,' Frank answered, momentarily putting the welfare of the unlucky academic before his own convenience, even though it might have delayed Aubrey's return. 'He might think that you have come to administer the last rites.'

'Frank, I am a clerk in holy orders. Of the Anglican Church.'

'You mean, you wouldn't do it because he's probably Russian Orthodox? Or, perhaps, a Marxist?'

'No, Frank, because I do not administer last rites.'

'No, but he probably doesn't know that. You'd probably scare him.'

'Do you think so, Frank? Well, perhaps I'll go in search of a cup of tea and if I see the Moderator I'll ask him… hang on a minute, would you, please?'

Frank waited for a few seconds, and then put the 'phone down. He returned to his computer and looked at what he had written on in his latest topic: the misrepresentation of court room scenes in television drama and soap operas. Ending it with the travesty of the judge in the full-bottomed wig seemed satisfactory enough. Perhaps a quick reread to see if he had missed anything. The 'phone rang again.

'Ah Frank, I don't know what happened there,' said Aubrey. 'We seemed to have been cut off. Er, the reason why I left you was because Mr Worthy, the Moderator, was just walking past. I suppose he was going to see if he could get some refreshment, although, in my haste, I omitted to make an enquiry of him as to whether there was any available; anyway, I did ask him if he thought that Dr Ivanov would appreciate a visit from me, both in my capacity as a clergyman and, dare I say it, as a colleague who shares the same interests; I don't think it would be appropriate to call myself a friend, or even an acquaintance, not on such a limited time that we had talking to each other although, in point of fact, it was I who did most, well actually, all of the talking when I was asking him my question...'

'And?'

'And? Oh, I see, well, the most mysterious thing. Perhaps not *the* most mysterious, after all, we are taught that the concept of mysteries is essential to our even beginning to set our feet on the path to understanding the Creator...'

'Aubrey,' said Frank, no longer trying to conceal his impatience. 'Do you know the expression 'cut to the chase' by any chance?'

'No, I can't say that I have ever come across it. Is that something else that you picked up in the Far East?

'No, Aubrey, it comes from the early days of Hollywood. It means: let's get to the exciting bit.'

'Oh, really, I had no idea that Hollywood contributed expressions to the vocabulary. No, I'm not correct there. I occasionally have had cause to rebuke my boys for using modernisms which I suspect they have garnered from American films on television. I heard Percival talking about a 'movie' the other day and was not altogether happy with it. But then, I don't suppose we can keep our young wholly immune from the influences to which they are exposed, particularly in the area of language. I gather from some of my parishioners that they have the greatest difficulty in communicating with their offspring because the young, they say, seem to talk a different language. You don't have children, do you, Frank? No of course not, how silly of me: I would have known if I were an uncle. Well, actually, I am, because my younger sister has children. But what I meant is that I would have known if you, being Celia's brother, had issue. I don't believe that you were previously married, were you?'

'No,' said Frank. 'Do you recall what I just said to you?'

'Er, about American films?'

'No, about getting to the point.'

'I was going to, Frank,' said the Team Vicar, offended. There was a pause.

'Well?'

'Oh. I see. Well, the most extraordinary thing. The Moderator seemed to be in a frightful hurry when he saw me looking in his direction, but I managed to catch him and asked him about visiting Dr Ivanov, and do you know what he told me?'

'How could I, Aubrey?'

'I don't follow. How could you what?'

Frank breathed deeply.

'How could I know what he told you? I am here at home and you are, where exactly?'

'The Madrigal Country House Hotel and Conference Centre. I imagine that you know it. It's that big white building set in park land about five miles outside Cheltenham. On the Evesham Road. It's a most impressive place, Frank. The facilities seem to be excellent. That is,' he added, 'for the conference. I haven't managed to explore the hotel proper, although I would have gone inside, of course, had I been to see Dr Ivanov.'

'Aubrey.'

'Yes.'

'What did this Mr Worth tell you?

'Worthy, his name is Worthy, Frank. Richard Worthy.'

'Good. And?'

'Oh, yes, well, he told me that he had already gone up to see Dr Ivanov. It wasn't he, but another speaker who had taken him, that is, Dr Ivanov, up to his room. A very pleasant lady, with a most forthright manner and an unusual name, and she told the Moderator that she had settled him, that is Dr Ivanov, not the Moderator, down on the bed and left him to have a lie down and given him her mobile telephone number – they really can be very useful things, can't they? Although sometimes they can be something of a nuisance, don't you think?'

'And?'

'Well, Mr Worthy had made sure that everything was

in order so that he could continue with the question and answer session after the short, unscheduled break that we had. It was, indubitably, sensible for the Moderator to have called for a five-minute break when Dr Ivanov collapsed. Well, collapsed might be too strong a word for what happened, but he certainly was not fit enough to continue. I noticed, even from a little distance away, that he had started to become rather pale when I was putting my question to him and I thought that I could detect, to put no finer point on it, a degree of perspiration on his brow, and I was, as I intimated to you, several feet away, at least fifteen feet I should estimate, although it might well have been further. And so, if I could see these symptoms from where I was he, undoubtedly, was not well; nobody should criticise him, Mr Worthy, that is, for taking the action that he did.'

'Has anyone done so?'

'Has anyone done what, Frank?'

'Criticised him. Otherwise, I don't know why you are telling me this.'

'No, no-body has, as far as I am aware. At least not to me. Or in my presence. And indeed, why should they?'

'Indeed, why?' said Frank, as usual, regretting his intervention. Every attempt to speed Aubrey up seemed to have the opposite effect.

'No, you are quite right,' said Aubrey. There was another pause during which Grinder battled inwardly with the urge to intercede between the Reverend's thoughts and his narrative so as to unblock the latter. He lost.

'Hollywood, Aubrey.'

'I beg your pardon.'

'You were going to tell me about what happened when this Richard chap went up to the Doctor.'

'Oh no, he didn't call a doctor. Did I say that he did? If so, I would have been quite wrong. At least, I think so... come to think of it, he may well have thought it the wisest thing to seek medical help. I suppose that the hotel might have a doctor upon whose services they may call in the event of an emergency. Oh I see what you mean, Dr Ivanov.'

'Bulls eye!'

'I'm sorry, Frank,' he said, 'I don't altogether follow you.'

Grinder groaned.

'Are you alright Frank? Are you sure that you haven't got someone with you. Because, you should say if I am interrupting something. I thought that you were saying something to somebody.'

'Please,' said Frank, 'just tell me what happened. The suspense is becoming too much for me.'

'Er, um, well,' Aubrey continued, 'the Moderator oversaw the rest of session. There were not many questions and, as I told you, I was not able to ask any more, myself. So he brought the proceedings to end and then went up to see Dr Ivanov. And do you know what he found?'

'No,' said Frank, and managed to check himself.

'*Well*, when he went up, the bedroom door was ajar, probably because the inside latch thing had been pulled across to stop it from closing. You can do that, you know, with hotel doors. I had to do it once when Celia and I were staying in a nice hotel in Eastbourne and I discovered, when we got into our room, that I didn't have the key.'

Grinder's self-protection mechanism failed again.

'Did you say *into* your room?'

'Yes. Why do you ask?'

'How on earth could you possibly have got into the room in the first place if you didn't have the key?'

'Ah well, that's an interesting story. I had found that I had mislaid the key when we returned to the hotel after our evening stroll and I assumed that I had left it in my other jacket which was in the bedroom. In fact I was so sure of it that, when I went down to reception and the young man, who came up again with me and let us in with a master key, wanted to wait until I had located it, I told him not to bother as I knew where it would be. So he went, and then I remembered that I had brought only one jacket with me. So Celia and I went down to the reception again and that is how I found that you could prop the door open.'

'And?'

'Well, the hotel was most obliging and issued us with replacement keys. Fortunately, they were those little card things that you slide into a slot. They took the precaution, which was most considerate of them, Celia and I both thought, of reprogramming the new key in case the old one were to be found by a miscreant, not that he would have been able to tell which room it was for, but it was still a sensible thing to do. Unfortunately, we couldn't get the new one to work, and so we had to go back to reception again. The nice young man couldn't understand why that was so and said that they had never encountered any problems like that before and came back up with us, and then he explained that it wouldn't work if the door was open, which it was, of course, although only slightly, because we had propped it open with that latch thing.'

'Aubrey.'

'Yes?'

'What about your Mr Worthless?'

'Worthy, Frank, you know it's Worthy.'

'O.K. Mr Richard Worthy. What did he find?'

'Well, he knocked, but there was no answer, so he went in and there was no sign of Dr Ivanov. He said that he knocked on the bathroom door but there was no reply, so he went in but he wasn't there. He noticed that it looked as if it hadn't been used since the room had been serviced, although when he went back into the bedroom he saw that the bed cover was a bit crumpled. So he went downstairs to the reception to ask if they knew where he was, the Doctor, that is, and do you know what they told him?'

'Aubrey, how could...No tell me.'

'They said that he had checked out, called for a taxi to take him to the station and gone. And it was just after that that I saw him?'

'Dr Ivanov?'

'No Frank, have you not been listening to what I have been telling you? I saw the Moderator when I was talking to you. Before we got cut off.'

'Right, I follow. Now what?'

'Well, I shall be with you, assuming that I manage to have some tea, in about half an hour.'

Frank put the 'phone down. He looked at his watch. Enough time for a really brief topic, he thought, unless Winnie and the others came back soon; they must have been enjoying themselves, as he had thought that they probably would have been back by now. It was surprising she had not called to say that she was on her way. Still, it was good to be able to take advantage of the quiet in the house. He flicked through the notes on his desk. Here was a good one: social networking.

Frank had just turned off the computer, when the 'phone rang.

'F'ank.'

'Hallo, Winnie, are you on your way?'

'No. I'm still in the seaside. Because ...Rambo and Alistair got arrested.'

CHAPTER 18

The heat under the Victorian iron canopy of the railway station was oppressive and Lev Semyonovich Ivanov was relieved when the London-bound train pulled in on time. Stepping up to the air-conditioned first-class compartment he felt a sense of relief; for the first time since realising that the mistake had been made about him, he began to relax. It had been his good fortune that the hotel reception did not ask him any penetrating questions about the reason for his premature departure but, then, this was England, and to someone brought up in the Soviet era, it was still a pleasant experience to deal with people who were what they seemed to be, and not another functionary of the state. The young lady at the desk had merely asked him whether he had taken anything from the minibar or had made any telephone calls that morning, assured him that everything else had been paid for in advance, expressed her concern that he had been taken ill, called a taxi for him, wished him a nice day and added that he should take care. At this last comment, his instincts had raised a momentary frisson, until he recalled that it was no more than a benevolent, if vacuous, form of goodbye, and not a warning. He put his black leather bag in the overhead rack and sank back into the comfort of his seat. He closed his eyes for a few moments then, smoothing his hair, took a note book from his pocket and, with a gold ballpoint pen, began to list the steps that he should take. His first task, of course, was to find a decent hotel, and his second was, urgently, to make contact with the principal and explain what had happened. He hoped that he had not lost too much time in Cheltenham and that he might still be able to do what he had come to England for, but, for him, the most important thing was to exculpate himself for not acting more quickly. He could, perhaps, imply that he had been kidnapped and, unaided and through his own skill, been able to escape; he might, possibly, hint that his safety was in peril. But, above all, he must ensure that his professional reputation was not jeopardised.

Maybe it would be better not to go to a hotel which was too flashy. Somewhere fairly inconspicuous would be more suitable. He would take a look near the station when he arrived. He made a few more notes and then put the book and pen away and watched as the countryside flashed past the train window.

Although he had been to London before, Lev Semyonovich was not familiar with the area round Paddington Station or, indeed, the station itself. He wondered whether there might be an information desk that would help him find somewhere to stay, but as he approached the ticket barrier he found the crowds too discouraging; it was not that he suffered from under-confidence, but that he did not want to be conspicuous and he felt that, with all these people around, it might take a while to locate a help desk, even supposing that there was one. Wandering around the concourse of a large railway station was the last thing he wanted to do, particularly as he had noticed the overhead cameras as soon as he stepped onto the platform. So he put his ticket into the machine and, as the barrier opened, walked with the throng straight out of the station and onto the street.

The traffic was at a standstill as he crossed the road. There were so many people on the pavement that it was difficult for him to stop and look around without causing an obstruction, so he walked down the first side street that he came to. It was much quieter there and he was able to stand with his back to a building and take in the character of the area. It did not look too promising. He was reluctant to return to the main road, so he went further down the street and turned into an alleyway. To his surprise, there was a sign on a building which, even at a distance, he could see was in Cyrillic script. He moved closer and saw that it was a hotel. A sombre building, but it looked discreet and unobtrusive. Strange that it had a Russian name. As he got closer, a smart, black Mercedes pulled up and an untidy-looking man with a beard climbed out of the back seat. He stopped for a few moments, talking through the window to the passenger in the front, adjusted his glasses and walked up the steps to the hotel. Lev Semyonovich followed him in, as the car pulled away.

The bearded man went to the desk and asked for his key. Then he went towards the gloomy depths of the hallway. Lev Semyonovich approached the desk. A flabby, shiny man was sitting behind it; he had just picked up a newspaper and seemed put out by another interruption. With an air of reluctance he conceded that, yes, they did have a room available tonight and for the next few days and, yes, it did overlook the street and, no, it wasn't necessary to produce a passport, only a credit card and no, there was no restaurant or bar in the hotel; and did he want the room or not? If so, fill in and sign this form.

Lev Semyonovich wondered whether it would be best, for the time being, not to use his own name, but realised that he would have to if he produced his credit card. He slid it from his slim, black leather wallet and passed it across to the fat clerk, who took an imprint from it. A look of curiosity crossed his face as he handed it back.'

CHAPTER 19

Frank Grinder was still in his study when he saw Aubrey's car pull up on the other side of the road. His heart sank and for a moment, just for a moment, he considered moving away from his desk so he could not be seen from the street. Then he remembered that Winnie's father was downstairs, and he might open the door when the bell rang and, limited though his command of English was, there was no escaping the fact that he would lead the Team Vicar to his quarry. A moment's thought later, and he appreciated that he needed Aubrey because Winnie had the car. So he got up and went downstairs and walked along the passage to the front door.

He could see an outline through the patterned glass at the top of the door but was reluctant to appear to be too welcoming by opening it before the bell rang. So he stood there and watched as the figure remained outside, not quite motionless, as Frank could see the head moving and could just make out a hand going towards the upper clothing. But still there was silence. Frank waited for the doorbell and wondered whether there might be a fault, but it had worked earlier that morning when Aubrey had come. Well, he'll knock, won't he, he thought, if the bell isn't working? Still silence, but an increase in the agitation outside: now both hands seemed to be rummaging through his coat or jacket. Then the figure moved away a few steps away so that Frank could not see him; then he came back and, through the glass, appeared to continue searching.

After a couple of minutes, he could bear it no longer, and opened the door.

'Oh, it is you,' said Aubrey.

'Of course it's me. I live here, you know.'

'Ah, yes, but I wasn't certain.'

'What do you mean you weren't certain. You came here this morning. You left what's-his-name here. You know, your son.'

'Alistair', reproved the Reverend M.A.

'Yes, him. What on earth were you doing outside?'

'Well,' he hesitated, 'I knew you lived here. That is to say, in this street. I knew that. And, as you so rightly observe, I came here this morning with my son, Alistair, whose name you seem to have forgotten, but I wasn't sure, in point of fact, that I had the correct house number. All the houses along this street seem to have – how shall I put it? – a certain sameness that makes it somewhat difficult trying to distinguish one from the other. That is, of course, not to imply…'

'Aubrey,' Frank interrupted, 'I hope that you aren't going to be offensive. These houses look alike because they were designed to. This is what is called Regency Symmetry. It's what Cheltenham is famous for. It is why the planners don't let people paint them in different colours or add bits on just so lost sheep might find it easier to locate their brothers-in-law.'

'No, of course I was not going to be offensive. I find this style of architecture particularly pleasing, although it has often been a source of puzzlement to me why it is relatively uncommon to find churches that are built in this fashion. I mean to say, there are so many Tudor, and earlier, churches and plenty of Victorian structures, particularly in urban areas, although there are also, in point of fact, quite a few in village settings, usually where they have replaced much older ecclesiastical buildings which had fallen into dereliction but not, unless I am very much mistaken, many in this style. Although, of course, I may be wrong.'

Frank, in spite of himself, threw his barb.

'You mean, there aren't many terraced churches? Yes, I suppose you're right. It would be interesting, though, wouldn't it: a row of churches, side by side? Difficult for the parishioners to choose which one to attend, though, I suppose. It would make more sense if it were multi-faith, come to think of it. Start, say, with C of E at one end, and then have Methodists and Baptists next to it then, perhaps, a Catholic church, then a synagogue and a mosque – no perhaps better to separate them, let's put the Unitarians there, then a Sikh temple perhaps, then Hindus then Jains, although I'm not sure whether they would get on as neighbours, so let's have the Mormons between them. It would be great. You could call it 'God-Botherers Row'.'

'Frank, I don't believe that you are being serious.'

'No, I'm not. But tell me, what was the problem? What were you doing outside?'

'Ah, unfortunately, although I could remember which street you live in, I could not recall the number. I had made a note of it, which I used when I brought Alistair here this morning, but I could not remember what I had written it on, or, indeed, where I had put it. I think I would have entered it in my list of addresses which I keep in my pocket diary but, I regret to say, I appear to have mislaid it. As I think I told you, there was an unfortunate incident, or, perhaps, it would be better to call it an unfortunate series of incidents, commencing when I was in the course of asking a question to one of the speakers at the conference and, I suppose, it is not entirely impossible that during the ensuing disorder of events and the puzzling *dénouement* that followed, I may have inadvertently dropped it, or – and there is a real chance, I must admit, that this might have occurred – it may have been knocked from my hand; not, I am sure, deliberately, because one would not expect, what I might term, rowdy behaviour at an assembly of such serious-minded people; but, whatever the explanation is, try as I might, I was not able to lay my hands on it when I was standing in the porchway of what I thought probably was your house; there was a certain familiarity which made me choose it but I was insufficiently sure to venture ringing the bell, which is why I was standing at your door, looking for it. Not of course,' and here he chuckled ecclesiastically, 'that I was looking for your door, although, in point of fact, I was looking for which one it was, because your door is by no means lost. No, I was looking for my diary, if the number is in my diary, although I might have found that I had written it on a separate piece of paper, in fact, yes, now that I come to recall it, I think that I did have it on a piece of paper, which I left on the dashboard of my car this morning when I came here. Shall I go and see if it's still in the car? No, I think not, as I am, after all, at the correct door as your presence here testifies. But here I am, rambling on in a manner which, I devoutly hope, is not typical of me. How are you Frank? Have you had a good day? Are they back?'

These sudden questions brought Grinder back from his mesmerised state.

'Oh, yes, thank you. I'm fine. But they're not back. In fact, there's a bit of problem,' he said. 'You had better come in. We're going to need your car.'

He ushered his brother-in-law into the living room, where the old man was still in front of the television set. The racing was finished and he was now absorbed in watching the Teletubbies, the Racing Post still on his knees. Frank had heard the rumour that one of the Teletubbies swore in Cantonese and wondered if Ah-leung was on to it.

'Are you all right?' he asked him.

The old man looked up and grinned.

'Can I get you something to drink?'

The old man shook his head and went back to the screen.

'You had better come upstairs to the study,' Frank said to Aubrey. 'I'm not sure how much English he understands and I don't want to get him upset.'

Aubrey followed him upstairs and took the seat that Frank proffered. Frank told him about the call that he had just had from Winnie; he explained that he knew no more than that they were all at the police station and that she had promised to wait until he got there. He did not even know what the boys had been arrested for, but it was plain that he would have to get there as soon as possible and that he needed Aubrey to drive him.

The vicar was shocked, but not into silence. He stood up and began pacing around the study, as he expressed a mixture of reactions and proposals, the underlying thesis of which was that there must have been a dreadful mistake as he knew that his son was incapable of wrongdoing (apart, of course, from the lapse involving the motor car); and that the best resolution was for him to present himself at the police station where, surely, the officers would accept the word of a man of the cloth. Once he had finished, or rather, paused for breath, Grinder suggested what he thought was a better solution. Although he was now retired, and that his years of legal practice spent in conveyancing commercial properties and taking part, with merchant banks, in the flotation of companies on the Stock Exchange of Hong Kong, and drafting partnership agreements, could hardly be said to have prepared him for police station interviews, he was sure that his training and experience as a lawyer would be rather more useful in this situation than that from which Aubrey had benefitted at theological college. He could see that he was upset and, almost, felt sorry for him and it was as much from a feeling of sympathy as from the tactical advantage of not letting

Aubrey make matters worse, that he tried to persuade him of the case for letting the solicitor rather than the vicar handle the affair. It was, perhaps, unfortunate that he added:

'Unless, of course, you expect some sort of divine intervention.'

Aubrey pursed his lips and inhaled, audibly, through his beaky nose, as if about to deliver a sermon to congregation of backsliders. Grinder forestalled him.

'Look, Aubrey,' he said, 'we haven't got time to sit around chatting.'

'You will, perhaps, have observed that I am not sitting,' replied the Team Vicar. 'For my part, I am taking this very seriously. It is a thoroughly regrettable turn of events and, the Lord only knows how frightening the experience must be for Alistair. I think that we must proceed as quickly as possible.'

'Not only the Lord,' said Frank, again, instantly regretting what he was about to say, but nevertheless, saying it. 'I imagine that Alistair also knows.'

'I am afraid that I don't follow you.'

'Never mind. Look, we're agreed that we should get moving. Is it alright to go in your car?'

'Have you any better suggestion, Frank?' replied Aubrey feeling, at last, that he had scored a blow against his – he had to admit it – somewhat conceited brother-in-law.

'No. So, I'll just give Winnie a call to say that you have arrived and that we are on our way. And I'll check that her father will be happy here on his own. '

They went downstairs and into the living room. The Teletubbies had finished and Ah-leung was now watching an Australian soap opera, a plate of sandwiches on his lap.

'Look,' said Frank, 'Aubrey and I have to go out. We won't be back for a few hours. Will you be O.K?'

The old man looked at him and smiled sweetly.

'Do you follow what I'm saying? We have to go and bring them back from the seaside. It's better if you stay here, but you can come with us if you're not going to be happy here. Would you rather come in the car?'

Ah-leung silently turned back to the screen.

'Help yourself to food, Ah-leung. Or beer. But are you sure that you'll be all right on your own?'

The old man, still smiling, gestured him away.

'*Mo fai-di,*' he said.

'O.K, then we'll be off,' and he walked towards the front door with Aubrey.

'What was that he just said?' asked Aubrey. 'Did you understand him?'

'Yes, he told us not to rush back.'

The Reverend M.A. opened the car and sat behind the wheel. He started the engine. Frank stood in the road by the passenger door; through the window he could see, on the dashboard, a piece of paper with his address written on it in large letters. Aubrey crashed the gears and slowly started to move away from the pavement, forcing Frank to leap out of the way.

'Hey!' he shouted.

The car stopped and Aubrey leant across and wound the window down: it was a very old car.

'I'm so sorry,' he said. 'I am afraid that I did not notice that you were not in the car. I must confess that I am somewhat preoccupied.'

'Somewhat!'

'Yes, I am not at all myself. But why don't you get in?'

'Because, because ...I can't do it.'

'Oh, my dear Frank, I am afraid that I took one or two of your earlier remarks as flippancy. I see now that you, too, are deeply affected by this turn of events. It is most remiss of me to have been thinking only of myself and not to have appreciated how disquieting the whole thing must be for you, too. That young man is, after all, your dear wife's brother and I can well see, now, how this must have come as a blow to you. If you find that it is all too much and that you cannot face the coming ordeal, I can well understand. If you would prefer it, I will travel down on my own and exercise what influence I might have with the police officers, as well as offering consolation and comfort to Winnie and her family. I have, after all, much experience of pastoral care and I'm sure that I will be able to cope. Perhaps you should go back inside – you are not looking at all well, in fact you have gone quite red in the face – and have a nice cup of tea. I am sure that I will be able to find my own way to the police station.'

'Aubrey.'

'Yes, my dear chap, what may I do for you.'

'Unlock the bloody door!'

'There is no need to resort to that sort of language, Frank, distressed though you may be. Wait a moment; I think it is stuck again. I'll have to unlock it from your side.'

A car came slowly down the road and squeezed through the gap left by Aubrey's projecting car; the driver glared at Frank, who forced himself against the door to avoid being crushed. Aubrey walked round the back of the car and opened the door, and Frank got in. He was next aware of the Team Vicar standing on the pavement, tugging at the driver's door. He bent down and spoke to Frank through the glass.

'I don't seem to be able to open this door. I can't think why.'

'Did you, by any chance, lock it just now when you got out?

'I don't think so. But I haven't got the keys. Are they still in the ignition, Frank?'

Grinder leant across the driver's seat and shook his head.

'They're not there.'

'Oh dear, that presents something of a problem. I can't think where they can be.'

'Have you checked your pockets, Aubrey? I wish you'd get a move on. I'm feeling very vulnerable, sitting here, stuck half-way across the road. Hang on a minute.'

He put his head out of the window, just as a van went past, sounding its horn.

'They're in the door on my side. Please hurry up, Aubrey.'

The vicar went back, retrieved the keys, unlocked the driver's door and got in. He looked ready for a chat.

'Aubrey.'

'Yes?'

'May I ask two favours of you?'

'Certainly, and, if it is all within my powers to grant them I shall try do so.'

'Well within your powers, Aubrey.'

'Good. I am so gratified that in a time, if not of crisis, certainly, one might say, of mutual concern, when there is every possibility that in our community of interests we may develop a fellowship, which – dare I say it? – may not altogether have been fully developed between us hitherto, I am able to render some assistance. What may I do for you?'

'The first thing,' replied Aubrey through half-closed teeth, 'is to start the car and move to the proper side of the road where I am less likely to get hit by passing traffic.'

'Of course. And the second?'

'I know that this is going to be a difficult one for you. But do you think that, for a half an hour or so, you might stop talking? I really would like to marshal my thoughts and try to work out how best to deal with the situation when we arrive at the police station.'

They drove off in silence. Frank was unsure whether he was now in a huff or merely co-operating, but the relief was outbalanced by his alarm at the way Aubrey drove. He had not been in a car with him before and was unfamiliar with the style of driving in which gear-changes seemed to result from whim rather than an organised progression. The engine alternatively roared and stuttered as, silently following Frank's direction, Aubrey drove through the terraced streets and then onto the wide road that led to the M5 motorway.

'Turn left at the roundabout,' said Frank. 'Towards Bristol. Not towards Birmingham'

'I know perfectly well which direction to take.' So, the silence had been pique.

Once on the motorway, Spindle gripped the steering wheel tightly, leant forward and stared ahead. The engine howled as he reached 60 miles per hour. Frank wondered whether he should suggest changing up a gear or two, or perhaps, three but then thought better of it. The noise had an obvious benefit: he had an excuse for not hearing Aubrey. After a while, the whine of the motor became an almost comforting background, and he sank back in his seat and his thoughts. How was he best going to deal with the problem?

An overbearing approach to the police was out of the question. Trying to bully someone who held all the aces was not going to work; in fact, browbeating was alien to his nature, although he was prepared to make an exception for his brother-in-law. Also, he knew that he would not be very effective at it. Nor would pleading for clemency be likely to succeed; they must listen to that sort of appeal every day and, he imagined, it probably would only harden their attitude towards the boys to hear them depicted as loveable, in need of kindness or deserving any form of sympathy. Alistair was, after all, a creepy little adolescent and Rambo was an over-confident oik who liked to convey the impression that he was an office-holder in a Triad society. He could, he supposed, announce himself as their solicitor and try to demonstrate to the police that it was illegal to detain them any longer, but he had to admit to himself that the youngest and least experienced PC would be infinitely more knowledgeable than he about this area of the law, and what they could and could not do to the boys. If only they showed signs of having been beaten-up, he thought wistfully, he might have something to go on. But then, being in a fight might be the reason why they were in custody, so that would not be much use. But, Alistair in a fight? Only as a victim. It would, at least, have given him something to go on if he knew what they had been arrested for. It couldn't be a driving offence; he knew that Winnie would not have allowed either of them to take the wheel of his car. What could they have done to have got themselves into this trouble? Might it, perhaps, be better, after all, to let the man of God take charge and persuade the officers to go gently on the boys? No, definitely not: ten minutes of Aubrey and they would all be locked up, for the protection of public sanity. He closed his eyes.

The change in the engine tone woke him. Aubrey was speaking to him again.

'Sorry, I didn't catch that.'

'I said that I am slowing down because I have seen a sign to Weston-super-Mare,' said Aubrey.

'Really, when was that?'

'A mile or two back. It said 'Weston 10 miles.' I thought it prudent to commence my deceleration now.'

A lorry, towing a battered caravan, hurtled past at about forty-five miles per hour.

'I believe that it is always wise to prepare to move into the correct lane and be ready to leave the motorway when one is some distance from the junction that one wishes to take, in order to avoid any unduly exigent manoeuvre as one approaches it.'

Exigent, thought Grinder, who uses that word in relation to driving? Instead, he said,

'Yes, you're quite right, Aubrey,' and wondered how many accidents the vicar had caused by driving so slowly. 'But don't you think that you should move into the slow lane if you are going at this pace?'

'In good time, my dear Frank, in good time. First, I want to achieve the appropriate speed before executing the manoeuvre of negotiating the vehicle into the inside lane.'

He put on his left indicator and drove with it flashing for about a mile.

'Now, I think,' he said and moved over.

There was the sound of a horn and a car went past them, its headlights flashing; the driver made a corkscrew gesture with his forefinger against the side of his head. Aubrey had a beatific smile on his face.

'There,' he said, 'now we are in position to turn.'

He continued down the motorway, the indicator still flashing, for another couple of miles until they came to the 'Exit' sign. He changed into second gear and pulled off. Two cars got to the slip road before him.

'Goodness, they must be in a hurry for something,' he said.

'They must,' said Frank. 'I don't suppose that you have any idea where the police station might be.'

'No. I have never had occasion to go to Weston-super-Mare police station. In point of fact, I've never visited a police station. Nor, have I been to Weston-super-Mare.'

Frank stopped himself as he was on the point of commenting on the sheltered nature of Aubrey's life. Having got this far in relative silence and with the ice in the atmosphere beginning to dissolve, he felt it would be better if they arrived in a degree of harmony.

'If you head for the town centre, there will probably be a sign,' he said instead.

They turned right at the roundabout and made for the centre of town. After much gear-crunching they found themselves on the road running beside the beach.

'Good God,' exclaimed Frank, 'there's my car! Quick pull up behind it.'

'Are you sure?'

'Of course I'm sure. I can recognise my own car.'

'Frank,' said Aubrey, tartly disapproving of the invective. 'I don't mean that. I was not, in any way, doubting that you knew your car. Plainly, you would know the registration number. Although, now I come to think of it, I am not altogether certain that I can remember my own. I know that there is an 'E' in it and I think the number 85, or it may be 86, although, now that I think about it, I am not entirely positive. Yes, it is 85, er, I think. No, what I meant was whether you are sure that this is a good place to park as we have yet to ascertain the precise location of the police station and we may well be a considerable distance from it and...'

'Aubrey.'

'Yes, Frank.'

'Do you remember I told you that Winnie had called me?'

'Called? Oh, you mean telephoned.'

'And do you remember that she said that she was at the police station?'

'Yes.'

'With her mother and sister?'

'Yes, of course I remember your telling me that.'

'Well, they have managed to get there from here, and so I am making an assumption that it wasn't too far for them.'

'They could have driven.'

'Aubrey, what is that thing that you've parked behind?'

'I don't follow. Oh, yes, I see what you mean. It's your car, so they couldn't have driven in it.'

'Bingo!'

'It's your legal training, Frank. You have an analytical mind.'

'You mean, I can understand the bloody obvious?'

'Frank, please try to repress your tendency towards profanity. And,' the vicar added smugly, 'you may have overlooked an important possibility.'

'What's might that be, Aubrey?'

'They may all have been taken to the police station.'

'What, you mean, Winnie and Winsome and their mother have all been carted off in a Black Maria with the boys?'

'Well, that is a possibility.'

'Two problems with that theory, Aubrey.'

'Really, I can think what they can be.'

'Number one: what arrestable offence do you think old Mrs Wong and her daughters have committed? Armed robbery, perhaps, or blackmail? What about piracy on the high seas? We're at the coast, after all. '

'Yes.'

'Number two: Winnie said that the Rambo and Alexander...'

'Alistair.'

'Yes, him, Winnie said that the boys had been arrested. She didn't say that she had been, or her mother or sister.'

'Well,' said Aubrey after a moment's pensiveness, 'I see the force in what you say. Indeed, you present a most persuasive argument, which is, I suppose, again the result of your legal training, but have you considered....?'

But Frank was already out of the car, in search of someone who did not look like a day-tripper.

The Police station was a square, ugly, concrete building, a short walk from where they had stopped. It stood on improbably flimsy-looking stilts. Frank and Aubrey walked up the steps to the main entrance and into the reception area. Along the wall, three Chinese ladies were sitting, on dark green plastic chairs.

'Oh, F'ank,' said Winnie, 'it's good you come. But you took a long time. We were all worry about you.'

'Well, we're here now. Any developments?'

'Yes that policeman says he wants to talk to you. I told him you were top lawyer. Oh, you got that wicar with you.'

'My dear Winnie,' interposed Aubrey, 'I have come in my capacity, not only as the father of one of the unfortunate boys, but also as a man of the cloth who may, ahem, though

I am most reluctant to assume for myself a position of influence, be able to – how might I put it? – intercede on their behalf and, so to speak, proffer some of that balm of mercy that might temper the majesty of the law...'

Frank interrupted him.

'I had to come with him because you've got the car.'

'Oh, but my dear Winnie, it was not just in the capacity of a chauffeur that I drove down with Frank. You see, I have in the past been called upon to provide a testimonial for some of my parishioners, not, I must say, usually in connection with the proceedings of the courts; no, more often than not it has been a reference for someone who was seeking employment of one kind or another, although there have occasionally been instances when they wanted my good opinion in written form in order to obtain the lease of premises, sometimes commercial and sometimes domestic, although, as I say, it was more usual in order to assist them in getting a job. It is, I believe, not altogether unheard of for a priest to provide something of the kind. We do still have some standing in society, I am happy to observe, although, in point of fact, one reads so frequently of the diminishing role of the Church in the modern world. Be that as it may, I am able to indulge in a small degree of pride when I contemplate the various instances where my help appears to have been, at least in part, instrumental in the obtaining of the desired object, whether it be accommodation or employment. And therefore, and bearing in mind that a representation made by a man in my position is very likely to be met with a sympathetic hearing by those who are empowered to make the sort of decisions that affect our lives in all its facets, Frank and I decided that it would probably be highly efficacious if I were to make an approach to the police not, as it were, in the form of a plea in mitigation, but more a conciliatory petition coupled with a revelation of a fact of which, it is not impossible, the police may not be aware, and that is that Alistair is the son of a clergyman and that whatever misdemeanour he may (or of course, and much more likely, may not – I have yet to hear his side of the story) have committed, it would, quite axiomatically, be alien to his character, and that once returned to the, ahem, bosom, of his family he will return to the studious and, I think I may make bold as to say, the exemplary life that heretofore he has led. So that is what we decided to do, isn't it Frank?'

But Grinder was no longer there. He was at the desk talking to the Station Sergeant. Aubrey walked towards them, just as Frank turned and started to come back. He gestured with his left hand upright, palm outwards to Aubrey. Aubrey looked perplexed, but waved back to Frank and continued towards him.

'Stop!' said Frank. 'Don't come any closer. Please.'

'I'm afraid that I do not understand,' said Aubrey, hurt replacing puzzlement on his face.

'Just don't talk to the officer.'

'Why ever not?'

Grinder took the vicar's arm fairly forcibly and turned him to face the ladies. They walked the remaining steps together.

'Please, let go of my arm, Frank,' said Aubrey. Frank did so.

'Please, tell me what is happening. I am bound to say that I find your behaviour quite mystifying. Not, I regret, altogether uncharacteristic; in fact, from time to time today I think you have verged on discourtesy. There, I have said it. But you have not previously resorted to violence. I can only be charitable and ascribe it to the pressure that you may be feeling because of the unhappy situation in which these two young people find themselves. It is precisely because I believe that you may be somewhat overwrought that I intend to take over and to talk to the authorities and make the case for them and you are, if I may so, impeding me in the pursuance of…'

'Aubrey, please, just for a moment, shut up.'

There was a shocked inhalation of breath.

'Aubrey, it was on a knife-edge whether or not the boys were going to charged.'

'With what offence, pray?'

'Did you really just say 'pray'?'

'Indeed, I did.'

'Well, it was criminal damage. But the station sergeant said that they would probably be prepared to let the boys go with a caution, as long as they admitted what they had done and as long as no attempt was made by *anyone* to try to paint them as young innocents who have never put a foot wrong before. You see, they hear a lot of that sort of thing and – I have to say this – when the sergeant saw you turn up wearing your dog collar he told me that his first thought was that if he heard yet another bleeding heart appeal, he would recommend to the CPS that they also charge them with riot, affray and manslaughter…'

'You can't mean that?'

'No, I made the manslaughter bit up. But do you get the drift? Just keep out of it, and the boys should be coming through in a few minutes. I told him that I – did you hear that, Aubrey ? – *I*, would go and talk to them if they needed any advice, but he said that, in the circumstances, and now that they have had time to sober up...'

'Sober up! Good gracious, have they been drinking? Surely, not Alistair!'

'...kids usually see the sense in accepting a caution. So I have promised him that, unless the boys want to talk to me – to *me*, Aubrey – we would all sit here patiently.'

'Well, I am not entirely sure whether or not that is the best manner of proceeding as you did say, I believe, that they would have to make a confession and I really cannot accept that Alistair could have committed any form of criminal offence. He is such a docile boy and he has always been taught to follow the path, not only of righteousness but, also, of lawfulness and to admit to a serious criminal offence which could blight his whole future when I cannot imagine that he could possibly be guilty of any such thing is not something that I could endorse without a great deal of prior contemplation and...'

'Aubrey, it is not your decision, it is theirs,' Frank interrupted. 'A caution is not a conviction; that's the whole point of it, so it's not going to affect their futures. And if anyone is going to have his life spoiled, it's me, as I have agreed, as part of the deal, that I will pay for the damage that they caused.' He thought of adding that the other way that his life was blighted was having him for brother-in-law, but instead, said 'So I ask you, please, not to interfere. Let's just wait here. If your son thinks that he is innocent or is being hard done by, no doubt he will say so or, at least, ask to see me. But please, just this once, let him make up his own mind.'

'Frank, I think it would be better if I went for some fresh air, rather than sit here with you. No doubt you will be happier waiting with your, er, Chinese family. Perhaps I will take a perambulation along the sea front.'

Grinder had heard that sort of comment before, in Hong Kong: an unsubtle hint at the superiority of the Englishman and the unspoken, uncomprehending disapproval of a westerner who had more than simply commercial links with the locals. 'Gone Bamboo' was the Antipodean term for it; 'Your Chinese Friends' was the English. He wondered whether his earlier jibe at Aubrey for being a racist, although meant in gest, had been nearer the mark than he had supposed. Now was not, though, the time to confront a professional Christian with his lack of Christianity. Although they were not showing it, Winnie and her family must be confused and upset and he did not want to make it worse for them by having a blazing row with Aubrey.

'Yes, well, we'll wait for you,' he said. 'But, please, don't be too long. I should think that the boys will want to get away from this place as soon as possible and we don't want to have to wait for you.'

Aubrey went off, without a word. At least I have achieved his silence, Frank thought. He asked Winnie and Winsome if they were all right. They both nodded and the younger woman gave him a half smile. Their mother was staring at the far wall.

'Is your mother O.K? Does she understand what's happening?' Frank asked.

Winnie told him that she was getting a little worried about her; she had said scarcely anything since coming to the police station to look for the boys and, although Winnie and Winsome had explained that they were in the building and had been taken here by the police, she was not sure that her mother had understood the position. Indeed, the only time that she had spoken was when the policeman, over there, had brought them all a cup of tea and she had complained that it was horrible and not sweet enough. Fortunately, when Frank asked, Winnie said that her mother had said it in Cantonese and he said that it was unlikely that the Station Sergeant would have understood her, but Winnie was not so sure.

'Because, she look as if she scold the policeman,' she said.

Frank tried speaking directly to Winnie's mother.

'Mrs Wong, I don't think that you need worry now. The boys are safe. They aren't going to be charged. They'll be coming home soon.'

She continued to stare ahead and gave no indication that she had understood him, or even heard him. Frank asked her daughters to translate what he had just said and Winsome did so. He caught and understood the odd expression, including '*Mo man tai*' – nothing to worry about. To his surprise, a tear rolled down the old lady's cheek, and then another and then, between quiet sobs, she spoke to Frank.

'How I tell his father Rambo go to prison?'

Frank started to explain again, then thought better of it. If the Station Sergeant was aware, and he glanced over his shoulder and saw that he was, indeed, looking at them, it could do no harm to the cause. Better a tearful mother than a pompous vicar. He sat down on one of the green chairs, beside his wife, and took her hand so that the Sergeant would have an unobstructed view.

The minutes passed slowly by. It seemed to be a quiet day at the station; no-one came in through the public entrance. Occasionally, a policeman appeared from somewhere behind the desk and put papers in front of the sergeant, who initialled them and gave them back. A young police woman in a white uniform blouse and dark blue trousers came from behind the desk, smiled at them and asked Frank if the ladies wanted anything, before continuing through and out towards the steps. A bluebottle flew erratically towards them; Winsome covered her mouth with one hand and waved it away with the other and it flew on and up and banged itself against the dusty window high in the wall above them. From outside came the sound of traffic and the scream of seagulls. A car started up nearby and drove away and, after that, a siren, very loud at first and then diminishing. The policewoman came back through the public entrance, smiled at them again, and went behind the counter.

The door swung open, and Aubrey came in and, without a word, sat down a couple of seats away from Frank, who was getting up to speak to him when another officer came from the back and had a muttered conversation with the sergeant, who then looked towards Frank and beckoned him over.

'All's well,' he said. 'It's all sorted. They've both accepted a caution. Good as gold. That young Chinese bloke speaks very good English, doesn't he? I had to go and check on them in their cells and he's quite a character, isn't he? I'm glad that it's gone this way: I took quite a shine to him.'

'It's the other one who might be the problem,' said Frank. 'Or rather, his father, the vicar over there. Are you satisfied that young Spindle understood what was involved before agreeing to the caution? It's been a hell of a job to keep the father off his back. Unfortunately, he's married to my sister.'

The policeman gave Frank a sympathetic grimace.

'I know the type only too well,' he said. 'But, no, nothing to worry about. It will all have been explained to the young lad, in fact, to both of them, and there's a form which sets it all out very clearly, what the effect of a caution is...Hang on a minute, I think they're coming through.'

Another door opened behind the desk and the same policeman came through, followed by a smiling Rambo and a subdued, pensive Alistair. The sergeant asked them to sign a document, and then spoke to Frank.

'There you are, they're all yours. You can take them back now; but I should drive with the windows open. That young one,' pointing to Alistair, 'still looks a bit green about the gills.'

He ushered them through a small gateway at the side

of the counter. Mrs Wong uttered a shriek and ran towards her son. She took his hand and held it against her cheek; he put his arm round his mother and embraced her, then he hugged his sisters. Alistair stood in the middle of the reception area as his father advanced.

'Alistair, I must talk to you. I really must. I don't know, quite, how to express my feelings. The first thing, I suppose, is to ask you if you are well. In point of fact, I do not mean physically well because, although you do, unquestionably, look somewhat pallid, I can see that you appear to be unharmed, that is to say,' and he glanced meaningfully towards the Station Sergeant, 'as far as I can tell without, ahem, examining your body. But I am concerned that you may have been put under pressure or, at least, that is to say, persuaded to confess to something of which you are not – I am afraid that I cannot choose a word that will not upset your feelings – of which you are not, in point of fact, erm, guilty. Your Uncle mentioned something about criminal damage and I find it not credible that a boy of your upbringing and, erm, background would have any part in anything so serious. So, if you have, in order to attain your liberty, admitted to something for which you are not responsible it is my opinion that we should, without further delay, consult a solici*tor*,' he emphasised the last syllable as if it were a hill somewhere in Devon. 'Not, perhaps,' and he lowered his voice, 'your Uncle Frank, so that he can take whatever steps may be necessary and, indeed, advisable, in order to rectify this most embarrassing, that is to say, unfortunate situation in which we find ourselves, not, of course, for the purpose of pursuing any claim for compensation, although that may also have to be considered, but in order clear your good name and also that of the rest of your family…'

'I did it,' Alistair interrupted him.

'Did what? Admitted the, er, misdemeanour?' I gather that you would have had to do so in order to obtain your bail, or whatever the technical term is. That was made clear to me.'

'I'm not on bail. It's finished. I've been released. But I'm trying to tell you, if you'll listen, that I did it. Both of us. Rambo and me…'

'Rambo and I.'

'Rambo and me, we did it. I haven't confessed to something that I didn't do. We smashed the amusement machine. I was tipping it over so that Rambo could cheat and grab a prize and I let it go and, oh, you should have seen the glass flying everywhere!'

'I am sorry,' said the Team Vicar, 'I am afraid that I am not following this. Are you saying that it was an accident? If it was an accident then, surely, you cannot be guilty of any, ahem, crime. I, of course, know little of the law but, surely, you must intend to do some damage to be – how shall I say? – culpable of such an offence.'

'There was something in the paper I signed about being reckless…'

'As I was endeavouring to explain to you, you must have intended to do some damage or, in point of fact, have been reckless.'

'Of course I was reckless. Beer makes you reckless.'

'Alistair, I can scarcely believe my ears. Although I was given some intimation by Frank that the police were suggesting that one of you had, indeed, been drinking I, naturally, assumed it not to have been you. Are you telling me that you were intoxicated? Are you telling me that you have wasted the pocket money that I gave you, in order that you should have an enjoyable and fulfilling day at the seaside, on alcohol? No, please do not answer me. I am sufficiently mortified by what you have already told me...'

He paused to collect his thoughts and then, in the voice of the pulpit, resumed.

'Your mother and I have devoted all our energies to the upbringing of you and your younger brother. Well, figuratively speaking, of course, because I have also had to give a portion of my time in the interests of my flock and also in the service of the wider Church, but you know very well what I mean. We have been, always, at pains to instil in you a strict – I say, strict, but in the kindest way possible – sense of morality and responsibility. We have been, without in any way indulging ourselves in unseemly hubris, able to hold our heads up high within our little community in that, conscious always of the need to be aware of the joys and, yes, troubles, of others in our fellowship, we have been able to demonstrate that our sons have been imbued with the qualities of responsibility and reliability and, in point of fact, sobriety. Today has been one of great travail for me and will, doubtless, prove to be for your dear mother when I am compelled to make her cognisant of that which has, er, transpired. Heaven alone knows how difficult it will be for me to tell her that your conduct has fallen below the standards that we have so painstakingly, and over all these years, endeavoured to implant in you. I am bound to say that I am appalled to learn that you have been drinking, that in drink you may have become intoxicated and,' his voice now rose to a high tenor, 'in your intoxicated state you and that young Chinaman behaved in an irresponsible and feckless manner. I suppose that his involvement, and probable bad example, may mitigate your responsibility, therefore and, in point of fact, soften the blow of what I, shortly, will have to impart to her when I telephone to explain our delay in returning but, the fact is that she is hardly prepared for this sort of thing. And, consider if you will, just for a moment, please, the effect that this will have on your younger brother, he who has hitherto looked up to you as a model of proper conduct in a young man. Did you consider, even for a minute, when you were damaging this, er, thing, this, er machine, whatever you call it...I am sorry, I still am unable to envisage what type of appliance it was...?'

'It was a gaming machine. In an arcade. On the pier,' Alistair explained.

'A gaming machine!'

'Well, a sort of crane thing.'

'I am sorry, I still cannot comprehend what it is. But you are diverting me. I ask you, perhaps rhetorically, and perhaps not, whether you gave a moment's thought to your mother and to your brother or to me although, perhaps, I should acknowledge that *I* am of little consequence in all this, but to the shame and distress it would cause her and the poor example that you would set to him? Did you? Well, did you?'

Alistair, who had up to this moment been examining his shoes, looked up at his father.

'Oh, fuck off, Dad, I just want to get home and go to bed.'

The journey back to Cheltenham was largely devoid of conversation. Alistair, who had refused to travel with his father, was in Frank's car. Winsome had offered to go in his place, but the vicar said that it would not look, ahem, fitting if he were to be seen driving with a very, in point of fact, attractive, young, erm, oriental lady alone in his car with him and the same would apply (although he, privately, thought to a lesser extent) to Winnie. Rambo, in his mind the instrument of his son's downfall, was not a suitable passenger for him either for, although he was, plainly, in need of moral guidance and likely to benefit from a couple of hours of his ministry, Aubrey felt that, until his own feelings subsided to a more manageable level, he would not be able to proffer a suitably ordered, erm, exegesis of the need for maturity and moral rectitude. So it had fallen to the still-confused Ah-Ma to travel back with him in his car

Alistair was in the back of Grinder's car between the two sisters, and Rambo sat beside Frank, saying very little except to give him occasional road directions which Frank ignored, not merely because of their fatuity. His mood was foul. He had wasted time; he had had to endure his brother-in-law's conversation and nerve-straining driving on the way down; he was hungry and, above all, in need of a drink; and he had, for the sake of his wife – although she did not yet know it – committed himself to paying for the repair or, more likely, replacement of the amusement machine. He did not expect that that would come cheaply: he must try to Google them when he got home to find out what he had let himself in for. It would be too late, by the time that they got back, to do anything useful on his book and, anyway, he was he was not in the mood for wit, however acerbic. As he watched the sky begin to darken ahead of him his only consolation was the thought of the tumbler of malt whisky which he would probably, no, certainly, take up to his study. Even the thought of what he supposed must be the atmosphere in Aubrey's car as he and Winnie's mother, in intense mutual incomprehension, drove, hearse-like, up the motorway was of little comfort; true, it had its amusement value, but it was very hard on the old lady to have to spend so much time in the company of the Reverend M.A. when she desperately wanted to be with her son.

Such conversation as there was in Frank's car was subdued. Rambo's attempts at ebullience failed to make headway; Frank was conscious that his own bad temper was palpable, but he did nothing to lighten the atmosphere. There was a certain satisfaction in silently communicating his mood to the others in the car and, almost, a sense of power; after a while none of them tried to speak to him, and they talked to each other in muted tones until, even including Rambo, they fell into silence. Frank put on the car radio and searched until he found something suitably funereal, which he thought that he recognised: was it Purcell's 'Music on the Death of Queen Mary'? He turned the volume up sufficiently to discourage any attempt to lighten the mood. Winnie was embarrassed and unhappy about the way that the day had turned out and, from past experience, he knew that she would be blaming herself for the annoyance that he had been subjected to; he guessed that, probably, Winsome, also was feeling unreasonably guilty. He was not at all sure that their brother or his new friend were sufficiently chastened, though. But what did it matter? His day had been wasted and there was nothing that he could do about it except, perhaps, to gain a few more merit marks with Winnie for having put himself out and for appearing to have effected the solution to a potentially serious problem. They were now approaching the Cheltenham exit and, at least, home was only a short distance away, the day was ending, and not much else could go wrong. And there was that whisky. Or, maybe, a gin and tonic: he was feeling quite thirsty.

As they drove through the suburban, evening streets, Frank appreciated, almost as if he was observing himself from outside, that his anger had subsided and had gradually been replaced by a feeling, if not yet of mellifluence , of something approaching contentment. He was beginning to look forward to his supper and he knew that Winnie could be relied upon to produce something satisfying and delicious with little fuss and delay, even in spite of the stressful day that she had had. When well-intentioned friends had, before they were married, warned of him of the risk of a cultural clash, he had thought, at the time, that the advantages outweighed any perceived disadvantages and one of the definite plusses was her Chinese cooking; she had never disappointed him in the years since. She was a sweet-natured, selfless woman who was very easy on the eye and, on top of that, a wonderful cook. That she, sometimes, struggled to express herself well in English was part of her charm, as were her peals of laughter when he tried to use his poor Cantonese and, more often than not, accidentally hit an inaccurate vocal tone and ended up saying something meaning something else, and even, sometimes, apparently indecent. Thinking of the prospect of a meal made him made him realise that, unusually, Rambo had not announced to the world, that he was starving to death. Perhaps he had taken on board that his behaviour had caused Frank a great deal of inconvenience and, with the dawn of introspection, was behaving, at last, in an appropriate manner. Another explanation, of course, was that he had fainted from hunger. Frank glanced at him; no, he was still conscious, just uncharacteristically silent.

There appeared to be something unusual about the house as Frank swung the car onto the driveway, which he could not, at first, identify. The headlights picked up the living-room windows and he could not see any change or damage to them. There was nothing that he was aware of in the small front garden that should, or should not, have been there. The house looked exactly as he had left it when they had driven off in Aubrey's car. But there was something odd. Yes, that was it: it was the same, but he and Aubrey had gone off in broad daylight and it was now dark and there were no lights on, even though Winnie's father was in the house. Perhaps he had fallen asleep in front of the television, except that there was no glow or reflected movement of light to be seen through the windows of the darkened lounge. Perhaps, Frank tried to convince himself, he is in the kitchen making himself something to eat.

They all got out of the car and Frank unlocked the front door. There was no light from the kitchen, or anywhere else; he could see from the hallway that the whole house was in darkness. He switched on a lamp on a side table and turned back to Winnie, who was holding the door open for the others.

'I think there may be a problem, love,' he said gently. 'There weren't any lights – I've just switched this one on; I think that your father may be ill.' Then he added, unnecessarily, 'I was a bit worried about him on our way from the airport on Sunday.'

Winnie said something to Winsome which Frank could not catch. Then they both shouted.

'Daddi-ah!'

They ran into the lounge, the dining room, the kitchen, turning lights on as they went.

'Perhaps he's having a lie-down. Perhaps he's asleep upstairs,' said Frank. But a sense of foreboding had already begun to take hold of him and he knew that he did not sound, remotely, as if he believed what he was saying. Winnie was already up the stairs calling her father and banging doors, with Winsome close behind her. After a few moments they ran down.

'No,' said Winnie, 'he not ill.'

'Oh, that's good,' Frank replied.

'No, because...he not here.'

'Oh shit!' said Frank.

'I'm starving,' said Rambo. 'Can we get something to eat. He'll be O.K.'

'How can he possibly be O.K.?' Frank asked, his mood rapidly descending again. 'He's never been out of this house since you all got here. I don't know how much English he speaks, but there's hardly likely to be anyone around here who speaks Cantonese.'

'My husband is right,' said Winnie. 'Better we look for him.'

'Wait a moment, please,' Winsome interjected. 'How about, maybe, he went into the garden for some fresh air. I'll go and look.'

She unlocked the kitchen back door and shouted for her father. The only sounds were of distant traffic and a neighbour's dog barking. A full moon was up and shone its reflected light onto the silver garden. Winnie pushed past her.

'No, not here,' she said. 'What shall we do?'

'One of you had better stay here,' said Frank, 'for when your mother comes back with Alistair's father. Perhaps it would be best if the rest of us split up.' In spite of his tiredness, the urgency of the moment had him thinking clearly and decisively. He rather relished taking charge; it had been a long time since he had exercised anything like control.

'This is what we'll do. Winnie, you stay here for your

mother. Winsome and Rambo, you two can look along the streets to the West, that is, from the front side of the house. Alistair, do you want to wait for your father to come back?'

'I'd rather not,' he replied, without hesitation.

'I thought that you wouldn't. Alright, you come with me and, Winnie, you tell Aubrey that I'll run Alistair back home after we've found the old man. That way,' he added to Alistair, 'we will be spared the pleasure of his company for the rest of the evening. Can you bear that?'

Alistair sniggered.

'I'll emphasise what an important mission you've been on and, if we work it properly, and get you back really late, you might not have to see him till tomorrow morning, by which time he will have slept on what you said to him. Come on, then, let's go.'

CHAPTER 20

Wednesday morning in the Hotel Medved was distinguishable from the other days only in that it was the fat receptionist's day off. Behind the desk that morning was a woman of an age that, although uncertain, was patently greater than that which she sought to project. Her bleached hair was cut in an awkward, page-boy style and her scarlet lips and long, vermilion finger nails battled with the electric-blue eye shadow which had been applied liberally to the lids and vaults of her eyes. Her cerise polyester blouse strained unsuccessfully to cover her cleavage, into the canyon of which plunged a gold pendant which spelled out at an angle and in cursive script – '*Sharon*'. There were multi-coloured bangles on both of her wrists and they clicked and clattered at the keyboard as she produced a bill.

Lev Semyonovich came from the direction of the stairwell and waited while the departing guest checked the bill, paid it and left. He was dressed that morning in a light-weight grey suit which was a perfect match for his dark blue silk tie. Somewhat to his surprise, he had passed an untroubled night and had slept well. There was plenty of time for coffee and a croissant in one of the cafés that he had noticed near the station. Another man was standing near the desk. He was bearded and untidily dressed; Lev noticed his scuffed shoes. He gestured to him with a twist of his outstretched hand, an invitation to go before him, but the other man shook his head, smiled, mumbled something and moved further away.

'Could you help me, please?' Lev Semyonovich asked the receptionist. 'I need to go to Baker Street. I have a meeting. Can I walk, or do I need a taxi? I am sorry to trouble you.'

She glanced up at him and her gaze lingered on the elegant, grey hair and the rimless glasses.

'Oh, I em only too gled to be of 'elp,' she simpered. 'I should say, but, of course, it's only may opinion, thet at this time of day, it would be advisable to walk. Texis do 'ave the raight to use the bus lane, but the congestion can be something awful. Besades, they can be rather pricey, especially if you get stuck in a treffic jem. Not, of course, thet I em implying thet you are short of cesh,' and she gave a withering smile. 'Would you lake me to show you on a mep?'

Ivanov nodded, and she took out of a drawer a map of the sort available in hotels around the world – two thirds covered with rectangles containing advertisements for services and shops that no sane person, other than a tourist with nothing else to spend his cash on, would want; and a small section of map in the middle, with red lines leading from the adverts to red dots shown on the map. Ivanov studied it for a moment and wondered why anyone, in London, would want to visit shops selling products from Australia or Peru. At least, Dr Amerjit Singh, emergency dentist and oral hygienist, might come in useful, perhaps after visiting the establishment which featured in another box, the Mississippi Rib Shack. He could see Paddington Station but had not found Baker Street, when Sharon took it back from him.

'Let me show you,' she said. 'Look, Baker Street is here, and let me draw on the mep the best way of getting to it.' With a felt-tip pen, she drew a thick line, obliterating most of the street names. 'Thet should be easy to follow,' she said.

Lev Semyonovich mumbled a word of thanks.

'Aim pleased to 'elp you, aim shoo-er.'

Ivanov took the map outside and studied it for a few moments. Then he turned out of the mews into the side street and then into Praed Street, where he hailed a taxi.

'Where to, guv?' the driver said. He really said it.

'Baker Street.'

'Where in Baker Street?'

'Just, please, Baker Street.'

'Well, if you're one of them Sherlock Holmes nuts, there ain't no 221b Baker Street.'

'I'm sorry?'

'How about Madame Two Swords? Is that where you want to go?'

'Please. Just Baker Street.'

'It's your shout,' and the driver set off in the wrong direction, taking a long loop before, £20 later, he stopped outside the Sherlock Holmes Museum.

Lev Semyonovich passed a £10 and a two £5 notes through the hatch.

'I pay you, although I think you have, perhaps, swindled me,' he said, and stepped out onto the pavement.

'Well you wouldn't tell me where you wanted to go,' said the taxi driver. 'And it's usual to give a tip. Oh well.' And he drove off.

Ivanov looked at the piece of paper on which he had jotted down the details the previous evening when he had been on the telephone. Then he set off in search of the travel agency with the blue sign outside. Jetoff was the name that he had been given. It sounded reassuringly Russian.

CHAPTER 21

The streets on either side of Suffolk Terrace were dark and empty. A chill had set in to the night air, and Frank was worried. If the old man had had a fall he might be lying, unnoticed, anywhere. Although Frank could not remember, exactly, what he had been wearing when he had last seen him, he knew that he was not likely to be adequately dressed to protect him from exposure to a damp night in a climate much colder than he was used to; people in Hong Kong put on anoraks and overcoats whenever it dropped below 20 degrees centigrade outside and an even relatively minor downward change in the temperature would result in a sudden outbreak of mink. He could not weigh more than 130 lbs. Frank was beginning to feel a bit cold himself and he regretted not having grabbed a jacket before leaving the house.

'Have you seen anything?' he called across to Alistair, who was progressing along the other side of the road, looking into the front gardens and alleyways.

'Not yet,' Alistair shouted. 'Do you think that he really could be in somebody's garden, Uncle Frank?'

'Not really. But I don't know where he might be. What could have happened to him?'

He called Alistair over. They would have to draw a line somewhere. It was pointless expanding their search to more streets further away; the radius would get longer and their task would become increasingly difficult. The old man might be in trouble and need help now.

'Do you think that we should go back to your house, Uncle,' asked Alistair, 'and see whether Rambo and Winsome have any news?'

'Good idea, Alistair.'

They got to the front door just before the others who, also, had nothing to report. Winsome was beginning to look scared.

'I don't know what has happened to my father,' she said. 'He is an old man and it's cold. He is probably lost and hungry. But why did he leave the house? He does not know anyone here. Where has he gone?'

'Maybe, perhaps, he's been kidnapped,' said Rambo, helpfully. 'So, it's easy. We just go in and wait for the 'phone to ring with the ransom demand. It happens all the time in Hong Kong.'

'Only in the movies,' said Winsome, crossly. 'Why would anyone want to kidnap Daddi-ah? We got no money.'

'Ah,' said Rambo with a wily look. 'They probably know his daughter married a rich *gweilo* lawyer. They've probably seen his big house. It's obvious to me that's what happened. Maybe better call the police, now, Frank. They got special policemen to deal with kidnapping.'

'I would have thought that you would already have had enough experience of the police for one day,' Grinder replied. 'Anyway, they would say that it's too soon. We've no idea how long ago your father left the house; he might have slipped out only shortly before we got back home. I don't think that they'll be interested in him, even as a missing person, if he might not have been gone for very long.'

'I agree with Uncle Frank.' Alistair looked alert, and rather pleased with himself, as if he had just had an inspiration. 'I've got a good idea. Is there a pub anywhere near here?'

'Well, yes, there's 'The Unicorn', replied Frank. 'Why?'

'Well, assuming that some of the customers walk there, they might have seen an old Chinaman in the street.'

'Chinese man,' Frank corrected him.

'An old Chinese man. Or they might see him when they walk back afterwards. Why don't we go there and ask, and perhaps try at other pubs as well?'

'That's a very good suggestion,' said Frank, combining approval with surprise. 'I'll just go in and tell Winnie what we're doing. Do you lot want to go with me, or do you want to wait inside?'

'I'll come with you, Uncle Frank, as it's my idea.'

'So will I,' said Winsome. 'If we see Daddi I can speak to him.'

'I'll wait in the house for when the kidnappers call,' said Rambo.

On the way to 'The Unicorn' Frank tried to consider what he would say and how he would say it. At this time in the evening, the pub was likely to be fairly full. How did you go about getting the attention of a crowd of drinkers, and what do you say to them? Do you tap on the side of a glass, like a master of ceremonies about to announce the guest speaker at a dinner of Rotarians or United Elks? Hardly: it would probably not be heard at the back of the bar above the loud chatter of the customers. Do you stand on a chair? Would it be better to go from table to table, and along the bar, saying the same thing over and over again, like a steward on a budget airline going along collecting up rubbish? And what do you say? 'Excuse me, has anyone seen an undersized, underdressed Chinese gentleman? If you have, would you please call this number.' No, you would probably be thrown out for annoying the customers. And even if anyone had seen one, how would he know that it was the right one? There must be other oriental families in this part of Cheltenham – in fact, he knew that there were, because Winnie had made friends with a few of them. So how could he describe her father so that he could be distinguished from anyone else? Maybe Alistair's idea was not so good after all. It could end up with Frank being barred from his local and the wrong elderly Chinese man being dragged round to Suffolk Terrace. With hesitation and an increasing sense of pointlessness, Frank pushed open the door of 'The Unicorn' and went in, followed by Winsome and Alistair.

The pub was unusually, and reassuringly, quiet. A few men stood against the bar, chatting to the landlord. Over at the table where Frank and Theo had first sat (was it only yesterday?) two men and two women, all in their forties, sat talking to someone else who was hidden from Frank's view.

'Daddi-ah!' shouted Winsome.

The two couples turned towards her, to reveal her father, who was half-hidden behind a mound of chips. His mouth, which was full of steak, dropped open. She rushed to the table and Frank and Alistair followed.

'These my friends,' said Ah-leung. 'This: Bill.' He pronounced the name as if it ended with a 'w', not 'll'. 'This his *tai-tai*. This Pete and Mrs Pete. They have drink with me.'

The others at the table looked up and smiled at the newcomers. Pete half-raised his glass of beer in salutation.

'How long have you been here?' Frank asked him.

'Perhaps, maybe, a hour. I don't know,' said the old man. 'You wan't a drink?'

'We've been looking for you. We were all worried. Your son wanted to call the police.'

'What?'

Winsome spoke in quick-fire Cantonese. He replied, very quickly, the only word that Grinder caught was 'sorri-ah'.

'He say,' a dimple appeared on Winsome's exasperated face, 'he said that he was hungry and didn't know when we were getting back and that there was nothing on tee-wee.'

'How did he know about this pub?' asked Frank.

Winsome translated the question and the answer.

'He says he did not. He says he was looking for a noodle shop or a *dai pai dong* but couldn't find one. And then he saw this place.'

As there appeared to be no other, reasonable, option

Frank went to the bar and came back with a round of drinks for Winsome, Alistair, the old man (this, after some hesitation on Frank's part) and Ah-leung's new friends, and they sat down at the next table to wait for him to finish eating. Grinder's anger, of earlier in the evening, had been replaced by anxiety, and then by exasperation. That had evaporated and the empty space in his emotional cannon was now filled filled with resignation. And fatigue. Then he remembered that Winnie and, by now, probably, her mother would be worrying themselves into a state of panic. He took out his mobile 'phone and called home. He could hear the dread in Winnie's voice when she answered and he was ashamed that he had not thought to reassure her as soon as he had seen her father.

'Good news, sweetheart,' he told her. 'We've found him. He's fine. He's eating. But there's some bad news.'

'What's that?'

'He says he wants to try the sticky toffee pudding with vanilla ice-cream when he's finished his steak.'

The blue sign above the window was there, sure enough, but Jetoff Travel seemed to be deserted. The street door was shut and did not seem to budge when Lev Semyonovich Ivanov pushed against it, and when he moved to the front and peered through the glass window he could see only an empty, unlit office with a rack of brochures and a few chairs against the opposite wall. He could just make out what looked like a counter with a computer on it, but there was no-one inside. He rapped on the glass but did not expect to be heard against the noise of the traffic. He went back to the entrance and noticed, for the first time, two backlit buttons set in the doorpost. A small panel beside the upper one read, simply, 'Jetoff'. He pressed it once, and then again, and waited. There was no sound from the speaker grille above it. He glanced down at the piece of paper; there was no doubt, he had been given that name and he had written down 'blue sign'. He took a step backwards and looked at the number above the door. Yes, it was the same number that he had been given on the 'phone, but had not wanted to tell the taxi driver. He pushed the button again and waited for a minute or so. Then he rang the lower, unnamed bell. A voice crackled.

'Who is it?'

'I am Ivanov. I am expected at Jetoff Travel, but no-one is there.'

There was no response, but he thought that he could just make out the sound of voices; it was hard to be sure, as a bus went past at the same time. Then he could see movement through the frosted glass, and the door opened. A thin man in an off-white shirt and ill-fitting, grey trousers was standing there. His bald head was partly covered by a few locks of dank hair which ran from a parting just above one ear. A smell of cigarette smoke hovered round him.

'Did you say 'Lev Ivanov'?'

'Yes, I am Lev Semyonovich Ivan*ov*,' he replied, supplying his patronymic and correcting the pronunciation of his surname.

'You're too soon,' and he began to close the door. This was, evidently, a man whose education had not included a term at charm school. Ivanov pushed the door back, firmly.

'I am here at the agreed time, or perhaps, possibly, just a few minutes early which, I believe, is courteous in your country. Do you want me to go away? And come back later?'

'No, I suppose you'd better come up. But you'll have to wait. Mr Li ain't here yet.'

'It was not I who suggested the time or place,' said Ivanov.

'Well, he isn't here yet and there's nothing I can do about it. Or you. Do you want to wait here or do you want to go away? It's up to you, mate, it's not my affair.'

Just then a silver Jaguar pulled up at the curb side and a tall, grey-haired, elegant, oriental man emerged from the rear door and walked slowly across the pavement. There was a perceptible hesitation in his gait.

'What is happening?' he asked the gaunt man. 'Who is this gentleman?'

'I am Ivanov, sir,' Lev said, conscious that he had come to report his failure and that a touch of deference was called for.

'Lev Ivanov?'

'Yes, sir.'

'You don't look anything like him. You are certainly not the man whom I met.'

'Well, I am Lev Ivanov, I can assure you.'

'Then I think that you and I need to have a little chat,' replied the Chinese man. 'Was it you who made contact with my, erm, organisation last evening to arrange a meeting?'

'It was I. Most certainly.'

'Then please come upstairs. But, Mr Skeggins,' this to the other man, 'I would be grateful if you would join us, and stay with us unless I ask you to leave.'

Somewhat to Lev's surprise, the staircase which was of uncarpeted wood, with scuff and scratch mark on the faded, white paintwork, led up to an elegant apartment. He had expected the floor above the travel agency to contain offices, but instead he was shown into a living room with two beige sofas, a rosewood coffee table and, in one corner, a plasma screen television set. An ultra-slim laptop computer lay on a rosewood desk, beneath a window which looked out onto Baker Street. Mr Li gestured towards one of the settees, a half twisting, half flowing movement of the right hand which indicated both courtesy and command. Ivanov immediately sat down and Mr Li sat opposite him. Skeggins stood beside the door.

'May I offer you some refreshment?' asked Mr Li. 'You will, perhaps, take some tea. We have Chinese and Ceylon, I believe. I regret not Russian. Or perhaps you would prefer some coffee?' Languidly, he crossed one leg over the other and adjusted the perfect crease of his trouser leg so that it did not stretch at the knee.

'No thank you. I have just had breakfast.'

'Then, if it is convenient you,' and Li glanced briefly at Skeggins, who had moved slightly so that the door handle was behind his back, 'you had, I think, better now explain to me who you are, what you are doing here and how and why you contacted my associates, yesterday evening. But, please, take your time. I am in no hurry; and Mr Skeggins has no other duties.'

Lev Ivanov had already decided that evasion would be the wrong course to take. These people would have enough contacts and resources to be able to check on a lot of what he said, and there was no way of knowing whether a falsification or a distorted half-truth might be exposed for what it was. One proven lie might be fatal to his professional reputation and, well, possibly fatal to him. There was something about Mr Li's elegant courtesy which was quietly threatening and, as for the other, he was too scrawny simply to be a muscle man; he looked just the sort who would keep a stiletto in his inside pocket with the same nonchalance as he would wear a wristwatch. There was no realistic choice; he would have to tell his story, truthfully and as it happened.

So, Ivanov began at the point when, before coming to England, he had received instructions to attend a meeting in Moscow, where he had been given some details of a new commission. Li asked him what he had been told about the nature of the assignment and he replied that all that had been vouchsafed to him at that time was that it concerned probable industrial espionage and that the object was to suppress the manufacture of some sort of condiment. Li asked him if he had been told nothing else. Ivanov replied that he was given a number of contacts, including the one which he had called last night, and was told that when he arrived in England he would be given more details of the process, enough for him to be able to carry out his work. At a second meeting he had been given airline tickets and cash and, of course, his fee had already been discussed and agreed upon. He could not now recall which, but at one or other meeting he had learned that what was being produced in England – and the target of the operation – threatened an existing monopoly.

Mr Li inclined his head, just enough to signify acknowledgement of the truth of what, so far, Ivanov had told him. He recrossed his legs, revealing dark blue silk socks between trouser turn-ups and lustrous black shoes. Skeggins shifted uncomfortably, but remained leaning against the door.

Lev Semyonovich continued, heartened by Mr Li's almost imperceptible sign of recognition. He told how, when he arrived at London Heathrow, he was surprised to find a driver waiting with his name on a placard, for he had been informed at the second meeting that arrangements would be made for him to stay in a hotel in London and that he would be given the details once he was in the arrival hall. He was even more surprised to be driven out of London, to a conference centre in the countryside near a town whose name he could not now quite recall, something like Cheltington and...

For the first time since he began his narrative, Mr Li spoke.

'Do you mean Cheltenham? My daughter was at school there.'

Lev agreed; it was almost certainly Cheltenham.

'I apologise for my interruption,' said Li. 'Please continue.'

He explained that he did not have any real suspicion,

however, that anything was seriously amiss until he heard himself being referred to as 'Dr Ivanov' – something that he had never been. He found that he was at some sort of agricultural conference and that he was expected to give a talk and he realised, then, that there must be another Lev Ivanov, at large somewhere, for whom he had been mistaken. He had never been in a situation like his before, so he had decided that there was nothing else for him to do but to pretend that he was Dr Ivanov in order, he added hastily, to protect the integrity of the operation for which his services had been enlisted. It was, therefore, essential that his real identity and purpose should not be discovered.

Mr Li nodded again, this time, possibly, to signify his approval.

'Doubtless, you also had in mind your own position, that is to say, your reputation as – how shall we put it? – an investigator. That too would have been compromised if your true persona were revealed.'

'Well, that came into it, to an extent. But my main purpose was not to compromise the mission, which seems to me to be very important and,' he added, 'justified.'

A quizzical smile lingered on Mr Li's lips. Ivanov could not make out whether it indicated approbation of his professional integrity or circumspection about his motives.

'So, how did you overcome the problem of the lecture?'

'As we say in Russia, 'with an iron heart and face of steel'. I made it up as I went along.'

'The expression in English is 'with a wing and a prayer', I believe,' said Mr Li.

Lev told him how he had filled out his allotted time by reminiscing about beetroot production in Russia. Mr Li uncrossed his legs and sat upright.

'Why beetroot?'

'Because I had already gathered enough to know that this conference was about beetroot as a means of curing Third World poverty.'

'No other reason?'

'No, of course not. I had no idea until the night before that that was the theme.'

'Please continue,' said Li, who was now staring intently at Ivanov as he continued with his story.

Lev Semyonovich told him how he thought that it was going reasonably smoothly and that he had managed to use up his allotted time without any obvious hitches, but then the session had been thrown open to questions and he knew that he could not answer anything technical or say anything which might reveal his ignorance of the subject; so he had feigned a sudden attack of illness and then he had been able to leave the conference hall and go back to his hotel room, pack hurriedly and get to the station, where he had caught the next train to London. Of course, he had immediately made contact with one of the telephone numbers that he had been given with the view, the sole view, of preventing the collapse of the operation.

'And why should it collapse?' Mr Li asked, displaying no sign of any concern.

'Because there is somebody else out there with a name very close to mine and he is, no doubt, accompanied by the people who should have met me and is being told what I was supposed to have been told and...'

'My God. That man with the beard,' interjected Li, now sitting bolt upright. 'You are correct. Skeggins, please go down to the office and call Mr Green. Find out what is happening.'

'Will you be all right with *him*?' asked Skeggins.

'Of course, of course. Now, hurry!'

Skeggins left the room and Ivanov could hear him clattering down the staircase.

'Mr Ivanov, I really am extremely grateful to you. You have acted most professionally and responsibly.' Li was standing now. 'Although you will appreciate that your exposure to view at the conference in Cheltenham – I take it that there would have been some coverage in the local press, not least because of your seeming to have been taken ill during it –means that my organisation can no longer use you in the capacity for which your services were retained, you may rest assured that you will not lose financially and nor will your reputation suffer. But may I, please, ask you to remain in London for a day or so. In the unlikely event that we have questions for you it would, I am sure that you will agree, be more convenient if you were on hand to answer them. Moreover, it would be inadvisable for you to pass through London Airport too soon after the events which you have just been good enough to describe. So, perhaps you will remain and take a short, quiet vacation in London. Do we have the details of how to contact you?'

Lev saw that, although all this was expressed with a charming smile, there was more than a suspicion of menace in his manner. Phrased as an invitation, there was no mistaking that it was an order.

'Of course, sir,' agreed Lev, perhaps a trifle too hurriedly.

There was the sound of feet running up the stairs and Skeggins burst into the room.

'It's too late. Green and Black have taken the bloke out somewhere. The guy I spoke to thought it might be Birmingham.'

'Can't they be reached on their mobiles?' said Li, impatiently.

'No,' replied Skeggins. 'They were told not to have them on so that their movements couldn't be tracked. Cell site recognition, or something like that.'

'I regret to say that I may have given that instruction myself,' said Mr Li. 'But I did not anticipate this situation arising. We shall just have to wait until they call in, if they do, or until they return.'

CHAPTER 22

In spite of the activities of the previous night, Frank Grinder woke early on Wednesday morning. He left the sleeping Winnie, and showered and shaved. Still feeling half-asleep, he went down to the kitchen and sat with a cup of black coffee, rubbing the crumbs of dried mucin from the corners of his eyes. The whole house was in silence. He had been finding the act of writing to be fairly exhilarating and he thought that, maybe, if he continued with his book now he might engage his brain better than by simply staring at his coffee. Even if it didn't work, he knew that Winnie treated his study as if it were a place of sacred meditation and she would ensure that he was not disturbed. So he could, at least, pass an hour or two without having to talk or listen to anyone else. He took his cup upstairs and turned on his computer.

The tantalising smell of toast wafted up to the study. It was curious, Frank mused, how the odour of bread transmogrifies. When dough has been kneaded and the yeast is rising, it gives off a faintly unpleasant smell, only to become paradisial when it is baking and then to smell of almost nothing at all when it is cold and ready to eat. Yet, as it is toasting, it becomes redolent of the comfort of childhood and when slightly, ever so slightly, it begins to burn it pervades a whole house with its siren call. He looked at his watch, remembered that he had had no breakfast, and went downstairs.

The whole family was sitting round the table with Alistair. With a jolt, Frank remembered that he had said, last night, that he would run him home. His bother-in-law would probably have alerted the police by now, if not air search and rescue.

'I'm sorry, Alistair,' he said. 'I was supposed to take you back to your house last night. It completely slipped my mind, probably because I was so tired. Have you spent the night here? Of course you have.'

'Because,' Winnie interjected, 'when you were looking for my father last night, that Audrey, she 'phoned.'

'Audrey? Who's she?'

'You know, your sister's husband: him.'

Poor Winnie, thought Frank, the absence of personal pronouns in Chinese has snagged her again.

'Yes,' he said, 'and what?'

'Because, she said maybe better Alistair not come home last night after what he said to her.'

'Sorry, love, who 'phoned? Aubrey or Celia?'

'I tell you already. She did. Audrey. The wicar.'

'Oh, and what else did she say, he say?'

'Only that she would collect Alistair this morning when she had calm down. And that she not want to see you.'

'Why not? What a nerve!'

'She said you were very rude to him yesterday.'

'Who said? Aubrey?'

'No, her wife. He came on to 'phone and tell me what you say to his husband.'

'Sorry, sweetheart, I'm losing this.'

'Look,' said Winnie in exasperation, 'it's very simple. Listen carefully. The wicar, her father,' indicating a smirking Alistair, 'she is coming to take Alistair back home but more better you not here.'

'When?'

'In about half hour, I think. You have breakfast then you go upstairs like a good boy. When they gone. I will take my family out and maybe for lunch. You deserve,' she added.

'Including your father?'

'Daddi also. Now eat.'

She put a plate of scrambled eggs on toast in front of him. Somehow she had deftly produced it without his noticing. Just as he was on his second cup of tea, there was the sound of clashing gears and a car engine stalling.

'That'll be him. Cheerioh Alistair. Say hello to your father from me. Or perhaps not. I'm off upstairs.'

He was not, in fact, yet on his way to Birmingham. Black and Green had arrived at the Medved Hotel just as a smartly dressed, grey-haired man came down the steps. Lev Petrovich was waiting for them in the lobby and they took him to the same car and went by the same route towards New Cross, and to the run-down industrial estate. This time, he was more aware of his surroundings. A small boy, who was kicking a tin can along the gutter, moved out of the way of the car as it pulled up near the gateway, turning to give it a curious look. They all got out of the car and had a hurried conference, Black and Green leaning on the roof, Ivanov standing on the pavement and looking about him in some puzzlement.

'O.K.' said Green. 'This is what we'll do. It's too conspicuous driving up to the factory and I don't think that John and I should put our faces on offer. After all, that's one of the reasons why you were brought over from Russia: no-one here knows who you are.'

Lev Petrovich was ruffled. 'Mnym, mnym, I think that I am well-known in my field. This is why I am brought to England, no?'

'No,' said Green. 'We're not saying that you're not a specialist – of course you are – and I'm sure that you're very well-known in the areas where you usually work; but I don't think that anyone would know you here, in this part of London. Or in Brum, for that matter.'

'Brum?'

'Birmingham. I shouldn't think that anyone knows you there.'

'But, mnym, Birmingham has very good university, no? They will know who I am there. And, mnym, Cheltenham.'

Green gave Black a quizzical glance. 'Sorry, I'm not with you. What is this thing you have about Cheltenham? Did you use to live there, or something?'

'No. Never been. But should go there.'

'Sorry,' said Green. 'We're losing time. Do you think

you'll be able to recognise the place we took you to before?'

'Mnym.'

'Well, you go off on your own and see if you can get in and bring back a sample. John and I will wait for you here.'

'Sample. Yes. Good. Now I understand. Mnym, you want analysis.'

'Something like that,' said Black.

Lev Petrovich walked the short distance along the street and through the open gates of the industrial estate. The boy paused in his can-kicking to stare after him. He remembered the place fairly clearly and it did not take him long to find himself outside Camberwell Light Engineering. He went up to one of the windows to see if he could get a view of the inside of the factory and was peering through the glass when he became aware of the sound of a vehicle behind him. He turned, to see an old lorry with soft, green canvas sides backing up to the entrance. The driver sounded the horn, gave Lev a cheery wave, got out of the cab and went round to the rear. He hauled on a rope which rolled up the tarpaulin at the back. A man in overalls came out of the building with a sack truck and, as the driver handed down large cardboard boxes, he stacked them and trundled them inside. After about thirty minutes the driver rolled down the back and secured it with leather straps.

'Fancy a coffee?' said the warehouseman.

'I could murder one.' The driver was in his late fifties, portly and with a jovial, red face.

'Come into the office and I'll make you one.'

Lev walked slowly round the side of the building and looked in at the entrance. Both men were chatting as they walked towards a partitioned corner at the rear. He could see a desk with a telephone on it. A light was on and he could make out a calendar, with a picture of a posturing, half-naked woman, fixed to the painted brick wall. The warehouseman led the lorry driver into the office and closed the door behind him.

Ivanov was not sure what he was supposed to do; but those men wanted him to analyse something and the cardboard boxes may have something to do with it. Making sure that he could not be seen from the office, he went a short distance into the factory and behind a pile of boxes. He picked up a loose one from the floor. It was quite heavy – too heavy for him comfortably to carry back to the car. There was some baling twine near the box and rolls of brown packaging tape; then he noticed something that he had not seen before, a black, plastic sleeve with a long, rectangular hole in the side, through which he could make out a dull metal. A yellow button was at one end of a narrow glide. He pressed the button and slid it and a blade appeared at the end of the sleeve. This was perfect. Working quickly, and with the excitement of taking part in something which his instincts told him might be illicit, he slit the tape securing the top of the box, reached in and took out a glass jar, then he folded the cardboard flaps down, took another box from the pile and put it on top of the one which he had opened. He looked round from behind the stack; the two men were still in the office and he could hear laughter. Putting the jar in his pocket, he went outside and, walking as quickly as he could, he got to the gates and onto the road. The black car was still there and he sat in the back, breathless.

'Did you get a look inside?' Black asked him.

'Yes. And got this for you,' and he produced the jar from his pocket. 'Boxes were just delivered. Hundreds. This from a box.'

Black leaned across and took it from him. 'Pickled beetroot,' he said.

'So far so good,' said Mike Green. 'Let's strike while the iron is hot.'

'Please?' asked Lev. 'What iron?'

'Are you alright for a bit of a journey?' asked Green.

'Yes. We go to Cheltenham?'

'Well, if you really want to see it, maybe afterwards. But I think now would be a good time for us to pay another visit to Birmingham. Are you up for it, Lev?'

'Yes. Am up,' he replied, not having the slightest idea what Green meant.

John Black started the car and turned it round in the entrance of the estate, then drove back they way they had come.

The house was delightfully peaceful. Frank Grinder breathed in the atmosphere, rather as one savours the air after a long car journey to the coast. There really was no sound: no conversation, no television, no clatter from the kitchen and, for the moment, no traffic noise. Just 100% proof quiet. It was the first time since Saturday that he had been alone in such blessed tranquillity. A sudden apprehension crossed his mind and he went downstairs; no, it was alright, the old man wasn't snoozing somewhere. They had all gone out.

He went to the kitchen and made himself a celebratory smoked salmon sandwich and poured a glass of white Macon Villages from the fridge. The luscious chill beaded the glass and for ten minutes he ate and sipped in blissful isolation. Then he made himself a black coffee and took it back up to the study. He selected a CD of Mozart which he put on at a low volume, stretched his back and began to write a chapter on wine snobbery.

That isn't bad, he thought. Perhaps, there is time for another short topic before they get back. He ruffled through his notes, stood up, stretched, walked a few paces round the room and sat down at the computer again. The culture of celebrity would be a promising target.

CHAPTER 23

They were back in the Balti Triangle by late lunchtime.

'God, that smells good,' said John Black as the aroma of spices wafted through the air vents of the black Mercedes Benz. 'Shall we stop at one these curry houses, Mike?'

'It's tempting,' Green replied. 'But I think that we'd better crack on. Knowing you, we wouldn't leave in under a couple of hours. You'd probably sample everything on the menu.'

'Perhaps you're right,' said Black. 'But, I must say, I'm a bit peckish. I could do with something to eat; it's been a long morning.'

'Well, we could grab a pie or a sandwich at that place we went to last time. It wasn't too bad, was it?'

'No, it wasn't bad; it was awful. But rather there than nothing to eat at all. I'm the one doing the driving,' said Black, as if to justify his need for sustenance.

They pulled up outside Proky's Café and all three went in. The fat owner was behind the counter. He came round, wiping his hands on a tea towel.

' 'Allo again, gents, you're becoomin' reklars.'

'Yeah', muttered John to Mike. 'Bloody reckless, coming back here again.'

'What brings yer 'ere again. Anytheenk special?'

'We've come to try your cheese sarnies,' replied Black. 'I read a review of them in 'Time Out'.'

'Narr,' said Porky, 'yer keedin'.'

'Yep, he's kidding,' said Green. 'A large plate of ham sandwiches and three teas, please,' without bothering to ask the others what they wanted.

Porky went back behind the counter and started spreading margarine onto sliced, white bread.

'Narr, what Oi meant was: what brings yer up here agin, to theess neck of the woo-oods?'

'Oh,' said Green, glancing out of the window, 'erm, we've some work being carried out by those printers.'

'Ooh,'eem? You wonnoo be careful of 'eem. 'E'll get yer nimes wrong if yer don't watch 'eem. What are yer nimes, boi the way?'

'I'm John White,' said Green.

'And I'm Mike Brown,' said Black.

Lev looked puzzled, but said, 'My name is Doctor Lev Petrovich Ivanov.'

'That's a beet of a mouthful,' said Porky, 'ent it? Day yer 'ave a shorter'n.'

'I beg pardon,' said Lev.

'Oi said, it's a beet...'

'Yes, mnym, is beet. I am specialist in beetroot.'

'Oi better call you Dr Beetroot, then.'

'No, is not my name...'

'How's the tea going?' Green interrupted. 'I could do with a cup. We've had a long drive.'

The fat café owner brought three cups of very strong

tea over to them and went back to making the sandwiches, using translucently thin slices of supermarket ham. They ate them in silence and in minutes; then they got up to leave.

'Tarra a beet, Gents and, er, Dr Beetroot,' Porky called after them, chuckling at his conviviality. 'See yer again soon.'

'Not soon,' muttered John Black. 'Not ever.'

As soon they were outside, Green asked Lev if he could remember where the building was that had interested them before. When he said that he thought that he could, Green asked him to go and take another look, on his own, and see if he could get some information, whilst he and John would wait in the car. Ivanov set off along the grubby roadway.

When he got to the factory, he immediately noticed a slight difference from how it had looked earlier; one of the front windows had been left open and a tattered curtain was flapping through it. Also, there were bundles of printed leaflets, wrapped in plastic covers, stacked against the door, as if a delivery had recently been made. He tried the door but it was locked, so he moved to the front of the building, pushed the curtain to one side and looked in. There was no sign of activity. It took him a few moments to accustom his eyes to the gloom, but gradually he began to discern a pile of flattened cardboard boxes, crates of glass jars, two gas rings mounted on what looked like a trestle table and several carboys standing on the floor. He could just make out the words 'Malt Vinegar' stamped on a brown label which was tied to the neck of the nearest carboy. Two large, white plastic drums were on a table just inside the window, one marked 'Sugar', the other 'Salt'. A metal sink with an oversized draining board slowly materialised against the far wall. A familiar, earthy smell began to come to him but he could not tell where from. He hitched himself up so that he could push the upper half of his torso through the window, his hands clinging to the ledge. As he did so, a breeze caught the dirty curtain and it wrapped itself around his face, making him let go of the window frame and drop down to the ground. Looking around to make sure that no-one was watching, he pushed the curtain to one side and hoisted himself up again. There, to his left, stacked in wooden vegetable crates against the wall nearest to the door, was the source of the unmistakeable smell: raw beetroot. The crates reached up nearly to the ceiling. So, he thought, this must be what these men had been talking about the other day.

He dropped back to the ground, scraping his hand as he did so, but hardly noticing it as the excitement overcame him. This was a real cloak and dagger adventure, the sort of thing that he had read in the cheap novels that he bought at airports to while away the time on long, tedious, domestic flights. Now he had something else to report back to Mike and John. Then another idea struck him and he looked through the window for any form of cutting implement, but he could see nothing. Walking briskly back to the car, he tapped on the window. Green slid it down.

'You have, perhaps, knife or something to cut?'

'Yes, there's a penknife in the glove compartment,' said Black.

'I borrow, please.'

Now running, Lev Petrovich went back to the factory, made sure again that he was not being observed, and pulled out from the centre of the pile a pack of the printed material. Carefully, he slit it open at the top, removed a leaflet and put the pack back with others on top of it. Looking around once more, he hurried back to the car and got in. Breathing heavily, he described what he had seen in the building and then, with an air of triumph, he brought out the leaflet and passed it to Green. Green looked at it and then began to read, aloud, first the heading.

'BEETSAREUS.'

'That sound like somewhere near Russia,' said John Black.

'No, you fool,' said Green. 'BEETS...ARE...US. It's a bloody flyer.'

He read on.

'ON BEET, WE CAN'T BE BEATEN.'

And then,

'THE FRENCH CALL IT 'BETTERAVE' SO YOU'D BETTER 'AVE SOME OF OURS.'

And,

'IN GERMAN IT'S 'ROTE BETE' AND THERE'S NOTHING MORE DELICIOUS WITH ROAST BEEF.'

He groaned as he read on,

'THE ITALIANS CALL IT 'BARBABIETELA'. WELL, THAT'S EASY FOR THEM TO SAY.'

'It's a bloody flyer,' he said again. 'They're not concocting some fake sauce. It's a beetroot bottling plant. It's kosher!'

Lev Ivanov was disappointed by what he could gather from Green's reaction; also, he was mystified.

'Kosher?' he said. 'Is there Jewish beetroot? Mnym, I not know that.'

'Christ,' said Green, who had turned pale. 'We've wasted all this time.'

'So we have finished here?' Lev asked, brightly.

'Yes,' Green sighed.

'Then, mnym, perhaps we go to Cheltenham now?'

'Might as well,' Green sighed. 'There's nothing else for us to do here. Or, probably, anywhere. Ever!'

CHAPTER 24

Frank Grinder sat back in his chair and stretched. He was conscious of an ache in his knee: it seemed impossible to cure himself of the habit of twisting his right leg behind his left when he was absorbed in writing. He pushed his glasses up onto his forehead and rubbed his strained eyes. There was a physical price to pay for all this work, a price which he had not considered before starting on his excoriation of modern life. Still, it was very satisfying to put in written form a selection of the more salient of the irritating stupidities that assailed him with increasing frequency. He got up from his desk and went to the window.

It was a sunny, quiet day and a woman taking advantage of it was being pulled along by her dog as it snuffled and sniffed from one revolting smell to the next in that excited, mindless, peculiarly canine way. His glance was caught by the slight twitch of a net curtain in a window across the street. It moved again as it was pulled to one side and, for a moment, revealed a face, with dark glasses and a ginger beard staring straight at him. A black baseball cap was pulled low over the brow.

He went down to the kitchen and made himself another coffee. He was about to take it back upstairs, but checked himself; there was no need for escape and he told himself that he must not become obsessive. This was not work, it was pleasure or therapy, or perhaps both. He was not a professional writer, although, who knew where this might lead? He took the mug over to the table and turned on the small television set which perched between a rarely-used, white terrine dish and a rack of cookery books. On Sky News a government minister was at the despatch box, and the shot was wide enough to show her colleagues on either side of and behind her, all exaggeratedly signalling their agreement. Frank topped up the coffee and took it upstairs, inspired to his next topic by irritation and nodding politicians.

The drive from Birmingham to Cheltenham was, mostly, in silence. Lev Petrovich had, as far as his natural mildness of character would allow him, made it clear to Mike and John that he really must get to this town called Cheltenham, that he was expected there, and that, if it was not too late, he had to attend some sort of meeting; but he had been very vague about the details. He explained that, before leaving the University of Volgograd, en route for Moscow and London Heathrow, he had been told that a car would be waiting for him to take him to the place where he had to be which was, he thought, mnym, mnym, part of a *khotel*, but he did not know the name of the *khotel*. It had probably been mentioned, but he had not though it necessary to write down the name, or, perhaps, he did write the name (he had been searching through his bag in the back of the car) but he did not seem have the paper with him. He told them how he had been surprised, and also disappointed, not to have been met and to have to find this hotel near Paddington Station.

At this point, Black had interjected,

'So you were told that you would be met at the airport by a driver? That's the first I've heard about it.' Green had nodded in concurrence.

'So, where in Cheltenham is this hotel? I don't suppose that you've got any idea at all?'

Lev nodded gloomily. 'Not know name, but is big *khotel* with lecture rooms. Must be.' And he thought, wistfully, of the occasional perk of academic life, being flown abroad and being put up in the comfort of the class of hotel that his own salary would never run to. He let slip his disappointment that it turned out to be the Medved.

'It's an odd name, that, for a hotel,' said Black. 'Does it mean anything?'

'*Medved* is Russian for bear. Is our, mnym, national animal.'

'Just as well it's in Paddington, then.'

'Please?'

'It's too complicated to explain.'

Neither Mike nor John had been to Cheltenham before. John said that he thought that it must be full of retired majors and colonial civil servants.

'And rubber planters,' said Mike. There could not be many places that fitted Lev's description. It would be worth cruising around the town to see if they could find the hotel; it might also be interesting going to have a look round somewhere new and it would give him and Black the chance to think, and to consider how they were going to break it to Mr Li that, from what they had seen of the two shabby premises, Camberwell Light Engineering had nothing to do with undermining a global monopoly, and everything to do with bottling beetroot.

They did not take as long as Mike Green had expected, and an hour after leaving the industrial estate in Sparkbrook, they were coming up to signs for Cheltenham on the motorway.

'Look at that, John,' he said, seeing a windsock blowing in a nearby field. 'There's an airport here. I never knew that. Did you?'

'No. I expect that they have direct flights to Bath and Harrogate. And K.L.'

'Cayle? Where's that?'

'Not Cayle. K.L. Kuala Lumpur. For the rubber plantations.'

The mood in the car had begun to lighten. It was almost as if Black and Green were relieved by the failure of their mission for, at least, they had some positive news for their employers, even though it was not what would have been expected. Green was also coming to realise that he had neither a plan nor any instruction about what to do, if they had uncovered a counterfeiting operation; he was conscious that he had put to the back of his mind the question of how they were supposed to deal with it. Arson? An explosion? Burglary? He had the uncomfortable impression that they would not have been expected to bother about such niceties as keeping within the criminal law. Yes, he was definitely feeling relieved. This was a result, after all: they had been sent out to discover whether the company was involved in the production of a fake, and they had found that it was not. So, a real result, without too much effort, and no risk of being charged with conspiracy to do something nasty. Mr Li could sleep at night, knowing that he still held the reins of the monopoly firmly in his grasp. No, not at all bad, when you came to think about it. It was just a question of reporting back, although not yet, because of the embargo on the use of mobile 'phones and, also, because a few extras hours before doing so would help make the work appear to have been more arduous than it actually had been.

A single-engine light aircraft flew low across the motorway and descended behind some trees.

'This airport,' Ivanov interrupted Green's thoughts, 'is called?'

'The sign said 'Gloucestershire Airport',' Black told him.

'And, how far from Cheltenham we are?'

'I reckon, about ten minutes.'

'Is good. Perhaps, when I finish, I catch airplane back to Volgograd?'

'I don't think that they'll have direct flights,' said Black. 'You'll probably have to go via Moscow.'

'So, mnym, you think that they fly from here direct to Moscow.'

'Oh, no question. Daily flights, I should imagine. Probably a couple per day.'

'Oh,' said Lev, beaming. 'That is very good. I came to London from Moscow. What is name of company?'

'Mickey Mouse Air,' Black replied.

'Minkle Maussair. I not have heard of this airline. Is new?'

'Yes, it is. I believe that it was started up recently. By the Disney Corporation. Look, this is the turn-off to Cheltenham.'

They parked in a bay beside a neatly laid out square. When they got out, Green noticed the imposing front of a hotel on the other side of the road, the Royal Hotel.

'Fancy some nice English tea and sandwiches?' he asked the others. 'It's about time we had something decent to eat. And perhaps a slice of cake. This could well be the hotel that you're looking for, Lev.'

In front of the hotel was a bronze memorial to the fallen of Sebastopol, set in a bed of beautiful, regular flowers. Green hoped that Ivanov did not notice the dedication. They walked through the revolving doors to a quiet lounge and Green went up and spoke to a young man behind the reception desk. He came back to Black and Lev Petrovich, who were already settled in comfortable leather chairs.

'Yes, they will serve tea here. But they don't have a conference centre and there are no meetings going on at the moment. The chap suggested that we try another hotel a few minutes' walk from here. It's new. He's given me a map and showed me where it is. We'll have our tea first and then go and find it. Look, he's also lent me the Yellow Pages.'

They moved to a table and Mike Green spread out the map of Cheltenham town centre. The familiar border of advertising boxes enclosed a street plan. John suggested that Lev might like to have a look at it, to see if any of the hotel names rang a bell, and slid it across to him. Lev Petrovich studied it for a while. Then he looked at the hotel section of the telephone directory, and flicked back a few pages, with a puzzled expression. Eventually, he spoke.

'You have agency special for one type of car. This, I find unusual. Mnym, in Russia we have garages sell all cars, or some cars, or show-place for automobile maker, foreign and Russian, but never I have seen for just one model. And this an old model of Ford, no? I am interested in Western cars. I once thought to buy one of these but not have saved enough money and now I thought they were not, mnym, manufactured any more.'

'What are you talking about?' asked Black. 'Show me.'

Lev pointed to a page of advertisements.

'Oh that,' said Black, 'I don't think that the models are very old. And, actually, some of them might come from Russia.'

'Russian? I not know of Russian cars in Cheltenham. I shall tell car shops in Volgograd that you can buy Russian cars in Cheltenham.'

Black was finding it difficult to conceal his laughter.

'What the hell are you two talking about?' Green interjected. 'You've lost me.'

'Mnym, mnym, I find, also, very interesting that they sell Russian cars in small town like Cheltenham. Yes, you are right, John, here says Russian models. Must be as well as agency for Escorts.'

'Look,' said Green to Lev. 'Just see if there are any names of hotels that you recognise in these advertisements. Or do any of the street names look familiar?'

Lev contemplated the map again.

'No. Can see nothing that reminds me. Nothing. I am sorry that I not keep the name. But, still...'

'Yes?' said Green.

'Mnym, still I find interesting that you may buy Russian car here.'

Tea and sandwiches and a pyramid stand of cakes were brought to them. They ate and drank in companiable silence, Black still grinning. When they had finished, they went out into the street, Green holding the folded map with the route to the other hotel marked on it. They crossed the road and made for a long row of shops, divided from each other by white-painted metal caryatids, staring blindly towards the traffic.

'It's somewhere behind here, I think,' said Mike Green. They walked along a terrace of Regency houses until he realised that they had gone too far and had missed a turning on the other side of the street; so they crossed over and walked back. As they did so, coming towards them, they saw a group of Chinese, three women and two men, who stopped and then went up the steps to the front door of one of the white, stuccoed houses. As the three men came level, the door was opened from the inside and they went in.

'There it is,' said Green, and he led them down the narrow lane. At the end they could see a large, newly-renovated building with a green dome and an empty courtyard covered with honey-coloured Cotswold stone chippings.

“‘The Caroline’,’ said Green. ‘This is it. It’s the other big hotel in town, according to the guy at that place we had tea. It’s brand new, apparently’

They went into a cool lounge area, minimalistic in that, amongst other things that were lacking, there was no seating.

‘Do you want to ask?’ Green said.

Lev mumbled his agreement and went up to the reception counter.

‘I am,’ he announced himself, ‘Dr Lev Petrovich Ivanov. You have, perhaps, room booked for me?’

‘No, sir,’ replied the young male receptionist, without looking up.

‘But, perhaps, mnym, mnym, you check your computer.’

‘No need, but thank you for the suggestion, sir. There is no room booked in your name.’

‘But perhaps you not understand how I say it. Let me write. Please give me piece of paper.’

The receptionist glanced up at him coldly, and with a barely perceptible sigh, pushed a pad and a ballpoint pen across the leather-topped counter. Lev Petrovich wrote ‘ИВАНÓВ’ and then ‘IVANOV’ and then, after a pause, ‘IVANOFF’.

‘Maybe, you check now to see my name on computer.’

Without deigning to look at the paper, the receptionist smiled, showing gleaming, perfect teeth, and said ‘No-one of that name is booked in.’

‘Well, mnym, perhaps I am booked in name of conference. You have conference room?’

'Yes, sir. We have.'

'You have, perhaps, conference on agriculture?'

'No, sir.' Again the teeth gleamed.

'On beetroot?'

'No, sir.'

'On, mnym, Hungry World?'

'No, sir.'

Lev felt an unaccustomed anger rising.

'Mnym, you say no room booked for me but you don't check. I show you how to spell my name, but you not bother to look. You tell me that you, mnym, mnym, have a conference room...'

'We have, in fact, several conference rooms, sir. We have a conference suite.'

'Good, yes, several, and you tell me you have no conference.'

'Yes, sir, that's quite right.'

'Well, how you can know? How you can be certain when you don't look.? Answer me that one.'

'Because, sir,' replied the receptionist, flicking a speck of dust from the sleeve of his black jacket, 'we don't open until next week.'

'Then why you here? Tell me this one.'

'Staff training, sir. Will that be all, or would you like to book a room for next week?'

CHAPTER 25

The unmistakeable sound of Cantonese voices in the street caught Frank's attention as he sat back in his chair, having just completed his short gripe on politicians. No other language or dialect, of which he was aware, sang the last syllable of an assertion or a question quite like that, or tacked on, solely, it seemed, because of its amenability to the upward inflection, the long 'ah' sound as in 'Mummi-ah', 'Daddi-ah' and that timeless expression of surprise and excitement, 'Aaayieeah', all of which came through the window of his study. It was a pity. He had notes for another topic and he was still in the mood; there was no sign of his creative energy flagging yet, but he really could not complain. Winnie, bless her, had had her family out of the house since soon after breakfast, and with such an assortment of conflicting appetites and needs to cater for it was quite an achievement for her to have kept them, apparently, together for so long. How had she managed to feed Rambo, shop with Winsome, rest her mother and, well, whatever interested her father (there, surely, would not have been time to take him racing) and bring them back, without losing any of them, and in high spirits? His heart swelled when he thought of what she had been prepared to do for him.

He went downstairs and opened the front door. Yes, they were all there, even Rambo, who was looking rather pleased with himself.

'We had a really good day, Frank,' he said. 'Winsome's been shopping,' and he pointed to several stiff carrier bags, all with expensive names printed on them, which she was trying to conceal behind her back.

'So, you like the shops here?' Frank asked her.

'Not too bad,' she smiled. 'Not as good as in Hong Kong, but some along the Promenade are quite good. And that place with all the white statues…'

'Montpellier.'

'Yes, that has good shops,' she sagely gave her verdict. 'I bought quite a lot, but could only manage to bring back these. The rest are too big to carry. They are going to deliver.'

'Are you having them shipped back home?'

'Yes, to your house. Delivery here tomorrow.'

A vision of his overloaded car on the way from Heathrow swam across Frank Grinder's mind.

'And my Mum's been, mostly, resting,' continued Rambo. 'We found some really nice gardens near here and she's been sitting there and taking a look. Except when we went for coffee. And lunch. And we came back to collect her for tea. We've just had it, in that big hotel. That was good. I like English sandwiches and cakes. They're better than Hong Kong cakes. The sandwiches aren't very big, though, are they? But plenty of them, when I asked for more.'

'What's your father been doing? He looks happy enough. But has he done something to his leg?'

'Oh, him. He's fine. Apart from when we were eating, he's spent his time in a shop. I thought it was an electrical shop, at first. It said something 'Power' outside.'

'Not 'Paddy Power', by any chance?'

'Yeah, that's it, I think.'

'Well, why is he limping?'

'Oh that. That's because he's got so much money stuffed in his trouser pocket. He had a good time at the shop.'

'And what about you, Rambo? What have you been doing?'

'I had a good day, too,' he replied. 'I didn't get arrested.'

They had all moved into the hallway now and were making for the kitchen, Winnie following the others. Frank put both his hands on her shoulders and turned her gently towards him.

'Sweetheart, I appreciate your giving me space today, I really do. But I don't know if it could have been all that much fun for you.'

'You're welcome,' she said. 'It's been good. I liked it. Looking after them. It's like a ship.'

'Ship? What ship?'

'No, silly, not ship. Ship.'

'Sorry, love, I'm not following you.'

'No, I follow them. Make sure they don't get lost.'

'But, what's that got to do with boats?'

'No boats. Who said boats?'

'You did.'

'I didn't. I said ship.'

'You just said 'not ship'.'

'No, not ship. Ship. Look, they like a ship and I like a shipdog,' and she laughed and patted his head to show him that she was not upset by his stupidity.

'Have you eaten?' she asked him.

'Yes, I made myself something at lunch time.'

'I better get some food ready.'

'I thought that you'd just had tea and sandwiches.'

'Yes, but that was, maybe, half hour ago. They'll want something now. Snack before supper.'

'Yes, I suppose it must have been exhausting work for them, all that shopping and betting and sitting between meals, and, especially for your younger brother, keeping out of the clutches of the constabulary.'

'What you mean, F'ank?'

'Look, love, you go and do the food. Do you mind if I go upstairs and finish off what I was doing?'

'No, course not.' She patted his head again and her eyes twinkled. 'You go and play.'

He went back up to his study and continued with an attack on slogans and taglines. When he had finished, he went on to a long-standing irritant: the overuse of first names.

CHAPTER 26

Mike Green could see that Lev was having some sort of difficulty. He could sense also, even from a distance, the hauteur of the overly immaculate member of staff. He walked briskly to the reception desk; Lev turned and gave him a grateful half-smile.

'Is there a problem?' he asked. 'If so, I will want to speak to the manager.'

'The manager is not here, sir,' the smile unswerving. 'But I am the assistant manager.'

'Well, what's the problem?'

'I was just explaining to this gentleman, sir, that the hotel is not yet open for business. I fear that he may have some difficulty in understanding me.'

'Listen,' said Green, his voice rising. 'He speaks excellent English.'

'Mnym, mnym, mnym,' concurred Lev Petrovich.

'He speaks *and* understands English.'

'I'm sure that he does, sir.' Was there, perhaps, a note of apprehension in the otherwise smooth tone as he glanced up to see that the other man who had come in with them was also walking towards the desk?

'Well,' continued Green, 'if you want to keep your job when the hotel does open for business, perhaps you would care to change your attitude.'

An image of incognito hotel inspectors rose from the depths of the assistant manager's soul.

'Of course, sir, of course. Would you permit to say that I deeply regret if there may have been any misunderstanding which, although unintentional, I am sure was all my fault.

'Mnym,' agreed Lev.

'So, how may I be of assistance?'

'Well, simply this,' said Green. 'My colleague here was supposed to have been booked in somewhere in Cheltenham but, due to a mix up, he wasn't collected from the airport and he doesn't know the name of the hotel.'

'No, well, it could not have been this hotel, sir, as I was endeavouring to…as I told the gentleman.'

'Alright, that's fair enough. But you might be able help. He should have attended some sort of conference. Do you, by any chance, know if there is one going on in Cheltenham? Something to do with agriculture.'

'Would it, perhaps, be this?' said the assistant manager, as he produced a leaflet from beneath the reception desk. '*Beetroot Production for a Hungry World.*' I have a few flyers here. Chef told me that he had thought of going as he likes cooking with beetroot. It seems to be quite the *légume du jour.*'

'Yes, mnym, that is, that is.' Lev Petrovich interrupted him. 'Where is?'

'It's being held at the Madrigal Hotel, a few miles out of town. Here, sir, there's a map on the back.'

'Thank you,' said Green.

'I am so pleased to have been able to be of assistance, sir. So very pleased. And if there is anything else that I may do for you, please do not hesitate to ask. Perhaps you gentlemen would accept some complimentary refreshment before you leave; I am sure that the kitchen would be able to produce something for you. No? Well, it has been a great pleasure to meet you. Have a safe journey,' and he added under his breath to the departing figure of Mike Green, 'Inspector.'

They walked back towards the car. The sky had become overcast and was the steely-grey colour which predicts rather than threatens rain. John Black suggested that they might take a stroll around the town centre, for the benefit of Lev, before going on to the Madrigal, but Ivanov said that he would prefer to get to the hotel as soon as possible, and Green agreed; he was keen to report what he now had come to consider to be good news but, because he could not use his mobile 'phone, he would have to wait until he got back to London, and he did not want to waste time. It struck him, not for the first time, how that once ubiquitous and, seemingly, permanent feature of the urban landscape, the public telephone box, had almost disappeared. So they went straight to the black Mercedes and got in.

The traffic was beginning to build up, rather to Black's surprise, whose idea of Cheltenham's rush-hour was a flock of retired colonels trying to get home in time for their tiffin, prepared by a Malay house-boy. They joined the flow until they saw the direction for the town that the assistant manager had said that they should head for and followed it. Within ten minutes they were out of the built-up area and in another ten they saw the signs to the Madrigal Hotel and Conference Centre. They turned in between the pillars of the gateway and onto a long, gravelled drive which lay between lawns, sloping towards a golf-course. The hotel was a white, stuccoed 1980's building. Scaffolding had been erected to the left of the entrance and a team of painters was burning off the top floor window frames. A few cars were parked on the otherwise empty car park, to the right.

'Doesn't look very busy,' said John.

'No, but there's a sign for the main car park. It's round the back. That's where they'll all be,' Green replied. 'I'm sure that we can leave the car here for a short while.'

They got out and went into the lobby. Two neatly uniformed young women were behind the desk; there was no-one else in the reception area. Green went up to them.

'Our Russian colleague, here, is attending the conference,' he said, glancing down at the leaflet, 'on beetroot in a hungry world. In fact, he is a speaker. I am afraid that he was delayed. Do you know where he should go to let the organiser know that he has arrived?'

The first young woman looked blankly at him, and then turned to the second and they spoke quietly to each other.

'I'm sorry. I've been off duty for a few days. But I know that the conference is over. They've all gone.'

Ivanov came up to the desk, beside Green.

'You've missed it, Lev,' he said. 'The conference has finished.'

'But there was room booked for me, yes?'

'What was your name, sir?'

'What was my name? I am sorry. I do not understand. I have not changed my name. It has, mnym mnym, always been the same.'

'I meant, what *is* your name, sir,' said the receptionist, smiling sweetly and not meaning it.

'I am Ivanov. Lev Petrovich Ivanov.'

She consulted the computer screen.

'Would that be *Dr* Ivanov?'

'It is. Mnym, it would be,' he added. Lev knew that there was a conditional tense in English, as in Russian, but he could not see why it should apply to his existence or his identity. In what circumstances would I be Dr Ivanov, he mused, and in what circumstances, not. The longer he had been among the English, the less he thought that he understood their language. His meditation was interrupted by the receptionist.

'But,' she said, 'Dr Ivanov has been here. He checked in for the conference on Sunday and I see that he stayed on Monday night. The conference was on Tuesday and I believe that he spoke at it because I see that he was part of the block booking that Mr Worthy made. Yes, he arranged for the bedrooms for the speakers and, oh yes, there's a note here that he was due to stay on Tuesday night as well, but he left suddenly on Tuesday evening. Yes, look, there's an item here: reception called a taxi to take him to the station, and it was charged to the bill.'

The other young woman leant forward.

'Yes, I was on duty and I arranged for the taxi. I

remember it because Mr Worthy was surprised that he had gone, but he did tell me that Dr Ivanov had been taken ill. But, excuse me, you don't look like him. Are you *sure* that you are Dr Ivanov?'

This may be, thought Lev Petrovich, why English people use the conditional tense: when they don't know if you are who you say you are. 'I am, mnym, Dr Lev Petrovich Ivanov,' he said stiffly. 'I know who I am. Certain.'

Green listened in silence to this exchange with growing concern. So there was another man, masquerading as Lev Ivanov, and attending a conference on the very vegetable that they had believed was at the root (the pun seemed not the slightest bit funny in the circumstances) of the knock-off condiment. Maybe he had jumped too soon, thinking that everything was above board and innocent and that there was no threat to his employers' business. And if he had, then the time that had been wasted and the failure to make any headway would get a chilly reception; in fact, that was the best that he could hope for, and it was pretty improbable. The people behind Mr Li could be callous, if not ruthless.

'Look,' he said. 'Thank you very much. We've got to get back to London now.'

'But please,' said Lev plaintively. 'This looks very nice khotel. Maybe, if room still held in my name, I stay here tonight. You have swimming pool?'

'Yes, indeed,' said the first receptionist.

'And, mnym, how you say, Jacuzzi?'

'Certainly,' smiled the second.

'And room service? And television?'

'Of course, sir.'

'Then maybe I not go to London, but catch airplane tomorrow to Moscow from local airport.'

'No,' said Green. 'We've got to go to London, now. All of us. Especially you. I may need you to back me up. Anyway, your luggage is in London.'

With a wistful backwards glance, Lev joined the others and got into the car.

CHAPTER 27

The whole family was sitting round the table in the kitchen, all of them contentedly full. In the short time that Frank Grinder had pounded out a couple of short chapters, Winnie had managed to produce a meal of eight Cantonese dishes, each more delicious than the last, which they had devoured, rice bowls held to the lips and chopsticks shovelling furiously, until almost everything was gone, and even Rambo had pushed away his plate containing the remnants of noodles in hoi-sin sauce, with a smile and sesame oil spread over his face. His father belched slightly and muttered something to Winsome.

'What did he say?' asked Frank.

'He said that this is proper food, at last. Not like in that pub or at lunch today. He said,' and she put her hand in front of her mouth as if wanting to hide the fact that it was she who was speaking, 'he said he does not understand how you *gwei-lo* can eat that muck. I think,' she added, again a dimple appearing with her shy smile, 'I think that maybe he is getting homesick.'

'Homesick?' expostulated Grinder, 'You've been here since Sunday and it's only Wednesday, today!'

'Well, that's what I think,' she replied. She looked

across at her mother and spoke in Cantonese. The old lady nodded.

Frank was not certain whether or not he should feel hurt. And what about Winnie? He wondered how she felt about all this. The old saying was that guests were like fish, going bad after three days but, surely, she could not feel like that about her own family. Come to think of it, in what societies did it take three days to notice that a fish had gone off? Certainly not the Chinese, where housewives' obsession with freshness was legendary. He would ask Winnie what she made of it, perhaps, later.

'That was a wonderful meal, sweetheart,' he said. 'Are you going to make some jasmine tea?'

Just then, the telephone rang. Winnie got up to answer it.

'Please, you wait a moment,' she said after a short time and, to Frank, 'Because, I don't understand him; he's speaking, maybe, Russian.'

'What?' said Frank. 'I don't know any Russians. Or any Russian. I had better take it in the hallway.'

'You wait a moment,' she said into the mouthpiece, as Frank left the kitchen and picked up the other downstairs telephone.

'Hallo. Frank Grinder here. Do...you...speak...English?'

'Of course Oi fockink spik English. *Stront*, mon, who did you think it voss?'

'Oh, hello Theo. I'm sorry. It's my wife. She thought that you were speaking Russian.'

'My Gorrd. Ess anyvun bin tokking to 'er? Any Rrussians? Dis could chenge thinks...'

'No, Theo' Frank reassured him. 'Not as far as I am aware. She just thought that, perhaps, you were Russian. She's not used to an accent like yours.'

'Exxcent? Vot exxcent? Oi effen't got en exxcent. You're de vun vit de exxcent, eff you orrsk me. Sometimes, Frrenk, Oi eff terr say, Oi corrn't onderrstand you. You perrnounce some forts in a ferry vunny vay – eff you vont moi opinion.'

'Look, I'm sorry, Theo. I didn't mean to be rude. It's just that Winnie hasn't come across many people other than Hong Kongers and Brits and Australians and Kiwis and Americans and...I'm sorry, what did you want?'

There was a palbable silence, while Nuthatch smoothed his feathers.

'Anyway, it's good to hear from you, Theo. How are you? I hope that your stay in England has been profitable.'

Still silence.

'Are you there, Theo?'

'Yiss.'

'Did you want something, or is this just a social call?'

A pause, then, 'Oi colled to tell you that Oi eff bin kipping moi arse on you.'

'Your what? Your arse?'

Another pained silence, and then a sigh.

'Oi eff bin wotching arrt ferr you,' said Theo, slowly and deliberately.

'Watching art? Why?'

'Not art. *Ach, die hel!* Arrt! Wotching arrt. Mekking sure no 'arrm vould come to you orr your family. End...'

This time the silence seemed to signify something portentious.

'Yes, Theo?'

'End, Oi em satisfied thet you arre oll seff. Therre iss no rrisk of any 'arrm to you. So, Oi'm orff.'

'Off where?'

'Orff beck 'ome. To Setheffrricker.'

'So, shall I see you again?'

'Iss better vee not mitt. Oi coll to say goodbye. *Tot siens* and *voerspoort* is vot ve say. It voss a pleasure. Oi think.'

'Well, Theo, I have enjoyed meeting you. It was very, er, interesting. And,' he added, 'thank you for watching out for me and my family.'

The 'phone clicked and Theo Van der Vyl Nuthatch went out of Frank Grinder's life. Possibly.

Very puzzling, thought Frank, and somewhat unsettling, in spite of everything. He went back to the kitchen.

'Who was that, F'ank?' Winnie asked him.

'Oh, just some Russian chap who I forgot that I'd met. Nothing important. Do you mind if I leave you all and go upstairs again? I've got something that I want to see to.'

He went upstairs to his desk and brought his, now developing, book up on the screen and then rearranged his notes.

It was already dusk when the black Mercedes came off the M40 and into the spread-out, dreary outskirts of London. What had once prided itself on being the greatest city on

Earth was now just another urban sprawl, in the long list of other huge conurbations, and not even near the top of the pecking order. Yellow street-lights were starting to come on, and the roads were packed with crawling traffic, the second of the daily migrations between home and work. When the 'plane had been coming in to land, Lev Petrovich, who was in a window seat, was astonished at the size of the man-made landscape, recognising nothing from the pictures in the guidebooks that he had bought for his trip to England until, eventually, he could make out the snaking glitter of a wide river, which he thought must be the *Temza*. There had been a huge, tent-like structure by a loop in the river, a giant, half tennis ball with spikes sticking out of it and he had intended (but later had forgotten) to ask someone what it was. Perhaps the big brown building further along might be the Parliament House. Now that they were at ground level and on the slow-moving edge of the city, the only thing to distinguish it from Volgograd, or Moscow, or Dusseldorf, where he had attended a seminar a year or so ago, was that the traffic was driving on the other side of the road. His eyes began to close, but he was startled awake by the sound of a siren and the flashing of blue lights as a police car overtook them on the inside. The traffic had now come to a standstill. As the car moved forward again, his eyelids felt heavy as he listened to the hum of the air-conditioning and the murmured conversation in the front.

He was aware that he was drifting in and out of wakefulness; not a particularly pleasant experience, because he wanted to look about him and see when the depressing, anodyne conurbation all around them would change to the exhilarating city depicted in the guidebook: soldiers in red coats and tall, fur hats; pubs with, elegant people sitting at outside tables; other, strangely-dressed, people riding horses in a big park; the royal family. He also thought that he should be awake to listen to Mike and John's conversation. They had driven a long way with him today and he had felt a certain cordiality growing between them. He had seen how, in particular, Mike Green's mood had changed to cheerfulness and then, quite suddenly and inexplicably, to concern and urgency in that last hotel that they had been to and, without understanding the reason for it, he sensed that it might have something to do with him. He might be able to help; he certainly wanted to. Perhaps he would be able to buy them both a drink when they got to wherever they were going. But, for the moment, all these streets through which the car was slowly progressing seemed to look the same – long queues of cars, lines of unvarying houses, small rows of shops and traffic lights, lots of traffic lights.

He woke up again as the car stopped outside the Hotel Medved.

'Lev', asked Green, 'have you noticed whether there is a 'phone booth in the reception?'

'What is?'

'Never mind,' said Green, 'we'll come in with you.'

As all three went into the hotel, Lev noticed a man, in his fifties, with rimless glasses and greying hair, in slacks and an open-necked shirt. He was sitting in easy chair, with a black leather shoulder bag on a chair beside him. He was reading a newspaper, but looked up as they came in. Lev Petrovich thought that he might have seen him before and nodded towards him; the other man acknowledged him with a hesitant half-smile. Green also saw him.

'Forget about the booth.'

'Mnym, booth?'

'Yes, forget about,' replied Green.

'Is gin, no? You wish to have a gin?'

'No, no,' said Green. 'Look, I need to make a call on a landline. Can we come up to your room?'

'Yes, and I bring gin for you.'

'No. No, thanks,' said Mike Green,

'Better, perhaps, vodka?'

'No, Lev, please, can you just take us up to your room? Do you need to collect the key?'

'Yes. From desk over there. Is very, mnym, mnym, up-to-date. In Russia, not allowed to take key. Is kept by, mnym, commissar who sits at table on landing and gives you key when you want unlock your door and you give it back to him, or her, (he pronounced it *xheem* or *xher*) when, mnym, leave your room. Here, is more modern system, and I like it, because you may just...'

'Lev, go and get your key, please.' There was a note of curtness in Green's voice that Lev Petrovich had not heard before.

'I just thought that, mnym, you would find interesting the cultural differences between our...'

'Lev, please!'

Lev went over to the desk and then they walked upstairs and he let Black and Green into his room.

'Telephone, there,' he said, pointing to the bedside table. 'Please, sit on bed.'

Green nodded his thanks, took out a note pad, turned the pages until he found the number, and pressed the buttons on the telephone. Lev noticed that his hand was trembling slightly and that, while he was waiting, he was standing staring at one of the hunting prints without really looking at it. Then the call was answered. Black moved away and sat down on the chair on the other side of the bed.

'Yes.'

'May I speak to Mr Li, please?' Green's voice was quieter than Lev had previously heard it.

'Who wants to speak to him?'

'Would you tell him that it is Mr Green, Mike Green.' Then he added, 'Please.'

'And with what is it in connection?'

'Could you just say, erm, a manufacturing process? He will understand. But I must speak to him personally. It is very urgent.'

A pause, and then:

'Yes, Mr Green, this is Mr Li.'

'Mr Li, I, erm, don't know how or where to begin. I wanted to contact you a while ago, when I was out in the field, but I had instructions not to use my mobile 'phone and this is the first chance that I've had to use a landline.'

'Where are you, Mr Green?'

'I'm in a hotel in Paddington. 'The Myedvyed', or something.'

'Medved,' Lev corrected him.

'The Medved. And, to be honest, I'm not certain how secure this is, as I have had to dial for an outside line, but...'

'Would you be good enough to get to the point.'

'Well, I thought that I had good news for you, at first. We've carried out an in-depth survey of the two premises, in London and...'

'I do not think it necessary, or advisable, for you to identify the locations over the telephone. I'm sure that you will agree.' Mr Li's tone did not concede that he allowed for dissent.

'Yes, erm, well, both of them, and I am quite satisfied that nothing...'

'Untoward?' Li inserted.

'Yes, thank you...that nothing untowards is going on. At either of them.'

'Yes, I see.'

'Yes, I, we, are sure that they're just bottling, er, vegetables.'

'Yes. It is, I think, unnecessary for you to indulge in taxonomy.'

'I'm sorry?'

'There is no need for a biological specification. I know what you are referring to.'

'Yes,' said Green. 'Oh, good. I see. Well, I thought that I was going to be able to report that your, er, enterprise had nothing to fear from the other, what-do-you-call-it, set-up.'

'Yes. And?' Even over the telephone, the crystals of ice were palpable. Mike Green swallowed.

'But then I, we, discovered that there had been some sort of mix-up, and that the gentleman who had come from…'

'Yes, let us say, from a country to the east of the United Kingdom. If, of course, that is what you mean.'

'Yes. There. Well, we, I, realised that we had got the wrong one. This one doesn't seem to have anything to do with, erm…'

'Shall we say, the solving of conundra?'

'Er, yes. Thank you. I think. Anyway, he's just an academic. Well, a pretty distinguished one, as far as I can gather,' and he looked towards Lev Petrovich, who smiled back with a shake of his head and a self-deprecatory gesture of the palm of his raised left hand.

'So, no harm done, would you say?' Mr Li's voice was the model of urbanity.

'Yes, well, I would have done, except, er, except that we have found out that another man has been masquerading as erm, our academic, using the same name and giving a talk at the conference that our man was supposed to be at and, apparently, then going on the run.'

'So,' said Mr Li, 'you have, would you not agree, failed in what you were employed to do?' The ice was hardening.

'No, not really. We found out that you had nothing to fear from the other…er… organisation and that, therefore, you would not have to get involved in taking any steps…'

'Please, Mr Green, please! Not over the telephone.'

'No. I'm sorry. But, actually, we have done what was wanted of us and…'

'Surely, Mr Green, you and your colleague do not expect to be paid your fee when, as you so rightly observe, there is serious unfinished business, namely, the tracing of this other person and the ascertainment of his purpose in behaving in the way that you have adumbrated.'

Green gulped unhappily. 'Yes, I see what you mean.'

'Then,' continued Li, 'as you do see what I mean – and I take it that you speak also for Mr Black who, I assume, is in the room with you – may I offer you a little comfort?'

Christ, thought Mike, what does this chilling man think of as comfort? John was staring at him with a worried look in his eyes; and Lev saw that his hand was shaking more and more and that the colour had drained from his face.

'Well, yes, Mr Li, sir, anything that would help us finish, I mean successfully finish, the job for you.'

'The gentleman, whom you have, in error, been taking about with you,' continued Li, 'is, I think that you will find, a Dr Lev *Petrovich* Ivanov. Perhaps you would like to ascertain that from him; I take it that he is with you, and that you and Mr Black are in his hotel room at the moment.'

Without pausing to consider how he could have known that, Green whispered, 'Are you Lev Petrovich Ivanov?' Lev nodded.

'Yes, sir, he is.'

'The person whom you are, if I may say so, unsuccessfully seeking, is a Lev *Semyonovich* Ivanov. He is *Mr*, not *Dr*, Ivanov. He is employed in the same sort of *métier* as are you and Mr Black but, and I hope that you will forgive me for saying so, at a much higher level. I have absolutely no doubt that that is the identity of the other Ivanov.'

'Excuse me, sir,' asked an impressed and perplexed Mike Green, 'may I ask you how you know that?'

'Ah,' replied Li. 'There are two reasons. Firstly, that is the name of the man whom you were supposed to make contact with and to take to those other, shall we say, establishments. It was, after all, I who arranged for his services.'

'Oh, I see,' said Green. 'And the other reason is, sir?'

'The second reason is that that Mr Ivanov has, I would venture to suggest, a thoroughly professional approach to his work.' Although the inflection in the quiet, cold voice was barely perceptible, Green understood the implied contrast with him and John Black. 'As soon as he could, after realising that he had been mistaken for your Dr Ivanov, he had the perspicacity to contact me. So I have known, for some time before your deductive powers led you to the same conclusion, that you were travelling around, uncontactable, I might add, with the wrong man.'

Green was about to rise to the bait and defend the implied accusation, but thought that humility would be better, and silence better still.

'And so,' Mr Li's suave tones continued, 'in the end, no harm has been done. Therefore, in all the circumstances, and bearing in mind that you and Mr Black have completed, at least, part of your assignment, I think that I will be able to see my way after, of course, consulting my associates, to letting you have your fee.'

'That's very, very good of you, sir,' said Mike Green, relief and colour rising in his face.

'So, would you be good enough to tell your Dr Ivanov that he may now return home. I do not suppose that he was aware of any restraints on his movements but,' again the chilling pause, 'I can assure you that there were.'

'Yes, of course, certainly, Mr Li, sir. I'll let him know; at least the bit about going home.'

'Yes, perhaps you should leave it at that. And one more thing.'

'Yes, sir?'

'Would you be interested to know where the other Lev Ivanov is?'

'Oh, certainly, I would, Mr Li.'

'He is staying at the same hotel from which you are speaking to me. Do give my regards to Mr Black. Goodbye.'

CHAPTER 28

Thursday morning passed in a haze of internet and telephone activity for Frank Grinder. He had been surprised when Winsome had, at dinner the previous evening, hinted that the family was considering cutting the holiday short and returning; but it was not until Winnie had come out of the bathroom and they were sitting next to each other on the bed, she in a pale blue, silk nightie he in his boxer shorts, that he understood the extent of the conspiracy that had been hatched during the day. She stroked his shoulder and rubbed the nape of his neck with her delicate, yet strong, fingers and kissed him on the cheek as she told him that they had decided that the visit had gone on long enough and, because she had not been back to Hong Kong for a long time, they had asked if she wanted to go with them; and she had told them that she couldn't leave her Frank on his own; although, she would like to go back, only for a short while, to see her old friends but, of course, she would not think of it, because it would mean his having to cope on his own, although it wouldn't be for more than a couple of weeks; unless, of course, he wanted to come with them, although that would mean either staying in the overcrowded apartment in Yuen Long in the New Territories, or having to book into a hotel; but she wouldn't want him to have to go that expense on top of the return air fares, although she had had a look on the internet, and Cathay Pacific was doing a very good deal in economy class, but, she knew that he didn't like travelling economy because he was very tall (as well as being so handsome), and he found it uncomfortable, so she couldn't expect him to put up with that; and, because, if he didn't mind her going without him she wouldn't expect to fly business class; but she didn't want to ask him and had told her family that it was, probably, not possible that he would want her to go, even though her husband was the kindest, sweetest man and he would know how much she would like to see her friends again, as well as some of the uncles and aunties; and it would only be for two weeks, and she would really, really miss him and shouldn't even think of worrying him with such a *lap-sap* idea, because, who would cook his supper and iron his shirts? She shouldn't even have mentioned it to him, but the family had said that it would be nice to have her back for a short holiday, because it really was such a long time since she had last been there; and are you ready to come to bed now, darling husband?

So that was why, after a couple of hours at his computer and on the telephone, Frank had managed to re-arrange the flights for the Wong family and to book a return for Winnie for the next day. Just as he had completed it all, he saw a delivery van stop in the road outside and unload the remainder of Winsome's shopping. Frank wondered how she was going to pack it all in her cases and how he was going to get all the cases into and onto his car. And now, Winnie's, of course, as well. Perhaps he could strap Ah-mah and Ah-leung, side-by-side, onto the roof rack. As long as, from time to time, someone would pass a couple of bowls of noodles up to them, they would probably be all right. Well, they would just all have to squeeze up tightly together in the car, with luggage and parcels on their laps.

Having completed the travel arrangements, he was tempted to spend the rest of the day in writing; but he could not. For one thing, he was unexpectedly tired. He had not slept well, because, after telling Winnie that, of course, it was right for her to spend some time with her family back home, and that he did not mind, it had struck him that this would be the first time, since their wedding, that they had been apart, and he was not at all sure that he was prepared for it. For another thing, he would have plenty of time on his own in the house over the next two weeks, so he hardly needed to grab the opportunity now. But, more importantly, much more importantly, he wanted to be with Winnie for the rest of the day, and if that meant being with her family as well, at least that might show her that he had not been deliberately stand-offish

So he took them all out to lunch and then piled them into the car and did an afternoon tour of the Cotswolds, to the gratifying cries of 'Waaaah!' and 'Aaaeeiyah!' – even from the old man – as they went from one honey-coloured village to the next. A sense of unreality began to set in, almost as if he were witnessing the last scene of a play rather than participating in actual events. Tomorrow, they would all be gone and this day would be just a memory.

He wished that it was Winnie, not Rambo, sitting in the front seat of the car next to him. He longed for bedtime, when she and he could lie beside each other, but he did not want the morning to come.

On Friday morning, Lev Petrovich came down, with his rucksack, to pay his bill. Standing at the desk was the man in the rimless glasses. Lev Petrovich heard him ask the receptionist to call him a taxi for the airport.

'Mnym, excuse me,' he said, are you going to the London airport now?'

'Yes, I am,' the other man replied. 'To Heathrow.'

'Perhaps, mnym, mnym, it is possible we can travel together. I also go to *Hissro*, and was going to ask for texi. We could share payment,' Lev added.

'An excellent idea,' said the other. 'Are you, by any chance, Russian?'

'Yes. From Russia.'

'I thought so, from your accent. Do you have to settle the bill? Yes, well, I'll wait for you, and then we can get the taxi together. Which terminal?'

'Three, I think.'

'Me, too.'

Frank pulled onto the short stay car park at Terminal 3 and walked with them, behind their overladen trolleys, as far as the check-in desk. There, he shook them, one by one, by the hand and hugged Winnie. Rambo slapped him on the back and pretended to punch his shoulder. He turned and walked away, hoping that none of them noticed the back of his hand going to his eye, and went to find his car.

Lev Petrovich stood in the queue next to the man he had shared a taxi with, and behind a Chinese family: an older couple, two women and a young man.

'She's very attractive,' said the man, discreetly nudging Lev's attention in the direction of the younger woman, as he took out his passport from his inside pocket. Lev glanced at it, surprised.

'Mnym, you Russian national also?'

'Yes,' replied the other. 'But perhaps we could continue to speak in English. At least until we are airside.'

'Airside?'

'Through passport control,' he explained.

Lev Petrovich was just about to ask why, when his attention was caught by a disturbance at the head of the adjacent queue.

'I am very sorry, sir,' the Border Agency officer was saying firmly. 'But I cannot let you pass. You don't look anything like the photograph in your passport. Are you, by any chance, wearing a wig?'

'*Die hel en stront*,' the man said. 'Diss iss 'ow I look today.

The Chinese family were through and Lev Petrovich followed the man in glasses.

'Have a good flight, Mr Ivanov,' said the officer.

'Thank you,' they both replied.

Frank was back at his empty house by early afternoon. He had stopped on the motorway for a sandwich which seemed to have been assembled from spam and damp cardboard and he was now feeling the leaden result, settling somewhere between his abdomen and sternum. Possibly, a topic on service-station food might be gestating within him; but there was another ache, also. Perhaps, he thought, a bit of writing will pick me up.

He made himself a cup of black coffee and took it up to his study. He could touch the silence. He turned on the computer, and whilst he was waiting for it to boot up, went through his notes. To his surprise, he had covered most of what he had wanted to write about. Perhaps a few more topics could be included. There was more on the assault on the English language, and he might have a go at Health and Safety.

The 'phone rang.

'Hello, darling husband… it's Winnie.'

'Yes, I guessed that it was you. No-one else calls me that.'

'I'm glad. I just call to say that we are about to go on the 'plane. I call you tomorrow, when it's morning in England.'

'O.k, my love. Let me know that you've arrived safely.'

There was a pause, then, 'I love you, F'ank.'

'And I love you.'

'I miss you, F'ank.'

She rang off, and he found himself staring at the mouthpiece, just like he had seen in television plays and thought that no-one did in real life. He felt quite cold.

He looked out of the window at the empty street. Then he remembered how difficult it had been to find his way out of the airport and to get onto the motorway, and how he had wondered how a jet-lagged, limited-English, car-hiring, first-time-in-Britain, traveller could possibly manage it. He might add another protest about how much better the road signs were in Hong Kong. Writing might make him feel better. He stared at the screen for a while, before starting to write again.

Frank was just finishing when the 'phone rang again. It was Alistair.

'Hello, Uncle Frank. Sorry to disturb you. Is Rambo available?' And, after a pause, 'How are you?'

'I'm fine,' replied Frank, feeling an unexpected warmth towards his nephew. Normally, he would probably, no, certainly, have been annoyed to have been disturbed, but he found, now, that he was quite grateful for the call. 'But, I'm sorry,' he continued, 'you've missed Rambo. I took them to the airport this morning.'

'That was quick.'

'Well, the old man wanted to go back and I suppose that the rest of them probably did, as well. I don't think that it was because they found Cheltenham too exciting for them; it wasn't that. I think, perhaps, it was because Winnie's parents had never been abroad before. Anyway, they've all gone back, including Winnie.'

'Oh, Uncle Frank, I'm so sorry.'

'No, no, she hasn't left me: she's having a holiday. She hasn't been back, you know, since we came here from Hong Kong. No, she'll be home again soon. It's a pity that you missed Rambo, though; it was all a bit hurried. They made the decision, and then we rearranged their flights yesterday, and now they're in the air. Winnie called me from the airport about an hour ago. I'm sure that he would have liked to have spoken to you before he went. But what was it you wanted? Just to have a chat with him?'

'Well, I just wanted to ask his advice.'

'Would that have been wise? I don't think that Rambo is necessarily the person I would turn to for guidance, particularly after what happened to you both at Weston.'

'Yes, I see what you mean, Uncle Frank. Perhaps you could help?'

'If I can.'

'Well, I'm about to apply for university places and I was just wondering whether there might be any chance of studying in Hong Kong.'

'Hong Kong? Why?'

'Because I've just been looking it up, and it seems that it's about six thousand miles from England.'

'Do you really mean,' asked Frank, 'six thousand miles from a certain vicar?'

'Yes, I suppose that's what I mean.'

'I'll make some enquiries from my old contacts there,' said Frank. 'Give me a day or so. But, for Heaven's sake, don't tell your mother that I helped you.'

'Oh, thanks, Uncle. Thanks very much. I'll call you again in a few days.'

'You can drop over to see me, if you like, Alistair.'

Frank put the 'phone down and went back to the computer to write his last chapter, an overview of everything that he had written. And to think about how he was going to spend the rest of the evening. Alone.

The book which, in the course of this story Frank Grinder wrote, eventually came out under the title 'The Little Book of Anger'. It is published by Matador, ISBN 978 1780882 208. Frank used the pseudonym 'Martin Wilson'.